LORD SUMNER OFFERED HIS HAND
TO AUGUSTINE

"So, my Defiant Angel, have you learned enough from me to go forth and discover my ideal?" he teased, but there was no barb hidden behind the words.

"Perhaps," Augustine answered, accepting his hand down. As soon as she was free of the block, she took back her hand, and wondered why the little touch of exertion that came from exiting the carriage had caused her heart to beat so? She shook off the thought, and looked up at him. "I do have a notion as to where we might be well served to seek our gem tomorrow."

"And where is that?" he asked, crossing his hands behind his back, his eyebrows raised in expectation.

"The lending library."

Lord Sumner raised a hand to his forehead, groaning. "Dear me, did I say I was seeking a bluestocking? If I did, I assure you it was merely an aberration of speech—"

"Tut, my lord! It is not only bluestockings who read, you know. Many ladies read. Many *unmarried* ladies, with time on their hands. . . ."

"Ah," he said, a dawning light of comprehension in his eyes.

"Ah, indeed," Augustine said with a smug nod of her head.

WATCH FOR THESE ZEBRA REGENCIES

LADY STEPHANIE   (0-8217-5341-X, $4.50)
by Jeanne Savery
Lady Stephanie Morris has only one true love: the family estate she has managed ever since her mother died. But then Lord Anthony Rider arrives on her estate, claiming he has plans for both the land and the woman. Stephanie soon realizes she's fallen in love with a man whose sensual caresses will plunge her into a world of peril and intrigue . . . a man as dangerous as he is irresistible.

BRIGHTON BEAUTY   (0-8217-5340-1, $4.50)
by Marilyn Clay
Chelsea Grant, pretty and poor, naively takes school friend Alayna Marchmont's place and spends a month in the country. The devastating man had sailed from Honduras to claim his promised bride, Miss Marchmont. An affair of the heart may lead to disaster . . . unless a resourceful Brighton beauty finds a way to stop a masquerade and keep a lord's love.

LORD DIABLO'S DEMISE   (0-8217-5338-X, $4.50)
by Meg-Lynn Roberts
The sinfully handsome Lord Harry Glendower was a gambler and the black sheep of his family. About to be forced into a marriage of convenience, the devilish fellow engineered his own demise, never having dreamed that faking his death would lead him to the heavenly refuge of spirited heiress Gwyn Morgan, the daughter of a physician.

A PERILOUS ATTRACTION   (0-8217-5339-8, $4.50)
by Dawn Aldridge Poore
Alissa Morgan is stunned when a frantic passenger thrusts her baby into Alissa's arms and flees, having heard rumors that a notorious highwayman posed a threat to their coach. Handsome stranger Hugh Sebastian secretly possesses the treasured necklace the highwayman seeks and volunteers to pose as Alissa's husband to save her reputation. With a lost baby and missing necklace in their care, the couple embarks on a journey into peril—and passion.

Available wherever paperbacks are sold, or order direct from the Publisher. Send cover price plus 50¢ per copy for mailing and handling to Penguin USA, P.O. Box 999, c/o Dept. 17109, Bergenfield, NJ 07621. Residents of New York and Tennessee must include sales tax. DO NOT SEND CASH.

The *Skeptical Heart*

Teresa DesJardien

ZEBRA BOOKS
KENSINGTON PUBLISHING CORP.

ZEBRA BOOKS are published by

Kensington Publishing Corp.
850 Third Avenue
New York, NY 10022

First Printing: July, 1996
10 9 8 7 6 5 4 3 2 1

Printed in the United States of America

*To the Brant cousins: Sommer, Jeffrey,
Amanda, & Kaitlin*

One

Augustine, Lady Wayfield, stared in chagrin at the calling cards in her hand. While the one brought no astonishment, the other certainly did. Mr. Prescott was a frequent caller, but Lord Sumner? *Lord Sumner* waited without to learn if she were at home and receiving?

Augustine looked up from her settee to her waiting butler, Mosby, and after a moment's pause nodded, indicating that the callers should be admitted. They would join the others who had already come to call at her home this morning.

"More callers?" the fresh-from-the-schoolroom Miss Stoakes asked at her side.

"Yes. Mr. Prescott," Augustine said. Rather reluctantly she added, "and Lord Sumner."

"Lord Sumner! Here?" Miss Stoakes' astonishment echoed Augustine's own. "But what can this mean?" the young woman asked the room at large. "Is he out of mourning yet? Oh surely not. No, I am quite sure it is not one whole year since Lady Sumner went to her reward? Surely he is not here seeking your talent, Lady Wayfield? But what else can his visit signify after your estrangement over all this time?"

Her words carried through the room, exciting a murmur from the three other morning callers. Lord Eubank, Mr. Sydney, and Miss Stoakes' mother, Lady

Calcomb, all sported astonished expressions to accompany their exclamations of surprise or curiosity.

Those very same exclamations were cut off abruptly as the two newly arrived gentlemen appeared at the threshold of the parlor. "Lord Sumner. Mr. Prescott," Mosby announced them.

Augustine nodded stiffly in greeting as the two gentlemen stepped into her parlor, her gaze going at once to Lord Sumner. She had meant to acknowledge Mr. Prescott first, but it seemed she was as curious as her other callers to learn what had brought Lord Sumner—Joseph, she had once been friend enough to call him Joseph—once again to her door. It did not matter, however, for Lord Sumner did not have the opportunity to look to her; instead he exchanged a nod with Lady Calcomb when the older woman tapped the sleeve of his charcoal-grey coat with the ivory handle of her parasol.

As the two exchanged greetings, the shorter, stouter Mr. Prescott moved to Augustine's side and made her a leg, a smile on his broad face. She inclined her head in acknowledgment, murmuring "Mr. Prescott" as he lifted her hand to execute an airy kiss over it.

"My dear Lady Wayfield," he greeted her in return.

Augustine's gaze wandered once again to her other caller, this time encountering Lord Sumner's gaze. With a shock she was reminded of the particular hue of his eyes, sky-blue, but the manner of blue seen only at the summit of the sky on a very clear, wintry day. They were that curious silver-blue that seemed all the lighter for being below the fringe of dark hair that ever fanned his forehead. Some had called them cold eyes, made to match the frequently satiric set of his mouth, and so they often were. But, as always, Augustine could not gaze into them without finding them quite literally breathtaking. It was as though she stood atop the mountains and touched the very sky—a foolish notion, but a very real sensation all the same.

He was handsome as ever. But she knew that quite well already, for was he not her immediate neighbor? Did she not frequently see him as he passed from his home to his carriage? Over the years she had learned to associate the name Joseph not with an old man of biblical teachings, but instead this dark-haired, light-eyed man in the prime of life. There was a potency to the name now, for her, a potency that had carried over from the man. He possessed that indefinable quality that made him impossible to ignore even though they had scarce spoken in ages. There was something in the way he held himself that defined confidence, or was it power? . . . but power purposefully held in check by grace of form and manner. She thought, as she had before, that he ought to have had dark eyes to finish the devil-take-you set to his mouth, the determined chin, the steady gaze, the often haughty stance.

Six years. It had been six years since Lord Sumner had entered her home, six years of strained relations between neighbors. They had scarcely spoken in those six years. Oh, sometimes they met at functions, murmuring polite greetings. He was always courteous, never directly cold or cutting to her, even though he certainly possessed the talent. No, he had never given her reason to avoid him, or to give him the cut direct, or to think him anything less than handsome in appearance and speech, yet she never stayed long in any room that also held his presence. He radiated an unspoken disapproval that she could not forget and would not forgive. Although, to be fair, she had to concede she had once done him a disservice. It was hardly to be wondered at that he had not forgiven her. Were she in his shoes, she could not imagine her involvement being forgot either.

And now here he was in her home, as unexpected as

cherry blossoms in December. There was something
about having his well-appointed person in her morning
parlor that was significantly more unsettling than
glimpses of him from afar, and now his steady gaze stole
any words that should have formed on her tongue. Instead she stared, unable not to.

There was an unreadable upward slant to his lips. She
would have preferred the more expected neutral half-
frown he usually reserved for her on those rare occasions they met face to face. This vaguely pleasant lift to
his mouth was too close to alarming. It gave her cause
to wonder if this call might prove to be as inauspicious
as it was unexpected.

"I believe I need not introduce Lord Sumner?" Mr.
Prescott said.

"Of course. Lord Sumner," she said at length, relieved
to hear how calm and ordered her voice sounded despite
her inner turmoil. "Of course we know one another."

"Lady Wayfield and I are acquaintances of long standing," Lord Sumner said to Mr. Prescott, just before he
also made an appropriately light salute over her hand.
"Good morning, madam."

Augustine stared a moment longer before turning to
the task of introducing the other occupants of the
room. Even as she performed the exercise, she fought
to keep her features calmly arranged, unable to think
why Lord Sumner chose now to kiss her hand when in
the past six years social conventions had failed to compel him to any such behavior?

The introductions completed, Augustine murmured
that the gentlemen should please find a seat. She
moved a little to one side on the settee, trying to re-
capture Mr. Prescott's eye and thereby silently invite
him to sit beside her, but to her dismay it was Lord
Sumner who took the seat at her side.

"Sumner and I have not come to call out of mere

idleness," Mr. Prescott said as soon as he was seated beside Lady Calcomb.

"Paul," Lord Sumner said. He spoke quietly, the words not a reprimand, but such was the timbre of his voice that the normally ebullient Mr. Prescott subsided at once, sitting back in his seat, his lower lip stilled between his teeth.

"Indeed, why have you come?" Miss Stoakes was quick to ask.

Lord Sumner gave the younger woman a brief smile, one that did not reach all the way to his silver-blue eyes. "My dear lady, you force me to get ahead of myself, but it seems I must reveal there is indeed a purpose to my call this morning."

"Pray tell," Miss Stoakes urged.

"Why, I have come for the most obvious reason," Lord Sumner replied, looking to his hostess rather than Miss Stoakes.

Augustine felt warmth invade her cheeks, even though he had said nothing untoward.

"I have come seeking Lady Wayfield's services as a matchmaker."

Augustine could not help the small gasp that escaped her, but perhaps no one noticed it over Miss Stoakes' squeal of delight.

"Told you that was why he came," Lord Eubank said to Mr. Sydney, smug with pleasure to have been proved right.

"My services?" Augustine repeated, feeling the warmth creep farther up her face. But how extraordinary that Lord Sumner should make such an announcement, and so publicly, too. He wished her to help him find a mate? *Her*, of all people? That thought was not just extraordinary, it was all but inconceivable! Why would he do such a thing?

"I assure you, I am no expert, not one to offer 'services'," Augustine stated.

"Oh pooh," Miss Stoakes declared, shaking her short, curly brown hair in dismissal. "Everyone says you are the best matchmaker in London."

"I assure you, it is not a profession I actively pursue—"

"Not for an income, certainly," Miss Stoakes agreed. "But rather because it is a particular talent of yours. Why, Lord and Lady Haldon are the darlings of Society, and all thanks to your ability in bringing them to one another's notice."

"I scarce did more than introduce them," Augustine hedged, throwing a quick glance at Lord Sumner from under her lashes. Had his faint smile turned into a sneer, or was that just what she expected to see?

"And what of Mister MacIntosh and his new bride? And Lord Block's betrothal to Cynthia Greenly?" Miss Stoakes went on.

"And there is your cousin Delilah," Lady Calcomb reminded her daughter.

"Of course. And Miss Alcroft to Sir Stephen."

"Yes, quite," Lord Sumner interrupted to say. "I daresay we all have heard tale of Lady Wayfield's gift for bringing likely couples together. That is, of course, why I am here today."

Now Lord Sumner gazed directly into Augustine's eyes, his own faintly mocking. "What say you, my lady? Will you have me as a client to your matchmaking skills?"

He did not have to say a word to remind her they had dealt together before over the matter of marriage. He did not have to utter anew how she had played a part in his unfortunate match, how she had fostered a relationship that had proven disastrous. His accusations were in his steady gaze, clear for her to see, so clear she could not answer for pondering why he came to her for assistance a second time, in *this* of all matters.

"There are others who offer such a service," she said, her voice uneven, reflecting her unease with the topic of conversation. However, she returned his gaze as steadily as she might.

"And those others are far less successful at their craft."

Her eyebrows rose in surprise at the implication that he had noted any 'success' she may have evinced in the area of matchmaking. It was the very last admission she would have thought to hear from his lips. "Whereas I am more capable at pairing happy couples?"

His mouth twitched in a very brief, darkly wry dance of amusement. "So I am told."

His words stung, but she deserved the sting for trying to solicit a tribute from him. It did not matter that the rest of London claimed she had the talent to help others form love matches, at least it would not matter to Lord Sumner. After all, in the instance of his first and only courtship, Augustine had proven a sorry Cupid when she had allowed Meribah Dempsey to set her cap in Lord Sumner's direction. Augustine had not followed her instincts, had not seen through Meribah's contrivances, and she could not deny it had led to Lord Sumner having to pay the price for the folly that was his marriage.

Of course I did not force *him to ask for Meribah's hand in marriage,* Augustine thought yet again, as she had a hundred times before, so any guilt she carried over the matter was surely ill-placed.

"My dear lady, you have not agreed to assist me," Lord Sumner pointed out, folding his hands against his waistcoat in a patient gesture. "Must I take it you demur?"

"Lord Sumner, how is it you are already free of mourning?" Lady Calcomb asked, saving Augustine from an awkward silence.

He did not bristle at the rude question, or at least gave no external gesture. "My dear lady, I am not free of mourning. Unfortunately there is no time for niceties.

I have determined to wed within the next six weeks, mourning or no." Now there was something in his gaze, a challenge that turned his eyes more silver than blue. They glistened like steel, defying Lady Calcomb to chide him.

Lady Calcomb lifted her chin, but did not offer the set down he might have earned. "Six weeks? Pray tell why so quickly, sir?"

"Indeed, why?" Miss Stoakes chimed in, echoing her mama.

"I must leave the country at that time. I cannot bring my son with me—he is too young, and the company too . . . unsuitable," Lord Sumner explained, his words perhaps chosen with care.

"Ah!" Lady Calcomb cried, her eyes glistening with comprehension. "At last your days at the Foreign Office serve you ill, I think. You have been assigned a task?"

"I have, madam." Lord Sumner inclined his head in acknowledgment.

"By whom?"

"A friend."

"The Prince, you mean!"

Augustine stood, not liking to have a guest grilled in her home, not even this unbidden guest. "Shall I ring for more refreshments—?"

"Am I correct?" Lady Calcomb interrupted her, looking only to Lord Sumner. "Come, come! 'Twas you who raised the matter."

"My friend, madam, asked me to accompany a mutual acquaintance to the Continent—"

"The Continent! With the war yet waging?" Lady Calcomb cried.

"Yes, madam. To friends across the channel."

"Prussia, you mean."

"To friends whose company would not well-suit my young son, nor would, as you indicate, the proximity

and possibility of danger from the war. Marcus, therefore, must remain behind, and he must have someone
to look after him. I require a wife to do that. That is
the sole reason I am here, Lady Calcomb. To solicit
Lady Wayfield's assistance in finding a mother for my
son, and quickly so."

"Surely you have servants who could mind the boy
while you are gone?"

Augustine gave a quick shake of her head, a motion
Lord Sumner may have noted although he did not look
directly to her. "Lady Wayfield only just recently sent
me a missive," he said, giving one quick sardonic twist
to his mouth, "that the aged nanny who sees to Marcus
is not quite as capable as once she was. I have yet to
find an assistant suitable to take her place. Lamentable,
but that is how the situation stands."

"Your father could keep the boy—"

"My father will not be caring for Marcus," Lord Sumner stated, and now there was steel in his voice as well
as his eyes.

"I see!" For just a moment Lady Calcomb appeared
taken aback, but then her usual aplomb settled about
her features. "Far be it from me to tell you how to conduct your affairs, Lord Sumner! I shall not even scold
you for leaving the black crepe behind you. London is
past all that is dull with the Little Season ending so
soon, and so I for one would welcome a wedding," Lady
Calcomb approved, the blue-dyed egret plume in her
turban swaying as she nodded. She turned to Augustine.
"Well, my girl, are you going to assist the man or not?"

"Not so quickly as that, Lady Calcomb," Lord Sumner interrupted, lifting a warning hand. "The lady
rightly waits to find out what I can offer her in repay-
ment for her services."

"I assure you, I have no interest in payment of any
sort," Augustine protested at once.

"Then you say you will assist me? And for nothing? Come, that is hardly equitable. I need someone to work quickly and work well, and such assistance ought not be expected for nothing," Lord Sumner drawled. The drawl was deceptive; she knew that just by the lightning hiding in the depths of his eyes.

"I have only ever helped those willing to help themselves," Augustine said, making her own gaze cool, half expecting sparks to leap from where their gazes locked. "I have only ever seen what was there but unsuspected by the participants. I have never caused anyone to fall in love, only helped them to see the possibility."

"Then this should be simple," he returned, "for I do not look for love. I, in fact, deny any aspiration to find it."

Augustine sharply drew in a breath, for his words were so cool as to almost seem a blasphemy—although her sister, Louise, would say it was so only to an incurable romantic such as herself. The rest of the world would not find it nearly so shocking.

"All I wish in a wife is someone who is decorous, gentle with children, and willing to be a hostess. I declare such a one must be easier to find than one with whom I could 'fall in love.' So, you see the task grows simpler, Lady Wayfield." He paused a moment, his gaze traveling over each occupant of the room until it landed on her once more. "And the compensation I have in mind is one I think might tempt you."

"I doubt there is anything—"

"I have learned, through my humble assistance at the Foreign Office, that a certain object has become available for sale. I propose to act as intermediary, to see that the object is brought from Italy, through Prussia, to England."

Augustine had been prepared to shake her head and decline any offer he could make, but now she froze, staring in genuine surprise. "Italy?"

He nodded. "The object being the marble *The Lady's Boat.*"

"The Lady of Shallot," Augustine said rather breathlessly, feeling her eyes grow round in her head.

"That is the subject matter, yes."

"But I thought that sculpture was not for sale?" Mr. Sydney said, his middle-aged face creased with puzzlement. "Certainly it was not when Lord Wayfield inquired after it three years ago."

"Fortunes change, Mr. Sydney," Lord Sumner replied. "The owner finds he now must locate a buyer, and I have assured him I know of an interested *parti.* He trusts my word and is willing to wait six weeks for a reasonable offer."

Augustine thought at once of the northwest garden at the country estate she had shared with her late husband. She could see the prepared footings that waited yet for the marble that had once been promised but never received. She remembered Christopher's scheme to make of his favorite garden an Arthurian triumph, a clever arrangement of stones and plants intended to evoke a medieval reverie.

She herself had never known any particularly resolute fancy for the scheme, instead merely taking a mild enjoyment from watching Christopher's satisfaction as the garden took shape and form. She knew it stung his pride that the property she had inherited from her maternal grandmama, a duchess in her own right, was better situated and certainly more grand than the one he owned in Sussex. If developing her garden to a new and more glorious degree was his way of assuaging that wounded pride, she had no quibble with that. The garden had become his passion, and Christopher brought it to near-fruition before his death over two years ago— all but for its centerpiece, *The Lady's Boat.*

That marble had been modeled from a painting, a

painting Augustine had adored upon first glimpse when it was presented to her from Christopher as a birthday gift. It had been the romantic in her, again, that had been so struck by the painting of the Lady of Shallot's final ride down the river toward Camelot. When Augustine had looked upon the lady's upturned profile and how the painted maiden leaned forward in the beautiful, gilded boat, one yearning arm stretched out toward the cold grey stone castle on the distant horizon, she had not seen the woman's eventual demise. No, when she had looked at the painting she had seen the woman's love for Launcelot shining through, making her face glow with a light Augustine chose to think of as hope, not grief. When she looked at the painting, she rewrote in her mind's eye an ending for the tale, one in which the Lady of Shallot lives and triumphs, winning the love of Launcelot. The lady would bring the too-inflexible knight to an even truer chivalry, awakening in him the capability of loving anew, of putting aside an unfortunate devotion that could do nothing but harm him and those he loved.

Now the missing marble, the only one planned for the garden that had ever engaged Augustine's whimsy, the final touch to complete Christopher's dying dream, had become available.

And Lord Sumner could act to procure it for her.

Again Augustine found herself speechless. It was not even so much that Lord Sumner had mentioned the one thing that might tempt her, but rather that he knew it would. It had been six years since he had set foot in her home, and yet he somehow knew to offer the one thing that gave her even a moment's pause. With such a gesture, it could be thought that perhaps Lord Sumner paid a trifle more attention to his neighbor's affairs than she ever would have guessed he did.

Or, someone had spoken to him of her affairs.

"Louise," Augustine announced flatly. "Louise told you of Lord Wayfield's attempts to acquire *The Lady's Boat.*"

Lord Sumner gave a brief shake of his head. "My dear lady, it was your husband himself who told me of his wishes. With the war ever raging on, he required the State's assistance if he were to have any hope of bringing the piece into England."

"Oh," Augustine said, chagrined at how she had so quickly thought to blame her sister. Although, it had been a logical conclusion to leap to, for timid Louise had, surprisingly, never echoed her sister's disassociation from Lord Sumner, had in fact declared his wit too droll to abandon. Louise had been the source of more than one awkward moment between the neighbors, and Augustine sometimes suspected her sister understood she was causing friction and for some perverse reason of her own, enjoyed that very fact. It was peculiar behavior for a woman who was in all other respects a rather shy and reticent sort.

"Of course, I do not know the piece, but I can only think you would wish to have it," Lady Calcomb pronounced to Augustine. "Certainly the garden at your Manningstone Hall is lacking its finishing piece, and such a central one, with the brook quite spoilt with those supports just jutting up as they do. I say Sumner names a fair price for your services as a matchmaker. What say you, Lady Wayfield?"

The completed garden had never been Augustine's dream, and yet she could only agree that the raw, unfinished supports awaiting the statue's supposed arrival spoilt the entire effect of her country garden. Still, it was but a garden, and Augustine was not about to be tempted into the folly of making a pact with Lord Sumner because of a mere material item. "I say, 'impossible,' " Augustine announced.

Miss Stoakes looked disappointed, and Lord Sumner grinned, even as his friend, Mr. Prescott, stuck out his lower lip in a decided pout.

The pout puzzled Augustine faintly, even as she decided that Lord Sumner's grin was a particularly unpleasant little grin. She lifted her brows at him, and could not quite keep from looking down her nose. "I am so pleased to see you are amused, my lord."

"Do I appear so? It is only that I always smile when I have won a wager."

"A wager, sir?"

Mr. Prescott's shoulders slumped forward to complete the picture of petulance. "I laid a wager with Sumner here that you would agree to the matter," he explained. "I told him you were the sort to help people. Said you had a talent, and good sense, too."

Augustine felt a flustered blush creep upward from her jawline. It was all she could do not to broaden the space on the settee between herself and Lord Sumner, whose open amusement went beyond vexing.

"Paul also told me you were a good Christian, ever ready to help the needy," he told her.

If she were wearing halfboots rather than mere kid slippers, Augustine would have been terribly tempted to kick Lord Sumner in the shin. That thought immediately alarmed her, for it was years since she had itched to do bodily harm on a provocateur—and it was certainly no proof of any Christian tendencies. The blush spread on her face, so that Augustine had to wonder if her aggravation might actually turn to steam and issue forth from her ears. That grin of his, that mocking, knowing smile!

But oh! Augustine thought of a sudden, *he ever expected me to refuse!* Not only expected it, but most likely counted upon it!

But why make the effort to suggest that which he did not want?

"You truly *do* want my assistance?" she asked, giving a small, puzzled shake of her head.

"I do, madam. I have little time to arrange a marriage before I must leave. I require assistance, especially now that London is so bare of eligible persons."

And you knew the only way I would come to agree was by declaring I would not, by challenging my personal honor, she thought, nearly saying the words aloud.

No matter. She did not need to speak. He knew what he had done, and that she was well aware of it. His smirk told her as much. Oh yes, he wanted her to react to his challenge. He wanted her to be riled into declaring her intention to accept his dare.

So, his need must be great. It was true, London after the Little Season's end would be far leaner when it came to Society. Families returned to their country estates to make the most of autumn's harvest and hunts, and to avoid the mire of winter roads. Those who frequented the marriage marts would have to wait until next spring to meet the newest crop of young ladies seeking betrothals. The populace in the parks reduced severely as the rains and winds of cooler months prevailed, chasing all sensible people within to sit before their fireplaces. In spring, six weeks might not seem too brief a time to secure a betrothal, but in autumn this allotted length of time seemed too restrictive. In winter there were fewer parties, fewer calls, fewer chances to casually meet.

Yes, she saw how he could come to feel his goal would never be achieved without assistance. So why not ask his friends for help? Why not send his acquaintances forth, setting them to bring any eligible *parti* to his notice? But so he had, if the tattlemongers had the right of it! Certainly it was no secret that Lord Sumner, in a manner quite unlike his usual self, was accepting nearly every invitation that came across his butler's salver. She had been told any number of times just this week past of his recent repartee, his cordiality, his willingness to squire ladies through the dance.

Obviously, he and his friends had attained no lasting success however. Lord Sumner, perhaps, had lost faith in his friends' abilities to find a likely candidate—nothing less than desperation, surely, would have brought him across her threshold to ask this favor of her. Of *her!* Of the very one who had brought him and Meribah Dempsey together in his first—and admittedly disastrous—marriage.

Augustine felt a tiny pull at the corners of her mouth, and just barely managed to keep a triumphant smile from forming there. She might have snapped her fingers to show how much she cared for Lord Sumner's schemes, for his 'need.' For once she would not let herself be swayed by her own romantic notions. She would not believe his folderol, nor allow herself to be manipulated into responding to any goads. It would be gratifying to see the surprise on his face when she refused him.

She parted her lips to inform him that his little ploy was not going to work, when he leaned toward her, placing his hand over hers where it rested against the fabric of the settee.

"Lady Wayfield, I do not ask this of you merely for my own sake, but for Marcus' sake especially. Marcus needs a mama."

She pressed her lips back together, her amusement fleeing. She pulled her hand free of his touch, folding it firmly with its mate in her lap.

Marcus. Her neighbor's son. The quiet child who had never resembled his mother but had rather been the miniature mirror of his father. The child had the same fallen-angel handsomeness as his sire, only his brows did not yet slant in derision nor his mouth *moué* in disapproval. The five-year-old had called upon her any number of times in this year past, providing a shy company for Augustine as she trifled in her garden or her kitchen. She could not have summed up the child's need more succinctly than Lord Sumner just had, for it was abundantly clear the lad needed a mother.

His ancient nanny bestowed affection upon the boy, but the woman simply was not adequate to see to the needs of a young child. Nanny took more naps than did the boy, leaving Marcus too free to roam, and her vision was so clouded that Master Marcus was known to wear the remains of his meal or the dust of his play to church. His shoes did not always match, and his hair was seldom combed, at least until his father came home and caught sight of the lad. The very fact Marcus spent hours in Augustine's company—his presence there apparently unknown to Lord Sumner's household except for the occasionally conscientious footman Bert—was a clear sign the boy was ill-attended. The child required someone to sit and read to him, to draw him out into speech. With a father who offered his services to the Foreign Office and so spent hours away from his house, the obvious conclusion was that Marcus indeed needed a mama, a woman far younger than Nanny. Lord Sumner did require a wife, for that reason if no other.

Augustine looked away from Lord Sumner, even as she felt her eyes narrowing in suspicion yet again. As he had acknowledged to Lady Calcomb, she had indeed recently sent Lord Sumner a missive. In it she had commended him for wishing to keep on an old and treasured servant, but also indicating the need for a new or additional nanny for Marcus. Lord Sumner had not deigned to respond to her note at the time, but now she knew for a certainty that he had received it.

Oh yes, Lord Sumner was aware she knew the child lacked in being looked after. He knew exactly how his words would strike her. *Marcus needs a mama* indeed!

Yet, it was only the truth.

"Lord Sumner," Augustine said, the words ending as a sigh. She shook her head, once. "You are quite right. Marcus *does* require a mama. For his sake, and that alone, I will agree to assist you in finding a wife."

Lord Sumner's maddening grin only widened. "Excellent! I promise once everything is settled, I will do everything possible to see your offer for *The Lady's Boat* is accepted, and the marble brought as promptly as may be to your estate in Kent."

"Excellent," she echoed, though with far less enthusiasm. The marble, after all, was only a secondary concern. It was dear, shy, little Marcus' future that was important. That sweet little face, so like Lord Sumner's, ought not be touched by derision, not yet, not at so young an age. A mama, a good woman, could ward away the little cruelties of the world, at least for a while yet.

Lord Sumner rose to his feet. "Then it is settled. I do not mean to be rude, Lady Wayfield, but I am afraid I must depart now—"

"No, you may not," Augustine interrupted, also standing, moving to tug the bellpull.

"Indeed not," Miss Stoakes put in, standing as well, as did the other occupants of the room.

"And why is that?" Lord Sumner asked, lifting an eyebrow in inquiry.

"First you must go through the cards," Miss Stoakes supplied.

"The cards?"

"The personality cards. They are Lady Wayfield's particular invention, and a marvelous tool to her. And to you, I might add."

"Personality cards?" He turned to Augustine, putting his weight back on one heel so that even his pose seemed questioning. "I do not recall any personality cards on that other occasion when I was thinking to wed."

"No," Augustine said, feeling her blush renew itself

at this, yet another reminder of her part in his first marriage. "I only fashioned them a year or so ago. So many people began asking how I knew some couples would suit," she explained at his continuing gaze. "I intended the cards as a way to explain how I compare attributes and needs, and, well, they became a bit of a parlor game, so that everyone came to know of them. It is only natural, now, that everyone expects them. . . ."

"I vow I am entranced. I must see them for myself," Lord Sumner said, looking utterly indifferent.

Augustine put up her chin. "Yes, you must. I believe Miss Stoakes is correct when she says you will find them a marvelous tool."

"Indeed, my lord," Miss Stoakes assured him.

Mosby arrived at the parlor's threshold, the callers' cloaks and hats in hand.

"Oh, but I had hoped to stay and—" Miss Stoakes began to protest at the sight of the coats.

"Come, Deirdre," Lady Calcomb said to her daughter. "I daresay Lord Sumner may have had no compunctions about revealing his matrimonial hopes, but I cannot believe he would wish us to be present when he selects the particulars of his soon-to-be-bride's attributes."

"The process is as painful as all that?" Lord Sumner questioned, looking anything but troubled as he bowed over each lady's hand.

"Silly!" Miss Stoakes said with a giggle. "Not at all! I only wish we could stay and—"

"Come along, Deirdre," Lady Calcomb said firmly. She nodded to Augustine, then turned to lead the way from the room.

Miss Stoakes gave a pretty little frown, but otherwise acquiesced by bidding her hostess *adieu.* Her murmured thank yous were echoed by Lord Eubank and Mr. Sydney as they gathered their belongings and made their departures as well. Mr. Prescott remained, having received a nod from his friend.

Lord Sumner turned from the open doorway to face Augustine, his arms folded before his chest. Augustine braced herself to hear some pithy remark or observation, but Lord Sumner contented himself by leveling on her the whole of his silent attention. She gazed back, feeling rather childish as they indulged in what increasingly felt very like the staring contests she had known as a child; all the same, she found she was unwilling to look away first.

Mr. Prescott cleared his throat, breaking the odd silent competition as both participants turned to him. "Well then?" he asked, lifting his shoulders.

"Let us move to the library," Augustine said. She shook her head, as if to clear it of dust, and made a gesture with her hand to indicate the direction. "The light is better there," she explained to Mr. Prescott.

"Of course," he answered with a smile. A pleasant smile, she observed, quite unlike Lord Sumner's odious grins.

The small party moved down the short hall to the library, where she gestured a second time, to indicate the two chairs arranged before the large writing desk. The gentlemen moved before the seats, standing until Augustine first sat, then settling themselves in the large wing chairs.

She opened the top drawer to pull out a stack of vellum papers, neatly trimmed to two inch by four inch rectangles and stiffened by a clear wax coating. She placed the stack of homemade cards before Lord Sumner, then folded her hands together, settling them on the top of the desk.

"Now, my lord," she said, meeting his dubious gaze, "You will tell us what manner of wife you require."

Two

"Ah, I see," Lord Sumner replied as he gathered the stack of cards in his hands, briefly fanning their edges as he glanced at the penned words upon them. "An attribute is written on each. I assume I select those to indicate which attributes I am seeking in a wife?"

"Exactly so," Mr. Prescott assured him, leaning forward to view the cards for himself.

"You have seen this done before, I presume?" Lord Sumner asked his friend.

"Quite. At parties and all, as Lady Wayfield said. I thought sure you would have heard of Lady Wayfield's cards?"

Lord Sumner shook his head.

"They are simple enough, my lord, even as you have indicated," Augustine said. "Just pick out the cards of those characteristics that would suit you. But do not be too quick to select," she cautioned as she reached in the drawer again, this time pulling forth some paper, a quill, and a fully stocked inkstand. "Occasionally someone will not see what he or she seeks, or there may be another word that would better suit. You must feel free to speak of anything I do not have listed."

"There cannot be much not listed—there must be fifty selections here!" Lord Sumner said. He set the stack down. "But this is not necessary. I have already stated my requirements. She is to be patient with children, content to serve as hostess, and I believe I also asked that she be decorous in her general behavior."

"But there is so much more to a marriage than children, parties, and a public persona, my lord!" Augustine chided him. She tested the point of her quill with her fingertip, finding it well enough trimmed, then reached to remove the stopper from the bottle of India ink. "I believe you will be surprised how much more thought ought to go into this decision. You will, God willing, be married many years, and so some common beliefs or interests are essential, you must realize."

"They might prove pleasant perhaps, but such commonality is not essential." He renewed his smile, although now the gesture had grown somewhat strained.

Augustine ignored his comment, dipping the quill's nib into the inkpot. She poised the readied quill over the paper before her. "Now, let us dispose of the basic requirements."

"Basic?"

"Such as those things which everyone requires. The basic attributes that make a person worthy of anyone's esteem," Augustine explained, putting ink to paper. "Your wife-to-be must, of course, be kind-hearted and trustworthy." She looked up, smiling slightly. "No one has ever wished to have a thief or a liar for a spouse."

"I am conventional enough to also wish any wife of mine would lack those particular characteristics," Lord Sumner said quietly. The smile faded from his face, but perhaps there remained yet a wry hint of it in his eyes all the same. Of course, Meribah Dempsey had proven to be a liar if not a thief, and he might well be pondering that very fact.

Augustine looked to her sheet of paper, avoiding his gaze. "She must be loyal—although I realize this word can mean many things to various people." Oh dear, *loyal.* Another word to bring unfortunate memories of the deceased Meribah to mind. Augustine cleared her throat ever so gently, still looking at the paper rather than at Lord Sumner. There was nothing for it but to go on. "And of course one's spouse is expected to be clean in their person and their habits, and of good health. There, that covers the expected items. Now as to education—"

"You surprise me," Lord Sumner interjected, glancing down at the top-most card and indicating its printed message with the touch of a finger. "Do you mean to say 'cheerful' is not one of the 'expected attributes'?"

"It is not, for you see, I have found some people find cheerful persons to be most exasperating, especially in the morning. But you remind me, I should have listed that a generally even temper is, of course, expected as well." She noted as much on her paper. "Now, let me ask again. As to education? Must she have attended a seminary for young ladies? How many languages must she be able to speak?"

"French, of course," he answered her last question first. "And some Italian would be well, if not essential. Otherwise, a standard education is all that is well and good," he stated crisply. "Just so she can read, do basic figures, and speak with some knowledge of historically important events. Nothing untoward, mind you, but it is important in my circles that one have at least some grasp of the past and of the state of current world events. Not a blue-stocking, of course, but someone with a notion of geography would be helpful, as she will sometimes need to entertain visitors to the Foreign Office. I should not care to have my wife confuse Austria with Australia."

Augustine felt a smile tug at her mouth at the thought. "No, that would never do. But that goes to my next question, as to social standing—I assume you do not care to marry outside the blood?"

"What? Do you mean a cit's daughter? Of course not! I do not require that my pockets be lined anew."

"I did not mean to imply any need in that regard, Lord Sumner, but these questions must be asked. Marriage is too important an estate for delicacy on my part to lead us astray."

"I dare say so," he said, and his pointed gaze could have bored a hole right through her. Meribah again! Did he not understand that Meribah had led her astray as much as she had him? No, of course not. He never accepted that Augustine, too, had also been duped by the clever but shallow young Meribah.

"Age?" she asked, doing her best not to acknowledge his speaking gaze.

He waved a hand. "Not so old she wishes to mother me. Not so young she wishes me to be her father."

Augustine took her quill away from the paper, making no note. She met his gaze, returning a level one of her own. "Religion?"

He gave a dismissive shake of his head. "Church of England, of course."

"Come, that will not do. You must tell me *something* more, my lord. After all, you have a young boy to raise and religion certainly plays a part in his training. Ought this wife to be devout? One to attend services regularly? Or is your household one that prefers a more, shall we say, *casual* attendance at services? Do you wish her to school your son in biblical teachings or—"

"No, I do not! Tutors may be hired for that manner of thing. I will not have any wife of mine preaching to my son or to me."

Augustine spread her hands. "I see. Go on."

Lord Sumner stared at her, flickers of annoyance flashing through his light eyes. He sat back and took a breath, thinking, until finally he sat forward again, making a shooing notion. "Put 'tranquil' on your list, Lady Wayfield," he stated. "And 'patient.' Those are the only words I can think of to describe how this paragon's religious virtues might be inscribed."

"Well enough," she informed him, her quill making its scratching noises as she noted the two words on her list. She looked up, indicating the stack of cards before him with the feathery tip of her quill pen. "Only the cards remain. If you would be so good?"

"Hmm," he said, looking once again to the card uppermost on the stack. " 'Cheerful.' I see what you mean. The company of someone who is too-consistently cheerful could quickly pall."

He put the card aside, looking at the next card, marked 'Loving.' He hesitated a moment longer, then that, too, was put aside. "Ah, here is one," he said, staring down at the next card in the pile, his lips pursed as he pondered its single word. He reached for it, handing 'Biddable' across the desk to her.

Augustine accepted the card, placing it on the desktop so that he might still read it, upside-down from her position behind the desk. She did not cluck her tongue, although she felt she wished to. 'Biddable' indeed! It was not the first time the card had been selected, and not for the first time did she wonder exactly what the word meant to the selector. It was certainly a word preferred by the gentlemen rather than the ladies. She noted it on her sheet, just keeping her lip from curling as she wrote.

He next turned up 'Decisive,' tossing it aside without second thought. The same happened for 'Inquisitive' and 'Helpful.'

"Not 'Helpful'?" Mr. Prescott asked, looking puzzled.

"That sounds far too much as though we were entering into a contract or a business together. I want a host-ess, not a partner."

"I thought a wife *was* a partner," Mr. Prescott observed. "Of sorts," he added when Lord Sumner fixed a cool eye on him. "You know, 'ye shall cleave one unto another.' That manner of biblical preachings and what all," he hurried on, his final words little more than mumbled.

"Feel free to select a wife of your own when I am done here," Lord Sumner told him, turning his gaze back to the next card in his hand. "Ah, 'Talkative'! I daresay that would suit you, Paul."

Mr. Prescott's response was to cross his arms and mutter, "Only meant to help."

"I do not require help in this particular matter," Lord Sumner replied. However, his tone had lost its cool edge, letting just enough humor into his words that any real sting was missing.

" 'Course not," Mr. Prescott agreed, looking mollified. "You must select to suit yourself. Of course."

Augustine raised an eyebrow. Lord Sumner treated his friends to a measure of consideration he did not grant those of whom he disapproved. She had become rather used to his eternally acerbic ways, and was faintly surprised to be reminded that he could take the frost from his tone if he wished to. She recalled that once she had thought of him in terms of being a suitable, even amusing, acquaintance. In all truthfulness, she had once thought to call him 'friend.' She reluctantly admitted that he had, at times, been gracious, even sweet. . . . Although, that had been years ago and with too few hints of those virtues since, she reminded herself.

"Go on," she said, indicating the cards.

He passed over many selections, scarcely glancing at them, although he did select 'Slow to Anger,' 'Well-

Read,' 'Motherly,' 'Gentle,' 'Courteous,' 'Considerate,' and 'Fond of Animals.'

Only the last surprised her in any way. "Well," she said slowly, reading the list over again. She raised her eyes to his. "Congratulations, Lord Sumner. You have just described a mother."

Did his skin darken with a flush for a moment, or was that her imagination? Certainly she could not claim he looked utterly pleased with her pronouncement. "That is rather to the point, would you not say?" he asked crisply.

"Yes," she admitted, "But it will not serve by itself. My good sir, will you not admit that this woman is to not only be mother to your child but also wife to you? Simply put, I could in the next hour find a dozen women willing to marry you, and of those, two might even suit as a parent to your son. However, none of them, I assure you, would suit you, sir. You have not asked me to find you a nanny, but a *wife!* You simply must cooperate with me, or else I will have to decline this commission!"

"And I have told you I am not seeking a 'love match'," he said from between tight lips.

"Have *I* said aught concerning a love match?" Augustine cried, one hand to her chest as if she would take an oath. "I can understand your need for haste. I can even understand your wish not to be devoted to this woman, but I cannot understand why you do not allow me to assist you in at least finding someone with whom you can bear to share a room!"

She stopped abruptly, having meant any room but belatedly realizing her words rather implied the sharing of a bedchamber. A flush of mingled embarrassment and irritation surged into her cheeks, one that only grew when he half-laughed and said, "Well! The kitten spits! No, no, Lady Wayfield, do not scold me for another moment! I am properly chastised. You are right, at least to the degree that any discord between his elders will be felt by my son. Of course I must make every effort to have a cordial alliance with this wife-to-be."

"Cordial alliance!" she echoed, frowning at him.

"I shall do as you bid. Meekly. Mildly. Look, here, I have selected an attribute just for me. 'Musical.' See? I have reformed. Do allow me to go through the stack again."

"I am being mocked," she said, her lips thinning.

"I assure you, no, not mocked. I cannot help it that I am not a True Believer in your cause of Romance, good lady, but at least allow me to enter the temple and attempt to believe, hmm?"

She glared at him, but then slowly, half-unwillingly, the anger that had been building inside her turned into something else. Determination perhaps. Certainly resolve. "You came here," she said clearly, tapping the desktop twice with her finger, "thinking you had nothing to lose. At last I understand how it is you could bring yourself to ask this service of me. You feel you risk nothing."

"Indeed, what do I risk, madam? I presume you are about to tell me," he said, oh-so-politely.

"Why, you smug, arrogant—!" She snapped her mouth closed, taking a quick, deep breath. "But no! I shall not fling insults at your head. No, my lord, I will do much more. I will find you the wife you seek, and one of whom you may be proud, mark me. *That,* my lord, is the risk you took when you entered my door: that I would be successful."

"I assure you, that is my every hope—"

"Stuff!"

"I wish you would explain what you mean by that," Lord Sumner said in a soft voice, and now it was his turn to frown at her.

Augustine gazed at Mr. Prescott, for he nodded every so often, as if he, for one, grasped the importance of this matter of marriage. She had an ally (if not a very vocal one) who at least made it clear she did not speak in some odd, foreign tongue. Certainly to measure by Lord Sumner's responses, she might as well do so. She sat back, putting the quill aside to primly fold her hands together.

"I do not explain," she stated succinctly, in the manner of one who is speaking to the daft. "That is not my purpose here, my lord." She unfolded her hands to reach and push the stack of cards another inch closer to him. "We will begin again. Select anew, this time with a wife—rather than a mother—in mind."

He remained still a moment, then executed a small, perhaps slightly mocking bow from his seat. "As it pleases my lady," he said, picking up the stack.

He selected 'Well-Spoken,' 'Sensible,' 'Logical,' 'Cordial,' and, after a moment's hesitation, 'Honorable.'

"This one as well," he said, flipping 'Amiable' toward her. His eyes had turned to steel again beneath half-lowered lids. "After all, one of her greatest duties will be to serve as hostess, to make my guests comfortable."

It was interesting, Augustine thought, that he had selected the additional term, for 'Amiable' could be said to be a word much like 'Cordial.' Yet, there was a subtle difference between the two words. Amiable implied a shade more tolerance; it was a trifle less constrained. Certainly Meribah had been amiable . . . too amiable. She was a woman who had wanted admirers, who did not know she ought to surrender some aspects of flirtation with other men once she was wed . . . did not know, or did not wish to know.

How curious that Lord Sumner did not shy from the word, that he thought it important any wife of his should be more than merely cordial. Could it be, as he claimed, a requirement of his office? Perhaps.

Some of the attributes he had passed over had not surprised her: 'Flirtatious,' 'Determined,' 'Frugal.' She had been faintly intrigued to see him dismiss for a second time the term 'Quiet.' She would have thought he would want someone of few words . . . but perhaps there had been too few words between him and Meribah in the last months of their marriage. Even Augustine, the shunned neighbor, had been aware of the strain running rampant between Lord and Lady Sumner. It had been a strain so acute that servants had scarce wept when that lady had succumbed to cholera.

Lady Sumner was almost a year gone, and an embittered Lord Sumner remained . . . as did a sweet and innocent boy named Marcus. So then, Marcus would have his new mama, and as for Lord Sumner—well! He would have a wife and, tease as he would, that wife would be more than Meribah had ever been to him. Augustine would see to it that this wife would be a good woman, a woman he would have to admire . . . and, perhaps, despite himself, even come to love. Silently Augustine vowed it . . . for Marcus' sake of course.

And, perhaps, just a little, for the cynical Lord Sumner's sake as well.

"I believe I am now free to take my leave?" he questioned, rising to his feet, as did Mr. Prescott.

"Except that we have yet to agree when we begin," Augustine told him.

"Of course. Paul here has no objection to my using his assembly tomorrow night as a device for launching this enterprise. Would you be able to attend, my lady?"

She looked to Mr. Prescott, who bowed toward her. "Please accept my invitation to attend, Lady Wayfield."

"Thank you, I do." She repaid his bow with a nod of her head. "That will suit admirably, as six weeks is very little time." She stood, motioning toward the door.

"Come, gentlemen. I will summon Mosby to see you out."

Mr. Prescott smiled, apparently pleased with the day's work, and led the way from the room. Augustine's butler was quick to see the callers were leaving, snapping his fingers at a footman to send the man after the gentlemen's cloaks. Their belongings were promptly restored, and then Mosby moved to open the door for them.

There was an immediate sound of multiple claws scraping against the floor tiles and a serenade of howls and yips as a pack of hounds leaped and tumbled through the open doorway.

"Out!" Lord Sumner said firmly, although not loudly, to the creatures.

The cacophony at once subsided, and each tail drooped behind a set of hind legs as the dogs turned tail and exited whence they had come. One, a short-legged terrier, was waggish enough to execute a circle balanced only on his hind legs, but with that completed and a unyielding stare from Lord Sumner, he, too, exited. Each of the six animals cast longing glances over their shoulders, their tails coming up to offer a few hopeful waves as they retreated.

"I beg your pardon. They must have got free of my houndsman. They are not always best behaved," Lord Sumner said, thereby verbally claiming ownership of the motley assemblage.

Augustine knew Lord Sumner chose to keep his hounds with him, and since he spent so much time in London to be near the Foreign Office, that meant the dogs were most times in the city as well. There were nights when the wind blew the wrong direction, carrying the animals' howls and yips to Augustine's window from the stalls Lord Sumner rented at the nearby mews. There were nights, too, when he let them have the run of the garden at the rear of his home, although she had to admit they were banished from there if they took to barking.

"Paul?" Lord Sumner asked as a liver-spotted setter crept back inside the house, "would you be so kind as to call Admiral out?"

Mr. Prescott did not take the request amiss, stepping outside to call the dog after him. The setter did not go at once, but after a softly growled "Go!" from Lord Sumner, the dog retreated.

"They mind you very well," Augustine said, half-inclined to call the dog back and offer its ears a caress or two to cause that saddened tail to rise again. A sudden image of Marcus leaped into her mind, and she could not help but think how quiet and unobtrusive the lad was when he came to call upon her. Had he, like the hounds, been trained to do exactly as Lord Sumner bid? Was his presence just as easily and summarily dismissed? Oh, hopefully not. A widower's only child? His son, his heir? Surely Lord Sumner had some time to give the boy? She had seen them together, of course, but could she honestly say she had seen a happy moment shared between the two?

"What company do you go to that is so unsuitable for Master Marcus?" Augustine asked abruptly.

Lord Sumner looked down at her, and she thought for a moment he would either make no answer at all or else tell her some taradiddle. Instead he sighed. "I suppose you have a right to know, that you might understand why I seek a hasty wedding. I swear you to silence, however. Quite simply and with little polish upon the truth of it: Lady Quiggmore's husband returns from his assignment to Vienna in six weeks, perhaps seven. He has got wind of the . . . indiscretions in which his wife has recently engaged with a certain member of a distinguished family. He has not taken the news well. The member whom she—"

"The Prince?"

"The member," he repeated, his tone making it quite clear no further representation on that matter would be forthcoming, "has requested that I escort Lady Quiggmore from the country. He feels she must be out of harm's way, at least until such time as her husband may be reassigned to further duties, and, hopefully, a lessening of his reputedly high emotion on the matter. It is believed that it will, in time, become evident to Lord Quiggmore that his wife is far removed from the source of . . . er, her temptation, and that his ire will cool."

"Ah," Augustine said.

"You need not purse your mouth at me, Lady Wayfield. I have not contrived the situation. I have only agreed to assist a friend in a matter about which he feels strongly. He is most concerned for the lady's wellbeing, even if their association no longer exists."

"Hmm."

He almost smiled, and made a sound that was a cross between a sigh and a laugh. "I do not exactly approve either, my lady, but the fact remains I am committed to the task. I am equally committed that Marcus shall not spend time with such company, nor in the court of those to whom Lady Quiggmore goes for succor. Think what you will of me for agreeing to be the errand boy in this matter, but at least agree with me that I do well not to involve my son."

"I do agree on that count!" she said at once, for she fully did. His frank words had the ring of truth about them, and they forced her to acknowledge he must, after all, harbor at least some measure of concern for his son's upbringing. Perhaps Lord Sumner did not indulge the boy, did not seek his son's company for its own sake, but neither was he wholly indifferent to the child's welfare.

"Good. Then you can understand my haste to marry,

given that I do not choose to place Marcus with any of my family while I am gone." He fell silent a moment, his steady gaze evaluating her even as a muscle along his jaw twitched. "My father . . . ," he said, the words obviously reluctant. "My father was not a man of any warmth, Lady Wayfield. He was a stern taskmaster. He has not softened with age, and I have deemed Marcus a lad who would not . . . prosper under his charge. My sister's house already runs to overflowing with her own infants, with another on the way. She has neither time nor patience for yet another child in her household. I cannot send Marcus to her."

"I see," Augustine said neutrally. She stood very still, in the way she always did when sensing a strong emotion emanating from another. She could tell he was not pleased to say these things to her, was not content to reveal any further personal aspects of his life, his requirements. It cost him, just a small measure, in pride to do so.

"Good. I am glad you see. You must understand the urgency of the matter," he stated firmly.

"I do," she said, and after a moment's hesitation, boldly added, "For why else would you have come to *me?*"

The muscle in his jaw stopped its twitching. In fact, his entire visage froze still as pond ice for the length of one heartbeat, but then something resembling a tight smile flitted across his mouth. "Exactly."

"Exactly," she echoed. "After Meribah—"

"Madam, we will not speak of Meribah."

"I believe you should know she manipulated me, my lord, much as you have manipulated my part in this scheme today—"

"We will not speak of her, Lady Wayfield. I will not allow it," he commanded, any hint of a smile once again gone. "Although your husband could never tell you nay—"

"So you have said in the past!" she snapped, well aware of his opinion that she had always bull-led Christopher. The comment had ever stung . . . in part because she could not categorically claim it was untrue.

"But *I* shall say you nay, and tell you this is one subject that will not be a part of our discussions in the future."

He did not give her any chance to respond, turning and striding out the open door.

"Well!" she exclaimed, rather wishing she had taken the opportunity to kick his shin when it had been presented. Instead she crossed her arms before her and tilted her head to one side as she watched his retreating back, a sportsman's back with wide shoulders finely clothed in charcoal-grey superfine. Truly, he was a finely made man . . . and one who could easily aggravate. He had not troubled himself to put any polish on how he felt about any future mention of the subject of Meribah. "My dear Lord Sumner," she said, her voice a mere whisper, not even intended for Mosby's ears, let alone those of Lord Sumner. "How can we never discuss her? Every attribute you chose this morning is Meribah all over again."

Augustine shook her head and stepped back, allowing Mosby to close the door. "But, my blustering, arrogant Lord Sumner," she murmured to the echo of his presence, "you do not realize that, do you?"

Three

Her sister, Louise, arrived no more than fifteen minutes later. "My dear Augustine," she cried, sweeping into the room almost before Mosby could announce her. "I have just heard!"

"Heard? Indeed, heard what?" Augustine asked, taking her sister's outstretched hands and leading her to the nearest settee. Louise looked well today, her light brown hair piled artfully atop her head, her fashionable gown proclaiming the healthy extent of her husband's purse and the return of her figure following the birth of her daughter. The reticent manner Louise sometimes adopted in public was nowhere to be seen today.

"Do not be coy with me! You know very well I can only be referring to Joseph's call this morning."

Augustine did not lift her eyebrows at the use of Lord Sumner's Christian name—after all, Louise had never ceased to call the man her friend. Instead Augustine merely wrinkled her nose at her sister. "Oh, pish. That."

"That? Yes, that. How long has it been? Five years since your little rift? No, six, for the little boy—"

"Marcus."

"Yes, Marcus must be nearing five already."

"He turned five this summer past."

Louise slid her gloves from her hands, and untied her bonnet, settling both on the sofa table. "Miss

Stoakes told all, or as much as she knows," she went on eagerly. "Is it true, Augustine? Did Joseph really come here to ask you to help him find a new wife? Miss Stoakes says they left when it was time to bring out your cards. Did Joseph go through them? What attributes is he looking for?"

"Louise, so many questions! It is quite unlike you to chatter on so," Augustine chided gently.

"But you know how fond I am of weddings! Even as you are."

"Not so much weddings, my dear, as the fact that two people have found each other and fallen in love."

"How unfashionable you are!" Louise said, giving a light laugh over the seasoned joke. "But how glad I am that you do not care tuppence for fashion, at least in the matter of marriage. With your help, I managed to marry a man Mama could approve of, and whom I could love."

Augustine smiled at her sister even as she experienced an old, expected pang. Yes, unlike herself, Louise had been far more than gratified with her groom, Mr. Andrew Sheffler, who had since inherited his father's title of Viscount Ruchert. Augustine acknowledged she had played a fair role in assisting that marriage of two hearts. In fact, her sister's on-going happiness had soon forced Augustine to admit to herself she did indeed have a talent for pairing couples. Alas, if only that talent had extended to her own affairs of the heart.

Augustine looked down at the wedding ring adorning her left ring finger. It was a simple gold band, round and one piece, meant to symbolize everlasting love and commitment, but now it served only as a mockery of that ideal. Oh, Christopher Laurence had been a fine husband to her. Really, there was shamefully little she could complain about regarding his person, his habits, or his demeanor during the four and a half years they were married. Following their wedding day, he had not proven to be utterly boorish, or unkind, or purely self-concerned. He had seldom embarrassed her in public, had never slighted her before guests (even if he increasingly had found no time for her in private) . . . and yet she had not loved him, not really, not even in the early days of their marriage.

It had taken only a few weeks for her to realize that. During their courtship, she had mistaken the strange tingling of physical attraction as a sign of love. In fact, it was not until she experienced that same tingling in the theater three months after her wedding that she understood a fascination with a person's physical being was not the same thing as love. The actor below their box excited in her the same flushed feeling she had known while being courted by Christopher. *What is this?* she remembered thinking, *I do not love that actor.* She was only attracted to his presence, to the role he played, entranced by the pretty lines he recited.

In horror she had recognized she was merely being assaulted by the actor's skill, his ability to cast forth an allure. Her response to him was nothing more than a physical ardor. In three short months she had come to know there was such a thing, that the body could create a buzz of excitement, acute, sharp, desirous. The brief longing she had experienced looking down at the handsome actor was the transitory kind, she knew that now. She had not, could not want the man in her life, of course not, not outside a daydream or two. But, oh, how familiar that enchantment had felt, how aware she had been of its brevity! It was the same thrill she had once known for the man who had become her husband.

Through a long, sleepless night she had at last admitted to herself that the burgeoning possibilities of courtship had been the intoxicant that had drawn her to Christopher Laurence. Unfortunately, in short order that intoxication had faded from their married state. At first Christopher's every difference, his maleness, his whiskered cheek, his deep voice, his large hands had been enough to hold her spellbound—they had all been so exotic to her. So unknown, so attractive because they had been unfamiliar. When he had decided to court her, the mere fact he fixed his attention on her, singled her out among the other misses making their debuts, served to turn her head, to make her fall in love with being in love. She was of an age to marry, of course, and with Louise due to make her come-out the following year, it behooved Augustine as the older sister to wed as soon as may be. The elder really ought to marry first, and Louise was so pretty that Augustine knew it would not be long before offers were made.

So Augustine was inclined to fall in love, or at least to seek a semblance of it. The spring flowers scented the air, the fascination of the routs and balls of her first season filled her eyes, and Christopher Laurence, Lord Wayfield, had been handsome and admiring of her.

So deeply had she been beneath the spell of infatuation, she had not awakened from it until the vows were said, the bargain sealed.

That awakening had proven a nightmare—a quiet, unspoken nightmare, for she knew Christopher was not a horrible man, was in fact someone that another someone might have wholly adored. For someone else the fact that he was quiet and introspective would have suited perfectly. His lack of decisiveness might have been the very thing for the kind of woman who prefers her own opinion over all others. His refusal to ever argue might be all that was charming for another—but for Augustine his ways were too quiet, too unassuming, too . . . lacking. To her horror, it had taken but a few weeks to realize that, although she found in Christopher a pleasant companion, she had not found a mate whom she could admire and adore.

She had never said one word to him of her feelings. How could she? Augustine had no one to reproach but herself. The matchmaker in her had shut her eyes, and it was not Christopher's fault that she had made such a colossal mistake. She could not love him, but she could try to be a good wife to him, especially if he never knew of her dissatisfaction with their union.

Many times Augustine thought to gain her freedom, to persuade Christopher to accept the cost, humiliation, and social stigma of a divorce by Parliamentary decree—except that Christopher never seemed unhappy. He accepted, seemingly as inevitable, the gradual cooling and distancing between them. He planned his garden, rode to his hounds, attended his clubs, and never evinced a single sign there might be more between husband and wife. He gave every indication of contentment . . . with, in the last months, one exception: he took a mistress.

Still, he had come to Augustine's bed at times—on quarter days, rather as though he were the landowner collecting the rent. She could not think of Michaelmas or Lady Day without a bittersweet bubble of humor at the thought of his punctual—and brief—returns to her bed.

He was dutiful to her, in his way, as much as she was to him. They threw their parties, gave their gifts, issued in their New Years, decorated their houses, and passed their days in proximity if not in love. Their greatest misfortune had been the lack of children, for the begetting of offspring had been the sole remaining hope that had prompted their metered reunions in the spousal bed. She had often wondered, especially in the early days, that if she had produced a child or two would it have made a difference? In loving her offspring, would she have come to love their father?

There would never be any answer to that question, for after two years and seven months of marriage, Christopher had died. The doctors assured her there had been no way to know his heart was weak. He had expired in his beloved not-quite-finished Arthurian garden, collapsing on one of the carved benches he had put in place himself. It was where he would have chosen, she supposed.

Louise patted Augustine's arm, startling her out of her reverie. "You are thinking of Christopher again," her sister said. "I can tell by the guilt on your face."

"Guilt?" Augustine shook her head. "Regret perhaps."

"You were good to him. He died of a weak heart, not a broken one," Louise scolded. "If anyone had a broken heart, it was you."

"I sometimes think you ought to have been born to a life in the theater, Louise. You are so dramatic." Augustine softened the words with a smile. Louise was not far from the mark, however. There had been times when Augustine had thought she would pack a valise and simply ride out into the night, simply leave behind the emptiness in her home and her heart.

Curious, then, to recall that it was Joseph—Lord Sumner—who had given her the strength to face her life, to maintain her marriage. She would never forget that night.

She remembered Christopher had been in his study, lost, as usual, to some distraction he had not chosen to share with her. Augustine had been abovestairs in her chamber, alone and lonely, idly penning a letter to Mama in Berkshire, or at least pretending at the task. It had been storming all day, the grey skies carrying over into a gloomy evening. Large drops of rain pat-

tered at her darkened windowpanes, tossed there by
errant winds. The flames on her bedroom grate danced
in primal celebration of the storm, while the occasional
puffs of smoke forced back down the chimney scented
the air with acrid gusts.

The storm made her restless, and she knew a strange
desire to howl as the wind did, to dash through the
streets of London, unfettered, unmindful of destination
or restriction. She gave up any pretense at writing, instead pacing before the fire. Even though she had ex-
amined her feelings a thousand times, she could not
keep from wondering, yet again, why this restlessness
must fill her soul. Her unhappiness did not extend from
anything Christopher did, for he was never cruel to
her . . . but was he ever truly kind? Did he ever exercise
an effort on her part beyond that he would extend to
any female? When he offered her his hand, he never
squeezed her fingers in support nor humor. When he
offered her a lap blanket, he never tucked it around
her with lingering hands. There had been a time when
his hands had tarried upon her, had there not? Or had
she just been too terribly naive and only imagined his
good manners to be a lover's caress?

Part of her had wished to go downstairs, to find Christopher. "Christopher, I demand something more than
a polite tolerance from you," she would state clearly,
calmly. "I demand that we find a way to go on that is
less distant, less detached. I demand that you . . ."
There her imagination always stopped, for what did she
wish to demand? Even if she could find the words to
express her longings, another part of her knew it was
unfair to demand that which she might never return.
But must that be true? Could she return his love? If
Christopher ever loved her, truly loved her, could her
initial attraction to him have turned into love?

Could he have yet, if he wished to, wooed and won

her heart? She had stood, half-convinced she would go to him, tell him what was in her thoughts, what she so craved, so hoped he could understand. . . . Only to sit down again before her writing table, her resolution dying even as it was made. It was not a new thought. It was an old hope, one that had never borne fruit before. How many times had she tried to compel love to grow? How many times had she attempted to bridge the fundamental gap in their union by exercising any talent she might possess at charm or sexual allure? Temporary interest had been the best result; indifference the worst.

Harping certainly never did any good, and it galled her almost as much as it surely did Christopher. She would not beg for that which he did not have the ability to give her. As things stood now, Christopher did not love her, but at least he could respect her; she would not lose the one consideration they possessed yet between them in their private life.

So she paced alone in her room, her steps tapping out a regulated pattern that the errant wind outside the window declined to imitate.

What had drawn her to the window? A sound? A shadow's movement in the darkness? Something had stopped her restless pacing and led her to look down from her bedchamber into the stormy night. Her window overlooked the cart path between her home and that of Lord Sumner. The path provided access to the mews they shared with four houses on the far side of the alley that ran behind their properties. She also had a partial view of the street before her house, but a better view of the small garden at the back of Lord Sumner's townhouse.

There was a light down there, in his garden, that of a flame leaping. Augustine caught her breath, fearing a tipped lantern or neglected candle. There were roofed shelters pressed up against the far wall, to provide some protection from the elements for the dogs; perhaps while working with the animals someone had forgot to take away their candle? Despite the rain, it was possible whatever wood or rugs were kept dry by the shelters themselves might take flame. Many a house had burned down in the midst of rainfall, a fire's appetite outstripping nature's attempt at fire control.

Augustine had thrown up her sash, leaning out into the night, hoping to see someone run to control the flame. A dash of rain struck her in the face, making her blink. She sighed with relief, however, when she saw the shape of a man below. She almost called to him, to be sure he knew of the fire, only to realize a second later that the flame was contained inside a lantern, and that the man was Lord Sumner. It was impossible to mistake his tall form even if the dogs had not scurried out into the rain to greet him with gleefully wagging tails. How odd—Lord Sumner wore no coat, having come out into the rain in his shirtsleeves and waistcoat only.

Augustine began to pull back inside the window frame when a strange keening sound struck her ears. It must be the dogs, those hounds of Lord Sumner's. And yes, it was, for they rushed about the man's feet, giving little yips of surprise and greeting, but it was something . . . no, someone else as well. It was Lord Sumner, mingling that haunting sound with those of the dogs. A shiver ran up Augustine's spine at the sound that was not quite a howl . . . perhaps something more like a wounded animal's warning snarl. Was this some greeting he gave his hounds? But no, Lord Sumner did not reach to pet a head or scratch behind an ear, nor did he kick out at the animals as his strange pained growl seemed to imply he might.

The swinging light from the lantern picked out odd details: the fisted hand at his side, the angry lift of his

chin, the whites of his eyes, the rigidity in his movements. Something seemed to crackle in the air, lightning perhaps, or perhaps it was the anger she felt even
across the distance, even despite the cover of the storm.
He moved with the stiff jerky movements of a man en-
raged, and now she recognized that keening sound as
a simple howl of fury.

Augustine gasped as Lord Sumner stopped abruptly,
dropping the lantern and plunging his face into the
cover of his hands. He stood still a moment, then slowly
sank to sit on a bench pressed against the house, his
elbows on his knees, the very picture of despair.

The sound—now no longer a howl and not quite a
sob, but having become something far more forlorn—
broke off into abrupt silence, leaving only the sounds
of the storm to be heard. Even the dogs became subdued, surrounding their master, trying to lick at his
face, padding in the mud at his feet. If they whimpered
in sympathy, the sound did not carry to Augustine's
ears.

But how wrong of her to observe his torment! He
obviously sought a private moment to come through
whatever interior storms racked him, and even though
he was clearly not aware of Augustine's observation, it
was wrong of her to invade his privacy. She pulled back
into her room and reached to close the window, only
to halt abruptly when the strange cry began again.

Augustine stood frozen, listening as the sound shifted
and rose and shaped itself into full-throated laughter,
a cautionless laugh of the sort she could easily imagine
Lucifer making from his desolate throne in Hades. This
was the sound of anger, not at others, but at one's self,
an anger too large to be confined to just one emotional
response, too great for simple wrath or sobs. Laughter
or tears or rage; this was the sound when all three
clashed together.

She moved closer to the open window, watching as Lord Sumner turned his face up to the stormy skies, his laughter fading from the air if not from Augustine's ears. He was uncaring of the rain splashing into his eyes, his mouth.

"How unhappy he looks," Augustine said to herself, shivering as rain and wind blew in to tangle the light fabric of her curtains with the hem of her skirt.

Just when she felt she could not bear to watch a moment longer, Lord Sumner lowered his face, glancing about himself, blinking like a man just awakening. He put out a hand, and one of the dogs stretched forward to meet his touch, its tail tentatively wagging as Lord Sumner caressed its ears. The man murmured something to the dog, and for a moment buried his face in the dog's ruff.

He must have spoken louder, or the wind shifted, for Lord Sumner's next words came clearly to her ears. "—know I have lost any affection I ever had for her!" he told the dog, all laughter gone, his voice turned strident, the hard, tight sound of disappointment. He looked about himself at the dogs, who lifted their ears in hopeful attention. "I try to enjoy her company. Everyone else seems to." His chest rose and fell, and she thought perhaps he sighed. "I do not love her. I do not even like her."

He hung his head for a moment, but then raised it again, reaching out a hand, tousling the ears of the nearest dog. "You know the humorous part of it? I find I cannot even blame her, not wholly. The fault is largely mine. She is beautiful and gracious. She never says a word wrong in company. She is . . . she seems to be all things she ought to be . . . most of the time . . . and still I cannot love her."

He said no more, simply sitting in the rain, uncaring of the gusting night around him. Augustine stared blindly down toward his unhappy figure, but she no longer really saw him, her vision turned inward to her own thoughts.

Joseph did not love Meribah! She had heard it from his very lips . . . although it was possible he meant someone else. . . . No. He meant Meribah.

Had the woman shown her husband her truer side, just as she had shown a snippet of her true nature to Augustine on the day of Meribah's wedding to Joseph? Augustine would never forget the girl's smirking smile, the superior laugh. Meribah had changed in an instant from a sweet, demure girl to a cool, calculating woman. Augustine could hear yet how Meribah had crowed, "Are you not jealous, Augustine? I am marrying a rich man, richer than my father certainly! Joseph need not even count the allotment he receives as his father's heir, not with the fortune he has made in his own right!" She had laughed, a deep, throaty laugh that was totally incongruous with her delicate beauty. "I am to be a viscountess, and one day a countess! And I have *you* to thank for making it all transpire exactly as I planned, my dear little matchmaking friend."

Augustine had not wished to believe what she saw then, what she heard, but time had proven the sharp-edged words showed more about Meribah's real disposition than anything she had said in all the previous months of their acquaintance.

Tonight Lord Sumner must surely have learned something irrefutable about his wife's nature—Augustine was only surprised it had not happened sooner. Meribah was a consummate actress, and well aware her own consequence stemmed from that of her husband. The woman knew she must keep him content, if only so he would choose to host or attend social occasions with her, would keep her firmly before society's eye. But Meribah's kind of poisonous disposition must find its outlet eventually, even with the one person she ought to keep it from forever. Joseph was not a soft man, not one to be easily led, not like—admit it—Christopher. Meribah was a fool if she thought as much. This woman ought never to have shown this man any face but her assumed, sweet-natured one, not even for a moment, not if she wanted to continue in the busy, almost frantic mode she had so far established.

How odd then, that mixed with the obvious fury that had driven Joseph out into the night—from his words, presumably something Meribah had said or done— there was also regret. He had taken the blame of any lacking love firmly on himself. Poor man. How much worse the years ahead would be for him, for surely this was only the beginning. The dike was cracked, the flood must follow. Where now he did not care for his wife's company, eventually he must come to loathe it.

Joseph did not love Meribah. The outwardly content marriage in the house next to hers was a sham, a deception, she now knew, practiced by both parties.

The knowledge, however, was not what had made her lips part in wonder, made her hands begin to shake. It was not what had rocked her, what had made her literally teeter on her feet. The possibility that Joseph had discovered his wife's false nature was not what had made her raise her unsteady fingertips to press against her mouth; the intimacy of marriage must surely, eventually, lead to his awareness. No, what had stunned Augustine was learning that Joseph suffered from the very same malady as herself: the unspoken horror of entrapment in a loveless arrangement.

"That keening sound he made," she whispered against her fingers. How well she knew that sound, even though she had never uttered it aloud herself. It reverberated through her chest, it pulsed in her blood, it haunted her sleep. That awful, terrible sound of quiet desperation. That wailing of a soul caught in the gentlest and yet cruelest snare. To have everything but the one thing you want; to desire exactly what you could not have. To know what is wanted, to see it on the horizon, to be unable to move toward it. It did not matter that she had the better mate, that Christopher's only sins were being too mild and too uninterested in her or in exploring a life together. She was greedy to want anything more than the simple contentment she already had, she knew. But, oh, how well she knew that mournful cry, that wailing of a heart denied.

Her gaze had focused once more on the scene below when Joseph moved, the dogs leaping around him. He had stepped forward, parting a wave in the sea of wagging tails, his hands only absently reaching to stroke an ear or a muzzle. His attention was not on the dogs, nor the storm, but now fixed instead on the house. What did he look to see behind the lighted windows there? What had Meribah done to drive him out in the cold, that kept him away from going inside to the promised light and warmth before him?

Augustine waited for Joseph to move toward the gate, to exit toward the mews, to escape whatever had brought him to this obvious outrage and despair. Instead, he moved slowly toward the house, his steps those of a prisoner mounting the gallows.

Why? Why return inside? What kept him from fleeing, to his club at least, if not to the country? Augustine stared down, one hand clutching the lace of her curtains. Did he go inside once more merely to fetch his traveling cloak? No, his were not the steps of a man determined to leave, but rather a man acquiescing to the need to stay. But why?

He stayed for Marcus, his newly born child. Of course the infant was the reason why.

Yet, an infant could be bundled into a carriage with

his wet nurse. Joseph could take the boy and could go to live at his country estate, far from London, far from Meribah. Many a wife had been left behind . . . Augustine herself was all but abandoned by Christopher, in every way but proximity. No, there was nothing remarkable about a separation of households, of lives. Joseph, so fortunate to be born a man, to have money and influence and freedom of movement, need not stay with a wife he could not admire, whose company so clearly chafed. Perhaps he meant to leave tomorrow? Or as soon as the boy might be readied for the journey to his estate in Oxfordshire?

Or perhaps Joseph had chosen not to leave at all, not to separate the child from its mother? She did not know how Joseph looked upon his role as father, but he would not be the first man to shy from the notion of separating an infant from its mama. Could it be he was not a man to ignore a marriage vow? Was he the rare manner of man who would not leave a wife behind, not seek comfort and affection in the arms of one woman while still married to another? Or perhaps he still loved his deceitful wife; perhaps he had chosen to forgive and forget as best he could?

Augustine could only guess. She might have sworn such depth of feeling, such rage, was beyond the usually composed Lord Sumner. Still, it was clear this could not have been the first-ever argument between husband and wife. The manner of volcanic wrath he had demonstrated came only after months of pressure, of heat and steam finally finding its way past all restraining barriers. The reason for his return was not important. The fact he decided to go back into his house, so recently filled with ill-will, was the significant thing.

Augustine had closed her window and her curtains, her movements slow and deliberate, a reflection of the stunned sensation inside her head. She blew out her lamp, disrobing for bed in the dark. She did not want company, not even the limited company of her lady's maid. She wanted to be alone with her realization that, as unhappy as she was, like Joseph she too must find a way to go on. Must decide to leave or to stay, to live no longer in a state of perpetual hope or to continually face the disappointment she knew when those hopes were not fulfilled. Even as Joseph had just done, she must weigh what was important against any emotional pull she might feel.

She had taken a sacred vow. She had made promises. It did not matter that Christopher had failed in his promise to love and cherish her. Both she and Christopher had also promised to honor one another, and they must do that if nothing else.

She had lain upon her bed, its sole occupant, the covers pulled up to her chin. She had stared at the barely illuminated canopy above her head, a kind of gratitude filling her. Gratitude directed toward Joseph for unintentionally showing her she was not alone in her unhappiness, her married isolation. She could bear it, somehow, just knowing at least one other person endured such feelings as well. And for that one other person to be Joseph, Lord Sumner! The proud, confident, sometimes arrogant, and seemingly imperturbable Lord Sumner!

That night's scene would play again and again in her head, even after Christopher was dead and buried. Strangely, the memory had often proven to be a source of strength, even when Meribah's death did nothing to repair the strained relations between the two households. Augustine never spoke of that night, not in all the months since, not to anyone. She certainly never spoke of it to Louise, who would have tried to dismiss the event as a mere lovers' tiff.

And here Louise sat today, eager to hear everything

there was to hear about Lord Sumner's morning call, seemingly not realizing how truly extraordinary it was that he should make such a call upon Augustine, of all people. While her little sister sometimes displayed a talent at arriving at sharp insights, she could also deliberately choose to ignore any awareness of strong emotion. Strong emotions unsettled her, especially the kind of rage Lord Sumner had shown that night toward Meribah, or the deepest shades of despair Augustine had learned to hide from her sister.

"We need tea if we are to have a good coze," Louise declared, rising to cross to the bellpull. She gave it three genteel tugs, then floated back to her sister's side. "Besides, then I might practice my pouring out, if you do not mind."

"Of course you must pour for us," Augustine said at once, happy to help Louise get over her bashfulness at performing the social nicety. If only their governess had not scolded Louise for every little drop that went amiss, then perhaps Louise might by now feel more secure in her ability to play hostess. There had been, unfortunately, one too many nerve-induced mishaps over the teapot in Louise's four years of marriage for that to have changed.

The tea tray arrived, and Louise poured with a steady hand, for her attention was fixed on Augustine rather than the tea. "So, tell me! Did you, as Miss Stoakes thought you would, bring out your attribute cards for Joseph to use?"

"I did."

Louise's eyes glittered. "Ah! Joseph truly means to find another wife then?" At Augustine's nod, Louise cradled her teacup between both hands and settled back among the settee pillows, prepared for a long chat. "You must tell me which attributes he selected."

"You must not speak of them to anyone—"

Louise waved the caution aside. "Of course, of course. As always, I shan't tell a soul. I know it is just between you and me. Have I ever told a soul before now? Of course not. Now, dear girl, do tell."

Augustine sighed and settled back among the pillows as well, already regretting that she had agreed to this particular matchmaking proposition.

Four

"Marcus!" Joseph called, walking into the nursery not ten minutes after leaving behind Lady Wayfield's library, and, happily, her damnable attribute cards.

Marcus looked up, a smile crossing his young features at once. Mrs. Rasmussen, his nurse, startled in the corner, blinking the sleep from her rheumy eyes. Marcus looked back at his collection of wooden sailors, set one piece in a gesture that implied the movement was extremely important in whatever game he played at, and then abandoned the figures to run to his father's side. "Papa!" Marcus cried, putting up his arms.

Joseph at once scooped the boy up, balancing the five-year-old on his hip. His own father would never have rumpled the lie of his coat by picking up a child, a fact Joseph had been only too aware of from a very early age. Joseph had long since decided that if one felt free to touch, it must follow that one would feel free to talk. Marcus would be raised to talk to his father, to tell of his hopes and dreams as Joseph had never been allowed to do with his own father. Decorum was important, yes, and comportment, but these were lessons that ought to be learned only following the more important establishment of affection and tolerance. "Good morning," Joseph said to his son.

"Morning," came the reply. For once, Marcus smiled.

He was a serious, thoughtful child, one who reserved his smiles for a selected few. There were biscuit crumbs in the corners of his mouth, indicating lessons had already been interrupted for a morning treat, not to mention Mrs. Rasmussen's doze.

Joseph turned his attention to the nurse. She smiled at him in a manner that always assured him she had never quite perceived him as having outgrown the short trousers in which she had once helped him dress. Mrs. Rasmussen was the only being on the earth who still referred to him as "Master Joey," despite his years, the courtesy title lent him by his father, and even his own rise into the realm of parentage.

Colleen, the new maid, sat in the light from the window, sorting Marcus' stockings. One of her duties was to look after Marcus whenever Mrs. Rasmussen faded into slumber, which was to say three or four times a day.

If Mrs. Rasmussen had not been Joseph's own nurse since some five-and-twenty years past, he would have long since replaced the old woman with a younger, more animated servant. As it was, she was as much a fixture of the household as the ancient paneling in the library, and certainly more beloved. The difficulty came in Mrs. Rasmussen's declining any talk of receiving her pension and retiring from duty. Colleen was a help, at least as much as Mrs. Rasmussen allowed her to be. Joseph had come to accept that only a new mama's devotion toward Marcus would convince the stubborn old woman that she would serve best by retiring to her sister's home. She would always be welcome to call, of course, and Joseph meant for his old nurse to remain a kind of foster grandmama to Marcus, but for now he could only sigh to know that she was not a vigilant attendant to his son.

Joseph did indeed sigh, thinking the old nurse's position was yet another reason he must remarry.

"Papa, want to see what I can do?" Marcus asked, his light-colored eyes, so like those Joseph saw each day in the mirror, sparkling with eagerness.

"Certainly I do." He set the boy down.

Marcus ran to the low table at which he sat for his lessons, and Joseph followed him more slowly, his hands crossing behind his back in a relaxed pose. Marcus reached for his slate and chalk, and with his tongue caught between his lips in utter concentration, painstakingly wrote out his entire name in a large, chalky script: Marcus Sebastian Gatewood.

"In script?" Joseph praised, ignoring the way the letters slanted downward on the slate in an unsteady curve instead of lining up in a straight line. "I knew you could print your letters, but now you have learned to write in script as well?"

"Only his name, my lord," Mrs. Rasmussen supplied, rising slowly from the oversized chair in which she had dozed. She shuffled toward the table, beaming at her charge. "He insisted he must learn it, even though I told him he will be learning nothing else of script until I am convinced he can properly print all his letters first." She spoke with that same mix of affection and resolve Joseph remembered from his own early days at lessons before he had moved on to a proper tutor.

"I cannot work for the Foreign Office like you, Papa, if I cannot write my name in script," Marcus explained.

Joseph smiled at his son, reaching to tousle the boy's hair. "Ah, I see! Well, you have done a good job of it, my lad."

Marcus frowned at his slate. "I do not think I could do it with ink, though."

"You have a few years to master the task," Joseph assured him, stooping down to be at his son's level. "Perhaps, when you are grown, you will find you do not care to work for the Foreign Office."

"Oh, I will," Marcus said with the absolute conviction of the very young.

Joseph said nothing to discourage the lad, but he could wish a different future for his son. In fact, neither Marcus nor himself need ever work a day if they chose not to employ themselves. It was not that Joseph wished his son to grow up as too many titled young men did, indulged and dangerously idle, but he would rather see Marcus find an interest outside the often deceitful and corrupted world of politics. For that was what the Foreign Office's duties too often came down to, petty little tasks borne of politics. Although, he had to admit to himself with a rueful shake of his head, this latest assignment could not even be deemed an affair of politics—it was the distasteful task of cleaning up after a mere affair of persons.

"When do you leave England, my lord?" Mrs. Rasmussen asked. She often exercised the uncanny capacity of the long-time retainer to speak to the matter uppermost in the master's thoughts.

He shook his head at her, but it was too late; Marcus had heard the words. The little boy stared up at his father, quietly thinking before he spoke.

"You are leaving England, Papa? Why?" Marcus asked, sounding too mature for his years. Had the boy always been this controlled, always had this quiet reticence? Or had Meribah's hot-and-cold affections taught him, so young, to be cautious and unwilling to display unbridled youthful emotion? Only the stick of chalk slipping from between the small fingers, the thrill of his new skill abruptly delegated to a secondary stature, revealed he might be upset by this news.

"Yes, Marcus, I must leave England, in a while. A few weeks."

"I will stay here?" Marcus asked.

A stab of physical pain lanced through Joseph, but as

much as he wanted to prove the boy wrong, to allow the child to stay with him, he could not take Marcus into the decadent world to which he must travel. "I am sorry, but, no, you may not go with me."

"Why can I not go? Where are you going? Will there be tigers there? Or natives?"

Joseph smiled ever so slightly, pleased with the childish questions, for they showed that the nights of tucking in the lad himself, of greeting Marcus first thing whenever he came home, of rumpling the lie of his coat to pull the child into his arms, all served to make the child believe at least some adults could be trusted in their promises. Marcus was able to believe his father would come home to him again. "You cannot go because you are too young. That is just the way it is. I am going to a little place in Prussia," he said.

He hoped Marcus would accept that nebulous explanation. Joseph was to tell no one of his exact destination, and certainly not a child, even a child such as his who could be expected to be shy and tight-lipped with anyone outside the home. "And no, there are no tigers there. The only natives are Prussians. No savages at all, I fear."

"Why are you going?" Marcus asked, as if the lack of savages made the journey pointless.

"I am going to help a friend."

"Is he sick? Is he dying? Is he being held as a prisoner by the Prussers—"

"Prussians. No, none of those things."

Marcus tipped his head to one side; it was the one gesture he had that ever put Joseph in mind of Meribah. However, when Meribah had done it, it had been a coquettish and conscious ploy for attention; when Marcus did it, it was a reflection of the child's questioning nature.

"You see," Joseph said, picking up a piece of chalk.

"I have to go because I have to help a beautiful maiden." He began sketching on the slate, making a rudimentary female figure with long and flowing hair, a pointy hat, and a happy smile on her round face. "I have to help her come away from an evil dragon, who likes nothing better than to gobble up beautiful maidens." He drew in a castle turret beneath the stick woman.

Marcus laughed, taking up a stick of chalk as well. "I am drawing the dragon," he announced.

"Please do. You see, there is a magic castle in Prussia, and if I can get the maiden there before the evil dragon catches her, then the magic castle will keep her safe from harm."

"The dragon cannot go in there?" Marcus asked eagerly, pointing at the drawn turret.

"Most certainly not." Joseph shook his head.

"So you are the brave knight? Do you have to let that maiden lady *kiss* you?" Marcus wrinkled up his nose.

"I am only the knight's friend. But the knight, you see, is off fighting other foes, so I must assist him, as any good friend would. Perhaps the lady will give me a token to give to her knight, but, no, I doubt she will want to kiss me."

"Good!" Marcus looked relieved on his father's behalf.

Joseph laughed.

"This dragon breathes fire," Marcus asserted, drawing squiggly lines coming from the general area of the many-fanged dragon's mouth.

Joseph began shading in the bricks of the turret with the blunt end of the chalk, the action more intended to encourage the boy to continue at the play than it was anything else. He looked at his son, musing as the boy quietly worked. No, he could not take this gentle child with him, not to a court ready to receive the cast-off mistress of the Prince Regent. Not to a group of people who knew little of restraint, and even less of prudent choices.

If anyone but his prince and regent had asked Joseph to escort the indiscreet Lady Quiggmore away from her husband's reported wrath, he would have refused. But how could he refuse His Royal Highness? How could he be received by the quietly weeping prince, be told he was the one man the prince could trust to see that "beloved Margaret" came safely away from the prince's "loving embrace into the caring bosom of our friends in Prussia," and yet, despite such praise and pressure, decline? In a way, Joseph almost had to admire the prince for not utterly abandoning the woman to her fate, even if he had chosen to give up the pleasure of her company. The prince swore there remained weeks until Lord Quiggmore could return to England, and even though his passion for the woman had cooled, the prince thought to see that she would not be at hand to bear the brunt of her husband's cuckolded outrage. It was a curious form of honor, and yet Joseph had to call the intent, if not the preceding deed, an honorable one. The thought at least made the duty slightly palatable.

At least he had time to get his own house in order. If he were gone from England for more than a month— and unfortunately, that seemed likely—it would be very difficult indeed for Marcus. How much better it would be for all involved if there were a new Lady Sumner in the house! Marcus would have a new mama to help him await the return of his father; Joseph would know some peace of mind, having instructed the new Lady Sumner to make sure the boy was better tended than he some- times had been in recent days; and Marcus' grandfather, Lord Tinsley, would not step forward and claim the boy must stay with him.

That must never happen. If Marcus was shy and quiet now, so little as a week in his grandfather's company

would reduce the child to a total and intimidated mute-
ness. It was not that his father was actively cruel, but he
spoke his mind, never thinking first if the words would
be ill-received by their intended target.

Joseph could hear the man now: "I can make a man
of the boy! No coddling. That is what the boy wants, a
lack of coddling! He will learn to speak at once upon
being spoken to, mind me. Well, boy, what do you have
to say for yourself? Nothing, eh? Then you can sit there
in that chair until you find your tongue and use it to
apologize for wasting my time! Sit there all night and
all day again, if you have to, if that is what it takes to
have you do as I say!"

Joseph would happily marry an ape-leader or a jade
before he would allow Marcus to wilt under the same
sharp-tongued mouth he had suffered as a boy. Any
woman, so long as she could be kind to children, would
do.

That was not what Augustine—Lady Wayfield—
thought, as she had been quick to let him know. *She*
thought he must marry for some manner of personal
contentment, and the advantages to his son were pe-
ripheral. Well, no, that was not quite true; it was her
consideration of Marcus' needs that had stopped the
refusal she had been obviously poised to make concerning Joseph's matrimonial ambitions. Despite her own
lack of children, there was presumably a soft spot in
Lady Wayfield's heart for the world's next generation.
Joseph knew Marcus sometimes called upon his neighbor, coming home with hair combed and hands
cleansed, except, that is, where either hand clasped a
jelly tart or warm buttered bread. So, obviously the child
was not discouraged from passing through her gate into
her garden, nor from receiving a treat or two. Joseph
would have thought Lady Wayfield's staff to be the in-
dulgent ones were it not for Marcus' free use of the

lady's Christian name, proving the lady herself was at hand during these calls.

"Auggie told me I sing very well," Marcus would say, or "Auggie showed me how to make a lavender stick."

"Lady Wayfield," Joseph would correct him. "You should call her Lady Wayfield."

"She lets me call her Auggie, 'cause I don't say her whole name too good. Auggersteen," Marcus demonstrated.

They had settled on "Lady Auggie," to avoid a constant correction on Joseph's part.

It was as well that Marcus had struck an accord with the lady, now that her particular talent was needed by the Sumner household. Certainly it had been the mention of Marcus' name and need for a mama that had tipped Lady Wayfield's scale in Joseph's favor.

Her reputation as a matchmaker was deserved, even if in Joseph's own case she had already failed once, miserably. His marriage had, from all reports and gossip, been the only true disaster among the many couples she was credited with bringing together. Some were obviously and deliriously, if rather fatuously, in love. Other couples exuded a happy contentment, if not rampaging adoration, with one another. Yet others seemed to have a flamboyant, even stormy union, but still managed to seem well-suited and gratified to find themselves caught in the throes of wedlock with their particular spouse. Even for the once-burned Joseph, it was impossible to declare Lady Wayfield's talent for matchmaking as anything less than extraordinary.

Of all the marriages she had played a part in, beside his own, there was only one other that had perhaps lacked in some important way: her own to Lord Wayfield. It was impossible to say exactly what that lack had been, but every once in a while Joseph had thought he saw some mirror-image of his own malcontent reflected in the woman's eyes. What had it been? A lack of sparkle in the woman who had once shone? A downturning of a mouth meant for smiling? Whatever it was, the first time he had seen it was the first time the two couples had begun to drift apart, becoming eventually virtual strangers who just happened to live next door to one another.

Ah, women! His history with the gender was not good, to say the least. There was no reason to think that course would change any time in the near future. Soon he must go through this matchmaking ordeal with Lady Wayfield. Then he must marry the selected female, whose motherly charms (despite Lady Wayfield's insistence otherwise) were the only ones he had any intention of admiring. The necessary evil of marriage behind him, he must follow that questionable pleasure with attending the frivolous and flighty Lady Quiggmore and her set. If he needed any more proof that he had difficulty allying himself with the female of the species, he had only to remind himself of Meribah, and even before her, his mother.

Mama, a name never earned by the stiff, too-formal woman who had been his mother. She had hugged him, now and again, when he was young and "adorable" as he remembered once upon a time being called. She had cooed at him when he was sick, even if she had covered her mouth and nose with a handkerchief and done so from the doorway of the nursery, refusing to enter the sickroom. She had, he was certain, preferred her daughter's company to her son's, although he never knew why. That reality was saved from being utterly crushing only by the fact that she obviously did not care for his father's company either. For years he attempted to please her, but her bouts of approval were overshadowed by the more frequent objections to his clothes, his friends, even his studies. He grew to assume she was not fond of men for some reason, but in truth his sister, preferred as she was, had fared little better in obtaining any lasting sign of their mama's approval.

Still, he would not have thought too poorly of his mama, thinking her very like the other ladies of the circles whose company she kept, if only he had not caught her betraying his father with her lover in bed one night. To the sixteen-year-old boy he had been, the shock came, yes, from the fact the man made love to his mama, but even more so from the fact his parent had chosen to act out her infidelity in her *marriage bed*. In the bed she shared with her husband. Even to the youth he had been, the sin of adultery had been made so much worse by the locale in which she had allowed it to occur.

And Joseph never forgot when his papa came home, how Mama had greeted her husband and turned up her cheek to accept Papa's greeting kiss.

That had been Joseph's first lesson in a woman's ability to deceive. If only that had been the end of his education on the matter; if only he had been quick to learn. But when it came to matters concerning women, folly had followed folly. Oh yes, others had surely found matrimonial joy, but Joseph had no reason to hope he ever would. He had only to look at the pattern of his days to see no lasting devotion for himself or those near to him. In his work, he saw that Lord Quiggmore did his duty for king and country, while Lady Quiggmore cavorted with the Prince who Lord Quiggmore served. In his youth, Mama had given her husband and family infrequent smiles even while she spent her afternoons moaning beneath a lover's weight. In his own marriage, it had been Meribah who had once and for all convinced Joseph there was something fundamentally wrong with the institution of matrimony, or at least his place in it. She had taught him there was no true binding of two hearts, no real lasting love as all the poets claimed there could be.

Meribah. How long had he been blind to her faults? Months. No, truthfully, nearly two years. Little things had disturbed him all along—a lie suspected; an inappropriate laugh; a charming pout to get her way, a pout that sometimes threatened to turn into childish petulance. At some point, some weeks before Marcus was born, Joseph began to really understand his wife was as light and frothy and uncaring as a bowl of whipped cream, that her lack of substance was no mere amusing coyness. He could have lived with that, with the knowledge that his wife was lacking depth—age and learning and patience could change that to some degree, surely?—but it was her unthinking little cruelties that at last destroyed any love he might have once known for her.

Even the cruelties toward himself might have been borne—but not those toward Marcus. Sweet, tiny baby that he was, how could she not have loved him instantly, without reservation? How could her tolerance for the tiny infant's presence be so short-lived, so easily abandoned at a moment's whim?

"Oh, take it away!" He had heard the words from her own mouth, had heard her call their newborn child 'it.' He had watched her turn away from the swaddled newborn child lying on the bed beside her. "Surely there is another wet nurse to be had somewhere in this city?" Meribah had demanded, glaring at the maid who had brought her the child to be nursed. "I have already told everyone I will not ruin my figure by nursing. How ill is the woman? Are you telling me she could not have a bed here as easily as at her home? Give her the baby in a bed here. All she would have to do is sit up long enough to nurse it!"

He had tried to forgive her—she was exhausted from

the birthing, of course. She needed sleep. And many women did not nurse, for the very reason Meribah stated. There was nothing unusual in that, but still . . . the way she refused to share his jubilation at the child's healthy birth . . . the way she had turned away from their child. . . .

Joseph felt a shiver run down his spine, knowing that was just the first of many little rejections Meribah had displayed for both her husband and her son. His son. The very boy who now looked up at Joseph inquiringly from his small stool before the nursery table.

"Yes? It is all right?" Marcus asked, peering at his father with an intensity of purpose that called Joseph back to the moment. His son's look was so eager, Joseph found himself nodding an assent to whatever it was the child had been nattering on about.

"Hurrah!" Marcus cried, leaping to his feet. He dashed to the door of the nursery, stopping just long enough to call back, "Come, Papa. You can come, too."

As the boy disappeared from sight, Joseph raised his gaze to meet that of Mrs. Rasmussen. "I was wool-gathering. What did I just agree he might do?"

"Master Marcus asked if he might go next door to visit Lady Wayfield," Mrs. Rasmussen told him.

Joseph dropped the chalk from his hand, dusting his hands together as he rose swiftly to his feet. "I had no idea that was what he asked," he grumbled. "I daresay Lady Wayfield does not wish to see any more members of this household today. I shall go and fetch him back."

"Shall I ring for a servant to go and fetch him?" Mrs. Rasmussen offered.

"No, I will go myself."

Joseph walked from the nursery, shrugging off a flash of annoyance that resulted from the way Mrs. Rasmussen had lifted her eyebrows in a questioning manner. He could retrieve his son himself from the neighbor's, if he chose, and there was no need for the speculative gleam that had leapt into Mrs. Rasmussen's eyes, no need whatsoever.

Five

Joseph's steps became increasingly unhurried as he moved down the stairs and out into the early afternoon light. Despite his exasperation at the way his old nurse could still vex him with but a look after all these years, now that he was outside the reach of her appraisal he had to admit he rather wished he had sent a footman in his place. His lack of haste was a reluctance to call yet again this day upon his neighbor, Lady Wayfield.

The six-year estrangement between his house and hers had been, after a fashion, a comfortable thing. Each of the participants had known the simple rule: ignore one another unless absolutely pressed by social conditions to smile and murmur polite nothings. If Joseph had not proved so thoroughly maladroit at finding a suitable mama for Marcus, he never would have done anything to disturb that estrangement. But facts were facts, and he only had six, maybe eight, weeks in which to find a willing woman for the position. Not only willing, but fitting.

The crux of the problem, of course, was the question what "fitting" female would marry a man after only a few weeks of courtship? Only one who had a reason to trust that a hasty wedding would not be utter folly, nor the bridegroom an idiot or a fool. Who could have such a reason, such faith that all would be well? Who would be willing to gamble on the future without any form of proof in the present? Only someone who had assurances from a third party, someone who could trust the word of another over that of the proposed groom. Joseph had quickly determined he needed a representative, someone to present his case for him: a matchmaker.

He could not, however, bring himself to hire a Covent Garden variety matchmaker. Not someone who earned her living by delving into such matters, not someone whose only interest was to collect a handful of coins for her efforts. He could not employ a person who took no real care for the results of their matchmaking attempts.

That left Lady Wayfield, the only woman in all London who did not make the "art" her trade, who did not bring couples together for any sort of monetary profit. Joseph could not say why she practiced her talent as she did. Did she do it that she might enjoy the glowing reputation it gained her? Did it help her while away the too-long hours of a widow's day? Was it a party game run amiss? No matter. What concerned him was the very real fact that she had a talent, and he had need of it. Still, it had not been an easy thing to walk the few yards across to her house, to ask her to lend her talent in support of his cause.

The ironic thing of it was he believed she would do her very best to find him a suitable wife, one, hopefully, far more engaging than the first had been. She might even look upon the opportunity as a chance to redeem her reputation in his eyes.

Joseph shook such ruminations from his head as he passed through a narrow opening on one side of the box hedges that surrounded her tiny front lawn. He took but a few steps, taking the four stairs two at a time, and found himself at her front door.

The butler responded almost at once, as soon as

Joseph had released the door knocker. The man escorted Joseph to the front parlor, ringing for refreshments before disappearing to inquire if Lady Wayfield were receiving.

Joseph turned to observe the trappings of the front parlor, and knew at once who had decorated it. Lord Wayfield had exercised dominion in the garden, but in all other aspects of their life together, Lady Wayfield had led the way. It was her taste reflected in the choices of color and style. Thankfully there were no Egyptian reclining sofas or sphinx-head carvings to be found among the assembled chairs and tables, and if Lady Wayfield had a penchant for Chinese touches, Joseph had to admit they were tastefully chosen. An opened silk fan on a filigreed stand here, a jade box on the table there . . . really, the choices were well-made, appropriate, and even of a nature to soothe a traveler's eye, just as they ought to be in a receiving room. A moment's reflection caused him to remember the other room he had recently entered, her library. It, too, had been a tastefully arranged room. Capital! He would take that as a sign that Lady Wayfield might, as everyone else attested, have a sense of the appropriate.

The butler returned. "Her ladyship wishes to know if my lord would be willing to meet with her in the kitchens?"

"The kitchens?" Joseph echoed. Had he come on a day when the household was making cordial or some other all-day task that required the mistress' overseeing? If so, that was surely where Marcus was to be found, in the midst of the commotion. Joseph made a motion with his hand signifying the servant should show him the way.

He was exactly right, for the first thing he saw upon going down the stairs and into Lady Wayfield's kitchens was his son, dressed in an oversized smock, standing on a chair before a large table, his hands thrust into a floury pile of dough. At his side stood Lady Wayfield, her attire also covered, albeit with a more appropriately sized apron. A quick glance provided the information that they were making bread, nothing special, just bread as would normally be made two or three times a week by the cook.

For a moment neither Marcus nor Lady Wayfield seemed to notice Joseph's arrival despite Mosby's announcement of it. Lady Wayfield smiled down at Marcus, her head turned at an angle, the very picture of attentiveness, and Marcus spoke some low, pleased words, following them with a smile for the lady in return. Late morning light shone down through the multiple basement windows, backlighting the woman and boy. Dust motes danced in the sunbeams, surrounding the two figures with an otherworldly nimbus. The servants working in the kitchen were outside the touch of the sun's light, lost to shadows, leaving only these two to look alive and beautiful and glowing. Joseph sucked in his breath, and wondered for one peculiarly fanciful moment if he had seen this pose before in some painting or other of the Madonna and Child.

"Marcus," Joseph said, his voice strangely thick. Marcus glanced up with the preoccupied air of the young, Lady Wayfield turned to offer Joseph a nodded greeting, and the sun shifted one degree in the sky, the world becoming normal again, the illusion fading. For it was but an illusion, Joseph reminded himself. Even if there were such a thing in this world as that imagined moment, that perfect picture of Motherly Devotion, Lady Wayfield had no reason to extend its touch to her neighbor's son.

"Lord Sumner, I apologize for bringing you down to the kitchens," Lady Wayfield said. It was curious that the rich, confident measure of her voice melded with the passing impression she had made in the sunlight's beam; he had half-expected her to speak with the whispers of

angels, but this was more fitting somehow. It seemed
right there was no meekness in the Madonna, but rather
the clear, nearly musical tones of a warrior-mother, the
voice of a defender against all evils.

"I assumed you might be seeking this fellow," she
went on, exchanging a smile with Marcus, who proceeded to squeeze the dough between his fingers. The
lad accompanied the action with growls of satisfaction.

The world tilted again, and Joseph almost wished to
stretch out his arms and stabilize his balance as he had
done when walking the narrow top board of a fence as
a child. His discomposure had something to do with
the smiles the woman and the boy exchanged, tied in
somehow with the suggestion of friendly intimacy. His
center of gravity shifted at learning his son had a secret
connection with another living, breathing person. How
strange it felt to know, as clearly as if Joseph had been
told, that Marcus had developed some degree of trust
in this neighbor, this woman. Their smiles spoke of confidences, of giggles and games, of moments shared of
which Joseph had not previously known. His son, it
seemed, had made a friend.

For a moment Joseph's breath was suspended, and
the lack of oxygen to his brain surely accounted for the
memory that floated before his mind's eye. A memory
of himself, a boy, standing next to Nanny, pressing the
edges of the tarts after Nanny filled each dough cup
with sugar-sweetened berries . . . gooseberries they had
picked together in a bright, warm summer light. He
remembered how he had looked up at her and wished
with all his soul that *she* might be his mother, not the
woman still asleep upstairs in her chambers. Wished
and wished . . . and it never came true.

But this woman was not Marcus' Nanny, and certainly
would never be his mother. If anything, this newly discovered camaraderie only proved how important it was

that Joseph hurry ahead with his intent to marry. Marcus must never know the sting of wishing for the impossible, of wanting the devotion of a woman who was in no position to play parent to him.

Joseph released his breath. "Indeed, I have come to retrieve the lad. Come, Marcus, dust off your hands and say farewell to the lady. We must go at once." He could not keep a cool edge from creeping into his voice.

Lady Wayfield's smile faded away, and her shoulders went back, even as her chin lifted. "Oh. It was not my intention to chase him away from his sport."

A flush of warmth filled Joseph's face, as if he had done something objectionable, when all he wished to do was to protect his child from the special hurt inflicted by unpredictably indifferent adults. "I feel sure you must have had enough of my household coming through your home today." Even to himself, the comment sounded stiff.

"Oh, never too much of Marcus," she said, equally as stiffly. Then it was her turn to blush, as she surely realized the implication of her words, that Marcus might be a welcome caller, but Marcus' papa was *not*.

"Nevertheless," Joseph said, crossing the room to reach and unbutton the topmost buttons of the smock. "Come, Marcus, we must go before the lady learns that all company galls after awhile, even that of a charming young rapscallion such as yourself."

For once Joseph was pleased to see his son respond beyond his years, as the boy acquiesced to the notion of returning home. Marcus gave the dough a final pat before turning to have his hands wiped in the cloth Lady Wayfield extended.

"Dear me, he is not quite coming clean. But there is water there in that bowl—"

"No, this is quite all right," Joseph assured her, scooping up the boy.

If before he had felt censure from the lady, now he sensed an aspect of approval—grudging perhaps, but there all the same—in the way Lady Wayfield looked at him over Marcus' head.

"Well. Thank you. We will not trouble you again to-day, I promise."

The lady murmured a farewell to Marcus, and to Joseph she said, "I shall see you tomorrow night at Mr. Prescott's party then, Lord Sumner."

He hesitated, then offered, "Should I bring my carriage around for you? It seems foolish to take two when we are neighbors. . . ."

She smiled, rather tightly he thought, at the belated offer. "That would be most sensible. A little before eight?" she suggested.

"That would be well."

She lowered her gaze, a gesture that had nothing to do with timidity and everything to do with ending a conversation. Joseph turned to leave without another word, not quite sure if he were relieved or annoyed at the lady's undisguised dismissal.

No, this woman was no madonna, and Marcus was not her beloved child. To her, Marcus could be no more than a diversion, an hour's company. Company whose familiarity, in Joseph's wide experience, must soon nettle even the most outwardly tolerant of women.

Colleen, Joseph determined, must receive new instructions and an increase in her wages, for after today she would be ordered to pay especial attention to making sure Master Marcus did not call quite so frequently upon their neighbor.

Augustine declined Cook's offer to finish kneading the dough, instead reaching for the mixture herself.

She flattened and folded the dough with all the energy that aggravation had put into her hands.

"What manner of father is Lord Sumner to snap at Marcus that way, to put such an abrupt end to his play?" she grumbled at the dough, giving it an extra slap of annoyance. Lord Sumner was arrogant, of course, as always, and she knew too well that he could be all too icy in his manner. If she had needed reminding of that fact, he had provided plenty: there had been the flash of knowing amusement in his eye when he had offered to secure *The Lady's Boat* sculpture, and that smile of his when he obtained her acquiescence by stating how much Marcus was in need of a mama. Both actions had been calculated and deliberate, not what one would expect of a doting parent. And he had been positively frosty when she had tried to speak to him of Meribah. The man was even firm with his dogs, despite the fact he insisted they were to live wherever he lived. Why would she expect any gentler display from him, even toward his son?

Although, she had to admit, her hands slowing in their motions of kneading the dough, there *were* some things about Lord Sumner that hinted at human emotions just behind those wintry-blue eyes of his. One was the very fact that Louise enjoyed his company—Louise who became flustered at the thought of planning a menu, let alone engaging in conversation with a handsome, overbearing man. Of course it was possible he had never shown anything but his charming side to Louise, that she did not know the real man. But it was true Augustine had seen him soften the cut of the words he tossed at his friend, Mr. Prescott, proving Lord Sumner had at least *some* kinder sensibilities. Even the fact he had chosen the attribute cards marked 'Fond of Animals' and 'Amiable' hinted that the stern nature might at times yield into a show of tolerance. And there was no denying Lord Sumner meant to protect his son by not taking the boy on his mission, and that he felt he also must protect the boy from his grandpapa, the earl, whom he had described as a stern taskmaster who lacked warmth.

"That was an interesting choice of phrase coming from *you*," Augustine muttered. She absently spread butter in a bowl to ready it to receive the kneaded dough. "You could be speaking of yourself, Joseph Gatewood."

"What is that, my lady?" Cook, wiping her hands on her apron, inquired of her mistress from across the wide table.

Augustine, well aware the tattle of why Lord Sumner had come to call had already spread among the belowstairs servants, hedged, "I was just thinking about the proper woman for Lord Sumner."

"Who would that be, my lady?"

Augustine picked up the ball of dough, putting it in the buttered bowl and covering it with a linen towel whose edges she had herself embroidered with tiny blue flowers. "She must be someone special, Cook. She must be someone who will make Lord Sumner smile, for he frowns and frets far too much to make a pleasant neighbor. And, even more importantly, she must be the manner of woman who would allow Master Marcus to continue to call upon us here."

"Very good, my lady," Cook said, looking dubious.

"Very good indeed," Augustine replied, feeling less confident than she sounded. Would a new mama keep Marcus closer to home? Would she deny Augustine the amusing observations and hard-won giggles Marcus brought into this large, empty house?

For the first time since Lord Sumner had walked into her parlor this morning, Augustine was suddenly glad she had been offered the chance to help Lord Sumner select his new bride.

Six

"Lady Duncliffe's daughter would suit, I should say," Augustine pronounced quietly to Lord Sumner, not wanting any of the crowd gathered at Mr. Prescott's assembly to hear her assessment. "She is even-tempered and has a talent at the harpsichord. I do not know how she might be with children, but it is difficult to imagine she would be harsh."

Augustine glanced up into Lord Sumner's face. She was not surprised to see, again, rejection writ there.

"She fawns," he said, dismissing the girl with a shake of his head. "Too grasping. Too concerned with naught but obtaining a title."

Augustine sighed inwardly, turning her gaze back to the crush of people. Lord Sumner had already summarily dismissed five females, without deigning to so much as be introduced to the ladies in question. "Miss Craig? She is no beauty, but her wit is clever, and her tongue not too tart."

" 'Not too tart'! That is hardly a recommendation, Lady Wayfield," he returned, sounding sour as he reached to pluck two glasses of champagne from the tray of a passing footman.

Augustine sighed aloud this time, allowing a measure of irritation to creep into the sound. "You will never marry if you never even speak to anyone," she pointed out crisply, accepting the glass he handed her.

"I will marry," he stated firmly. He took a sip of his champagne, and then glanced down at her. "Do not tell me you are ready to give up the search? We have only just begun."

"We have not begun anything at all, rather. Truly, my lord, you have employed me to be your guide, so I wish you would allow me to do my duty. There is a fine showing tonight of those families remaining yet in London. If you dismiss all these candidates here out of hand, I shall have precious few others to draw upon. Dance with a lady before you reject her, that is all I ask. Besides, it will make your entry on to the marriage mart all the more noticeable if you are seen dancing with all and sundry."

"It has not worked to date," he replied dryly, but then he nodded. "But it is even as you say. I must put aside my prejudices and attempt to see if there is more to these ladies than meets the eye or is rattled off of others' tongues."

"Precisely! And here we have a lovely nominee: Miss Sarah Moncraft. She is graceful and agreeable, and her father's title is lofty enough to save her from being grasping." Augustine tilted her fan in the lady's direction until she saw by the clearing expression on Lord Sumner's face that he had managed to find the woman in the press of people.

"Miss Moncraft is lovely indeed," he said, a hint of enthusiasm at last lightening his tone. "You need not even be put to the effort of introducing me to her. Miss Moncraft and I are already acquainted, via her brother." He turned to set his glass on another passing tray, then took a deep breath, as might a jockey before climbing up on his steed for the big race. He gave a short nod to Augustine. "So then, I go forth to cast my fortunes to the winds of fate."

Augustine found that a small smile curved her lips as he walked away. She was a trifle surprised he had given her that brief display of nervousness, for she had grown used to a lack of divulgences from him. There had been nothing in their shared ride to the assembly that had suggested things would ever be otherwise—in fact, he had been positively taciturn. His grunted replies to her few brief questions had not boded well for the future of this endeavor, and she had begun to fear that perhaps her grasp had exceeded her reach. If he would give her no assistance, how was she to find suitable prospects to complete her task?

Yet, she would not fault him for his anxious display, and was in fact pleased to see it. If a man could be made unsettled, he could also be made contented. She had not taken on the impossible . . . merely the next to impossible.

She laughed a little at her own jest, and a measure of her own nervousness faded. Even before word of her fame at the art of matchmaking had spread, she had seen for herself that she had a gift for pairing people— why should it be any different for Lord Sumner? Just because she had failed him once before did not mean she need fail again. Still, it was an easy thing to promise to find a good match for someone, something else altogether to find a person who possessed the required attributes.

There was no point in thinking along uncertain lines. She had accepted, she was good at her vocation, and that was an end to the matter.

"Lady Wayfield?"

Augustine turned, smiling as she saw who was at her elbow. "Mr. Prescott."

"Would you care to dance this next set with me?" her host offered.

"Of course," she replied at once, putting aside her glass and placing her hand on the arm he offered her. He led her to join the other couples assembling in the parallel lines of a progressive dance, the long line of men facing the long line of women opposite. She and Mr. Prescott were only a few feet apart, but still she needed to raise her voice a trifle to be heard over the bustle of dancers and tuning musicians. "I saw you danced the opening minuet with Lady Hume. I thought that a rather clever decision for a bachelor to have made."

"Yes. What better way to allay any rumors of an imminent marriage than to partake of the first dance with the oldest, longest-married woman in the room, eh?"

"That is exactly the impression I had of the event," Augustine said, smiling as she lifted her hand that he might take it in the beginning movement of the dance.

"I noticed my good friend, Joseph, did not choose to dance the first dance at all," Mr. Prescott said when they drew near, his voice kept low, meant only for her. "Have you been slothful in your duty? No, no! Do not scowl at me—I but repeat the question buzzing throughout the entire assembly tonight!"

"So it has already been noted that I am assisting Lord Sumner?" Augustine asked, but it was not truly a question, for she had not missed the raised eyebrows and shared whispers when Lord Sumner had handed her down from his carriage. Their mutual and former rebuff of one another's company had never gone unnoted, so that their entrance tonight, with her hand on Lord Sumner's arm, could hardly have hoped for anything less than a circuit among the tattlemongers. Lord Sumner had let it be known he was seeking a wife, and Augustine knew herself to be reputed as the *ton's* unofficial matchmaker—what could anyone think but the obvious?

"Only tell me, please, that no one believes it is *me* Lord Sumner means to marry?" she asked on a plaintive note when the dance brought them back together.

Mr. Prescott was quick to realize her complaint was offered in humor. "Every one of 'em, ma'am!" he said, grinning. "Every tongue is singing words of the love match of the Season."

"And so they will," she said, still smiling although she allowed authority to ring in her words. "It is only that it will not be for myself, but for the charmer I intend to find for Lord Sumner."

"A charmer, you say? Are we back to speaking of yourself?"

Augustine laughed and shook her head.

"Or can it be Miss Moncraft is to be that charmer?" Mr. Prescott asked, nodding to where Lord Sumner and the young miss danced together.

Augustine gazed upon the couple, noting how well Miss Moncraft's blond locks appeared poised near to Lord Sumner's dark good looks. The two of them swayed gracefully through the movements of the dance, exchanging words when they stepped together. Miss Moncraft's shy smiles upward indicated a return of notice, and she surely could only be too aware she had gained a particular status at being the first lady asked by Lord Sumner to dance this evening.

"I should hope Lord Sumner would be pleased to offer for Miss Moncraft, but a knowledge of the gentleman's disposition keeps me from making any predictions," she belatedly answered Mr. Prescott's question.

"You mean to say he is fickle!" Mr. Prescott laughed.

"I do not believe I mean fickle exactly, but I must say he seems inclined to be contrary. He asks that I find him acceptable females to court, and then he flatly refuses to make their acquaintance."

Mr. Prescott shook his head, a smile lingering in his gaze. "That is Joseph to a certainty! Contradictory as a mule. You are wise to realize he will not be pushed, especially into a liaison not of his choosing."

Augustine gazed at Mr. Prescott, considering the obvious regard that lingered behind his words. "I should think Lord Sumner would not be an easy man to have as a friend."

"Oh, but he is the very best sort of friend. Contrary, certainly. Stubborn, without a doubt. But faithful as a hound, and generous to a fault."

"Lord Sumner?" Augustine asked dubiously.

Mr. Prescott laughed. "I know. He does not seem that way to the casual acquaintance, but I assure you, once he calls you his friend you are a friend for life. So long as you are half so fair and forthright as he is himself, he is a most forgiving, lenient sort."

Augustine looked away, not wanting Mr. Prescott to see the sudden, sharp pain she experienced. If what the man said was true—and not merely a friend's blind devotion—it was clear that Lord Sumner had found her own nature wanting, for she was one person he had ceased to claim as friend. They had been estranged for years, yet how oddly painful it was to learn how deep his dislike of her must run.

The dance ended, and Augustine forced aside her upset, summoning forth a smile as she made her curtsy to Mr. Prescott's bow. She looked up from under her lashes to where Lord Sumner also offered his closing bow to Miss Moncraft. Part of her was pleased to see he lingered at the young lady's side, no doubt making polite chatter as he ought, and part of her knew a re-occurring flash of distress to think he never bothered to engage *her* in little niceties. With her he was curt, and demanding, and sometimes even rude. If she had thought, even for a moment, that their burnt bridges had been mended, she was very much mistaken. He had come to her out of desperation only, not because he was willing to forgive her for being the fulcrum that had levered him into his duplicitous marriage with Meribah.

She was pulled from her ruminations when Lord Sumner bowed again to Miss Moncraft and left the lady's side. His long legs carried him in short order to Augustine's side, where he turned, looking anywhere but at Miss Moncraft. He rested his hands together behind his back, and lifted his chin. "No," he said quietly, firmly.

"Miss Moncraft will not do? Are you sure you do not wish another dance or perhaps to see her at a card party or—"

"I am quite sure she will not suit."

"Whyever not? No, do not give me such a look! I need to know why, or else I shall be forever starting over," Augustine said, trying not to sound as curt as he did.

"She is too young," he said, fighting back a frown. "Too silly." He looked directly at Augustine, and said in a carefully neutral voice, "In too many ways, like my first wife."

Augustine rolled her eyes, perhaps to draw attention away from the guilty blush that heated her cheeks. "You said this woman is to be gentle, and cordial, and, ah yes, biddable, as I recall. What is there in Miss Moncraft that does not meet those expectations?"

"I will concede that Miss Moncraft is quiet and biddable in a way my first wife never truly was, but I did not mean I desired the company of someone so biddable that she never has an opinion of her own. I made several conflicting statements about the weather and the gathering tonight, and Miss Moncraft managed to agree I was quite right on every point." He shook his head in disgust.

"Perhaps she was merely being polite, for she could scarcely call you a liar or a fool," Augustine pointed out.

"Better that she should than to suffer me as either. Besides, as I said, she is naught but a babe. I should think a woman of more years would be more the thing for this endeavor."

"Very well then. I will make a note that our paragon is to have opinions and is to be aged."

He looked down his nose at her. "If this is how you treat all your followers, however did you become the darling of the *ton?*"

"By having good manners, unlike others I could name," she said pointedly. "And may I say how flattered I am to learn that you include yourself in any group that can be named my followers!"

His eyes flashed and his lips thinned, just before he parted them to respond.

She cut him off before he could speak. "But we are not here to exchange barbed comments, my lord. You said you wanted someone who was biddable. Well, Miss Moncraft certainly is biddable, if she is nothing else."

"The problem, my dear lady, lies in the very fact that she is nothing else *but* biddable," he said in crisp tones. "We may argue about her suitability all night, but, as you say, that is not our purpose. Let us see who else attends."

Augustine inclined her head in what she hoped passed for graciousness rather than vexation, and surveyed the crush anew. She clucked her tongue, dismissing four ladies at once without bothering to offer their names for consideration. Two were too young, at least according to Lord Sumner's dictates; one Augustine knew to have a quick temper; and the fourth had the reputation of being too forward. The latter two would never suit to serve as Marcus' mama. Marcus' mama must be a lady of fine manners, gentle ways, and generous heart.

"This will never do. We have been going about this whole matter all wrong," Augustine declared, putting her shoulders back. "As we seem to be having no luck at bringing the mountain to Mohammed—"

"So Mohammed must go to the mountain?" Lord Sumner finished for her. "Are you proposing I let the ladies decide among themselves who would be best suited to marry me?" He actually shuddered.

Augustine, to her surprise, grinned, and for one wicked moment contemplated the horror that would cross his face if Lord Sumner were presented with the winner of a competition or lottery for the position of his wife. She ducked her head, forcing down the unexpected smile, chiding herself that such self-amusement was inappropriate in the midst of a business dealing. Their association was a simple arrangement: one wife for one rare statue. She must remember tonight and any other nights served no other purpose than that, not even mending an old breach. "No such folly as that," she assured him. "Instead, I suggest we learn more about *you*, my lord."

"Do not tell me you are going to make me sit down like a schoolboy and write an essay entitled 'Fifty Important Facts to Know About Me,' " he said, and she would have wagered there was real alarm in his voice.

"No," she said, and now she laughed aloud, one hand pressed to her throat as though that might hold back her mirth.

He did not laugh with her. "I am pleased to hear your denial. But you must be more explicit."

"Over the years I have noticed there are Seven Indications of Love," she said, her smile fading. She did not look at him, did not want to see a bored or skeptical look come across his handsome face. "I know you do not seek a love match, never fear, but much of what one seeks in an affair of the heart serves as well in a union for other, more prosaic purposes." She did not say aloud that of course this was only what she had observed, since she had never achieved such harmony in her own home.

"Hmm," he said, the sound perhaps faintly encouraging.

"But I make it a point never to tell a prospective groom or bride all seven at once," she hurried on, making a play of gazing about the room as though she were searching for a suitable *parti*.

"Whyever not?"

She dared a glance up at him, and was emboldened by the lack of censure she found there. He might find her words foolish, but if he did, he chose not to let her see as much. "The first Indication is a simple and rather obvious one, I must say."

"And it is?"

Was that a long-suffering sigh he smothered? "I daresay you will not care for the wording, as it relates to a love match, but any alliance must start with mutual respect, for with mutual respect—"

"Yes, yes, the lady and I shall therefore deal together smoothly and contentedly, et cetera and so forth! All that being understood: what is this first Indication of yours? What affected trait must I exhibit to attract the nonpareil we seek?" He crossed his arms over his chest, beginning to look bored.

She opened the reticule that had been dangling from her wrist, and presented him with a card. Despite the fact he could read it for himself, she explained, "It is simply that if you love someone, you will be willing to give something up for them."

"I can see that is what you have writ here. You are a lady much given over to cards, are you not, Lady Wayfield?"

"To have something writ before you that you may consult is often very helpful for the act of retention, my lord. It can be very beneficial to read a thing several times, until the meaning of it is absorbed—"

"That is all very well, Lady Wayfield, only I do not love anyone, nor care to," he interrupted, attempting to hand the card back to her.

She ignored it, so that he drew back his hand and tucked the card in his waistcoat pocket. "My lord—"

"No, do not scold me! I only protest because I cannot see how your Indication of Love applies to my situation."

"Really, my lord, I sometimes believe you positively choose to be doltish! If you meet a young lady tonight whose company you believe you might enjoy, ask what you would be willing to surrender to retain her company. Could it be you would never wear blue again if she asked it of you? Or if she said your dogs must stay in the country, would you forsake their company or rather hers? I declare there will be any number of ladies for whom you would surrender nothing at all, but there might be one who makes you hesitate and think perhaps, because she cannot bear cooked fruit, you could do without ever having another cherry tart served at your table again."

Lord Sumner's stance relaxed a degree, and he considered her words. Finally he nodded. "You make good sense. I will apply myself to looking upon the ladies with such consideration in mind. But understand, please, that I am already quite convinced there is nothing at all I would care to surrender for Miss Moncraft's sake—particularly not intelligent conversation."

Augustine bit back an unexpected smile. "Understood. But only see who has just entered!" she said instead, experiencing an actual sense of satisfaction at the sight of the woman being escorted into the room on the arm of the lady's papa. "She is Lady Christina. Her family name is Ross."

"The Earl of Scribner's eldest?"

"Exactly. She is a trifle older—this is her third Season, I believe—but that must not be counted against her in any measure. I am afraid it is her lack of beauty that has kept her on the shelf, not her disposition. I can tell you I have found her to be sweet and kind, and she has a clever mind. Look there, she is in the pale pink with mulberry ribbons." She discreetly indicated the direction again with her fan.

Augustine watched Lord Sumner's face, waiting for the moment of disappointment she expected to cross his face when he caught sight of the uncomely Lady Christina. Truly, the woman possessed no outward beauty, owning as she did a long face and a receding chin, with no softer feature lent by eye or mouth to improve her visage.

He did not display open disappointment, not beyond one thoughtful blink. "Ah yes, I recall Lady Christina. Come then, Lady Wayfield, introduce us, for I admit to being so lowly as to have never taken the chance to meet the lady in seasons past."

Lord Sumner, Augustine admitted, had moved a degree higher in her estimation for being able to look to a woman for something more than physical beauty. He might have moved several degrees higher yet if only she could believe he did so from some greater nobility of mind rather than from a desire for haste in achieving his goal of marriage. All the same, his manners were cordial and impeccable as he requested a dance of Lady Christina, and the woman was clearly, if shyly, delighted to be asked. That alone made the evening a success in Augustine's eyes, even if Lord Sumner should find Lady Christina as unsuitable as all the others he had dismissed this night.

Augustine frowned at the thought . . . but her attention need not linger on Lord Sumner, not while the dance went forward anyway, she firmly told herself. While the couple danced, she might take a few minutes to enjoy herself, and what better way to enjoy an evening than by putting two other like hearts together? Lord Sumner might not cooperate in that regard, but Miss Moncraft was looking decidedly crestfallen where she stood unasked to dance again, and was that not young Ned Tredlemeyer just come in through the door?

Seven

Joseph bowed to Lady Christina at the end of their dance, pleased to find he did not need to force a smile to his lips. The uncomely lady was easily flustered, with an odd habit of making exaggerated movements—the back of her hand to her brow to indicate fatigue, and her curtsies were too deep—but she otherwise seemed the embodiment of a gentlewoman. She agreed with nearly everything he said, but when he contradicted himself by saying once that the assembly was ill-attended and then later that he found it to be a crush, she had the good sense to ask him which he meant.

He stayed to chat after returning her to her father's side, as was only polite. She did not offer much in the way of conversation until prompted by questions, but she at least gave more than monosyllabic replies when she did.

"And how is it you know Mr. Prescott?" he asked, aware of how Lady Christina's father eyed him. The cautious look the earl gave Joseph seemed a mix of suspicion and wishfulness . . . a look echoed by the daughter.

"Mr. Prescott's father is an acquaintance of Papa's," Lady Christina replied. Joseph was a little surprised when she ventured a question of her own, "And how do you know Mr. Prescott, Lord Sumner?"

"Eton. We met our first year there," Joseph said, smiling encouragement down at her.

"How pleasant to have a friend for so long a time."

"Indeed." Joseph nodded, and sipped his champagne, and searched about in his mind for another question to keep the conversation from withering. The only one that came to mind ("Have you no long-standing friendships then, Lady Christina?") could hardly be asked. An awkward silence grew, causing Joseph to blurt out the next thing that came to mind. "Lord Scribner, I wonder if I might have the honor of riding out in Hyde Park tomorrow afternoon with Lady Christina?"

Lord Scribner stared at Joseph, unblinking, then suddenly cried out a little too loudly, "Certainly, sir!" Belatedly he added, "Er, that is, if my daughter has no prior engagement tomorrow afternoon. Christina?"

Lady Christina had long since looked to the floor, bright red spots decorating her cheeks. "I would be honored," she said in a very small, slightly squeaky voice.

The specifics were determined—Joseph was to call for her and her father at half past four tomorrow—and then he bowed himself from the lady's side.

He absently moved toward where the rose-tinted feathers adorning Lady Wayfield's pearl-and-diamond studded bandeau bobbed as she spoke with a group of uniformed gentlemen. As he made his way, he considered the strange sensations in his chest. Part of him was greatly relieved to have begun, for even if nothing were to come of his association with Lady Christina, at least he had made the first real attempt at securing himself a new wife. Another part of him objected that, having begun, this pursuit felt too very much like a foxhunt.

Bedamned! It did not matter that this was the way things were done, that marriage ought to be a decision made by the head and not the heart. If he had allowed his head to rule some six years ago, he might have seen beyond Meribah's facade, might not have been fooled by her pretty face and affected ways . . . but, then too, would any other marriage have turned out differently? Did he not have his own parents as a perfect example of what marriage became when dictated by practical and mercenary concerns? Was there any way to win the game of love, or was love all merely an illusion?

No, not that, not an illusion. Love was real enough, Marcus had shown him that. Too, Joseph loved his sister, and even his well-meaning if stern father, after a fashion. It was best to assume what had long been obvious to him: that the kind of love he sought, a devoted marital love, was outside Joseph's ability to engender. If his courtship of Lady Christina, or any other Lady Christinas to follow, felt like a foxhunt, he must accept that was how it must be.

He stepped to one side of the circle of gentlemen gathered around Lady Wayfield, and knew a faint annoyance when he was unable to catch her eye before she accepted a dance with Lieutenant McDougall. He watched her move into the set, noting how well her deep coquelicot gown suited her coloring. It brought out the hidden tones of red in her dark brown hair, colorations he knew usually were only noted in sunlight. Those red highlights had been hidden when she was dressed in her widow's weeds; rose suited her far better than black ever had. He wondered if it was through design or accident that the coral ribbons decorating her small puffed sleeves were almost exactly the same shade as her lips? Design, most likely; what woman had he ever known who did not see to such details?

Design or no, the world would be an easier place if only more females could conduct themselves as did Lady Wayfield tonight, he thought. Except for displaying a brief flash of aggravation at his rejections of the females she had pointed out to him, Lady Wayfield had largely chosen to behave logically, with a smooth efficiency that showed she took seriously her charge to assist him. She gave his words thought, considering how best to satisfy his requirements. Her manner was unaffected, lacking any coquetry or plays at gaining his attention. She behaved quite sensibly, in fact, not attempting to inject emotion into a business arrangement. He must remember to compliment her on the fact.

Joseph looked up to find Lady Wayfield no longer danced with Lieutenant McDougall. She was now part of a whole other set, smiling up at some fellow whose name escaped him. Joseph glanced about, reviewing the nearest ladies, thinking rather sourly that he may have been too quick to hand compliments out to Lady Wayfield; she was perilously close to neglecting him. This was a second dance in which he ought to have had a partner—never mind that he could ask any number of ladies to dance on his own. Of course, he could scarcely disallow Lady Wayfield to dance, but she had agreed to be his guide in this matter of marriage and knew how short his time was. She had an obligation to him, by her own decree. So why was she lingering with the people from the set just ended? Need she chat so long with the same small group, when she could be moving about, acquiring suggestions for him?

Just as he thought this, a couple moved away from the group, positioning to be the first to line up for the next set. Lady Wayfield looked on indulgently, nodding at several comments thrown her way and smiling. A buzz of conversation crescendoed in the room, and all eyes turned to gape at the couple who had first moved on to the floor, all except Lady Wayfield. She took the moment to look up, sweeping the room with her gaze, perhaps looking for Joseph. Her glance missed him however, causing him to have to resist the impulse to lift his hand and wave to gain her attention. Instead he settled on moving forward into a slight clearing in the crush, keeping his gaze on her so that they might make eye contact should she ever look his way again.

The buzz of conversation abated, but not before Joseph heard the words "Third dance!" repeated several times around him. He glanced at the couple, both with bright red cheeks, and recognized first the girl. Why, it was Miss Moncraft! And, by Jove, that was Ned Tredlemeyer who lifted her hand. What was this talk of a third dance? Was Foxy Tredlemeyer dancing a third dance this evening with Miss Moncraft? Surely not. Three dances in the same evening with the same lady? It simply was not done, not unless the couple were betrothed.

Joseph looked away from the debatable question of this occurrence, only then locking gazes with Lady Wayfield. She smiled, appearing as pleased as the cat that has caught the bird it stalked. She nodded at him once, and began to make her way in his direction.

"What do you think?" she asked as she stepped to his side, turning to look out at the dance floor again. There was that self-satisfied smile again.

"I presume you are asking what I think of Mr. Tredlemeyer and Miss Moncraft sharing a third dance?"

"Of course I am. They favored one another from the very moment I introduced them, but even I must confess I am a trifle startled to see them standing up together again. He might as well propose!" she said, still smiling, shaking her head.

"I can scarce believe it. What must her chaperone be thinking of?" Joseph shook his head.

"She is thinking her young miss has made a grand splash tonight! First Miss Moncraft dances with Lord Sumner—who has done his best to make it clear he seeks a wife—and then her charge is sought for the dance repeatedly by yet another eligible swain. I have no doubt Miss Moncraft's chaperone can scarce wait to report her protege's success to Mama and Papa Moncraft at home!"

"Nonsense. The creature stands in danger of losing her position for allowing Miss Moncraft to make such a spectacle of herself."

Lady Wayfield glanced up at Joseph, revealing the sly amusement writ across her features. "Should we request another dance from Miss Moncraft before she promises herself to another?"

"No!" He repressed a growl. "I only reveal my surprise at such forward behavior, especially given the two have been aware of each other for, what? Thirty minutes? They know nothing of their respective characters to act so besot with one another! Can you imagine how foolish Foxy will feel once he realizes Miss Moncraft detests foxhunting? He adores it, you know. Lives for the sport. But she told me herself not an hour ago that she finds the hunt barbaric and cruel. What of this imprudent display of attraction then, eh?"

"The First Indication of Love," Lady Wayfield said, her pleased smile softening, becoming perhaps a shade wistful. "If he loves her, he will be willing to give it up."

"But he treasures the hunt! It is his namesake, his passion. He would not give it up for any female!"

"Then he does not love her."

She spoke with such assurance, Joseph's only response was to clamp his lips together and give a small shake of the head.

Augustine glanced up at him. "We shall have to wait and see if he comes to love her in truth, will we not?" she said, shrugging. "You may be entirely correct, for, as you say, they have but met. But as soon as I saw Mr. Tredlemeyer enter the room, I remembered how he blusters to hide a fundamental bashfulness. What better manner of female for him than one who will not say boo to his opinions, who will, over time, draw out his true feelings as only another shy, quiet person could? Mr. Tredlemeyer is all false sound and fury, and it will take a soothing, gentle nature to set him at his ease, to help him put aside his bombastic pretentions and bring the best of the man forward. I think Miss Moncraft is such a one. Too meek for you, my lord, but perfectly mollifying for a man such as Mr. Tredlemeyer."

Joseph stared down at her, too astonished by her evaluation to hide his amazement from her. He then looked up at Foxy, a fellow he had known ten years if not more, and at the demurely smiling Miss Moncraft, and back at Lady Wayfield. "I never would have thought to describe Foxy that way, but I daresay you may be right! He *is* all bluff and blow, and would not care to have a lady at his side who was as ready to spout steam as he is himself. Brava, Lady Wayfield." The word stuck in his throat a moment, but when a person was right, they were right, and he saw no sense in refusing to acknowledge as much. "You have proven your worth, once and for all, as a matchmaker."

"How easily impressed you are, my lord! You may speak too soon, for these two may find yet there are too many obstacles to overcome, or their families may object, or a dozen other things might cause love to never grow there. But not if they build on tonight's infatuation, not if they truly come to love one another. Then nothing, no one, will turn them from each other."

She sighed, and for a moment the wistful look crossed her face again. He found himself wondering: had her marriage been a happy one, or at least one free of distress or dissatisfaction? Difficult to say for sure of Lady Wayfield, whose company he had avoided for so long. Certainly Lord Wayfield had never seemed discontent . . . not outside the fact he made little secret of his mistress, traveling together as they did to the theatre, to disreputable places such as Vauxhall Gardens, and obviously to the chambers in which he housed the woman. How much happiness could the presence of a mistress—known to all, and surely to Lady Wayfield as well—denote? There were a hundred other matters that made up a marriage besides the activities of the bed-chamber, but how pleased could a couple be with one another if such intimacies were not a part of that marriage?

Thoughts of her satisfaction—or lack thereof—with her marriage led him inexorably back to her own pronouncement that there were Indications of Love. If Lady Wayfield had ever loved her husband, what had she given up for him? Children?

He mentally shook himself, erasing a frown that had formed to crease his brow. "I have arranged to take up Lady Christina for a drive tomorrow afternoon," he said abruptly, for she looked up at him with a questioning gaze.

"Splendid! Our plans march forward." She nodded. "Now, you have had ample opportunity to review more of the attending ladies—"

"Oh, is that what I was to be doing while you waltzed away the evening?"

"Certainly!" She did not look the least contrite. "I suppose I could stand at your side all night and continue to point to various ladies, but that would scarcely suit, now would it? There is being frank in one's public dealings, and there is being gauche. I prefer not to be gauche. Tell me, to whom do you require an introduction?"

He sighed, trying not to let her hear the chagrin that prompted it, and answered, "That lady over near the punch."

"The one in green?" Lady Wayfield made a face.

"How ungracious of you. But, no, the far younger female behind her, the blond one in white with gold bows."

Lady Wayfield moved in front of him, the fluttering ribbons of her sleeve tickling over his hand as she did so. It had been a long time, he suddenly realized, since something so feminine as a ribbon had brushed his skin, creating a tingle. The sensation, unexpected as it was, caused him to jerk away his hand. He raised his chin, hoping the motion covered the involuntary action.

"The blond? Oh, yes, I see her now," Lady Wayfield said, apparently oblivious to his reaction. "I do not know her. You must wait here while I see if I might contrive an introduction. If you see me tap my fan against my cheek, like this," she demonstrated, "you should join me at once, and I will make the most of the moment to include you in the introductions."

He nodded, crossing his hands together before him, the one overlaying the spot where her ribbon had touched. The tingle had gone, but not so the awareness that he had been too long away from womankind. What else could explain his over-reaction to that gentle, unplanned touch?

A young lady glanced his way then turned abruptly aside, causing him to think he must be frowning again. As he worked to erase the expression from his face, he considered this new complication: was all this talk of marriage and love raising old, useless hopes in him? Had he not learned the lesson that he was never made for the lasting love of a woman?

Well, perhaps he had learned it well enough, after all, for as he saw Lady Wayfield gently pat her cheek with her fan, he could not miss the sinking feeling in his stomach. Where another man might have been cheered to know he was to make the introduction of a lovely young lady, Joseph only knew a sense of tired resignation. He crossed the room, drawing on any talent for acting he might possess to display a smidgen of eagerness. No, this game of hearts and kisses was not a sport for him, and if he had known a moment's reaction to an errant, feminine touch, it was only because he had been too long celibate.

Perhaps he ought to have taken a mistress while Meribah was yet alive, for following her death it had seemed, at best, disrespectful. It did not matter that Meribah had never earned his respect, that she herself had twice taken men other than himself briefly as lovers, proving herself inconstant even in her infidelities. He supposed it was the idea of marriage itself that he honored. Maybe he had not wished to stoop to his wife's level, did not want to engage in one of the very activities he condemned in her. It was certainly not society's disapproval he had sought to avoid . . . maybe he had just never quite summoned the enthusiasm necessary to seek a mistress, not even once Meribah was gone.

If he was not soon to marry, he considered, he might have had to bestir himself to find some female companionship, if only to avoid any other jolter-headed responses—jumping like a green boy! And to think it had been a reaction to Lady Wayfield, of all people! Yet another reason to marry. In fact, Lady Wayfield might even approve such a carnal impulse were he coarse enough to mention his thought to her, for she would say he had at last found a reason of his own for marriage.

He smiled as he was introduced to the woman in white with gold bows—Miss Collins by name—and thought perhaps his smile was broader than it might have been, for he had formed another thought that quite amused him. Would Lady Wayfield indeed approve if he were to say he had decided that, yes, it was time to marry, if for no other reason than to slake his masculine appetites?

He stifled a guffaw, instead asking Miss Collins if she would honor him with a dance.

Eight

Late the next afternoon, Augustine lifted the small watch pinned to her bodice, seeing it was half past six already. She glanced at her sister, sitting at her side on this bench in Hyde Park, and was glad Louise had asked to accompany her on the outing. There would have been little enough impropriety for her, a widow, to meet Lord Sumner for a brief discussion in the open air of the park, but Louise's company had kept her from taking too many glances at her watch . . . until now.

"I have not seen Lord Sumner and Lady Christina since they drove off this path over an hour ago," Louise said, as if reading her sister's mind. "I thought they would circle past at least once again, but we have been denied that chance to spy." Louise was seemingly unaffected by the hour-and-a-half they had waited and watched on this bench, tossing shelled chestnuts to the park squirrels who boldly scampered near the two sisters' feet.

"They have not been gone too long, not really," Augustine said, although privately she thought exactly the opposite. "They had their drive together, and although it is not crowded on the walks today, that takes some time. And then he must return Lady Christina and her papa home before ever returning here to speak with me . . . with us."

"I hope all goes well. Poor Lady Christina, she is so ill-favored. I cannot like to say it, but—"

"But it is true. The happy news is that Lord Sumner does not seem, unlike most men, to require great beauty in a woman to be able to admire any other virtues she might possess."

"I daresay he has had to learn a difficult lesson about a pleasant surface concealing an inferior nature."

Augustine turned to Louise in surprise. "You knew of Meribah? How she . . . ?"

"How she broke that poor man's heart? Yes."

"But you never said a word to me!"

"And what was I to say? 'Oh, have I mentioned that Lord Sumner's wife is a termagant and a brass-faced hussy?' I think not." Louise threw more chestnuts to the squirrels from the twisted cone of paper she had purchased from a hawker strolling the park. She glanced up from under her lashes, then back to the squirrels. "You see, one night I am afraid he had imbibed a bit too freely, and allowed a measure of frustration and injury to show in his eyes. Naturally I asked him if everything was well, and he briefly and reluctantly confided it was not. I could scarce betray his confidence, Augustine. Besides, what purpose would it have served? I certainly never told him of your own unhappiness."

"He would not have wanted to hear it," Augustine said, knowing how blind she had been to anyone else's misery until she had been confronted with it the night of the storm.

Louise sighed. "I suppose not. Your houses were certainly estranged by that time. It is my experience that, contrary to the saying, misery does not always love company. People are extraordinarily sensitive about revealing matters of the heart, particularly unhappy matters."

Augustine lifted her eyebrows—but that was Louise,

not one to chatter on for hours, and when she spoke it was to the point—and considered the truth of her sister's statement. Even after she, Augustine, had known of Lord Sumner's unstable marriage, had she gone to him to commiserate, to let him know he was not the only person ever to struggle against the matrimonial bond, to fear a future of ever-increasing disappointments? No, indeed. Mired in her own misery, she had taken no steps to alleviate his burden. Her last inclination at that time was to share her own wretchedness with her quietly hostile neighbor.

Louise threw the last of the chestnuts to the squirrels, and announced, "Lord Sumner returns."

Augustine raised her gaze, seeing the approaching carriage with Lord Sumner at the reins, a groom up behind.

He pulled the horses to a stop on the nearest spot of the driving path, and tossed the reins to the groom. "Give the horses a slow, cooling walk," he instructed the man, receiving a nod in return.

As the carriage moved away, Lord Sumner crossed the grass to their bench, briefly doffing his hat in salute.

"Joseph," Louise greeted him, offering him her hand. He bowed over it, sketching a kiss above her glove.

"Louise," he greeted in return, then turned to Augustine. She belatedly raised her hand for a similar salute, and wondered why it felt so exceptional to have his hand touching hers, his mouth so near her glove. He had offered the same tribute only two days ago in her front parlor; there was no reason to allow the simple courtesy to fluster her. "Lady Wayfield," he said, releasing her hand.

It might have been perfectly natural to tell him he need not be so formal with her, but the truth was, unlike with Louise, he and she were not friends. Nothing had occurred to thaw the freeze that had long since robbed them of the warmth of familiarity.

"You did not tarry at Lady Christina's side in Lord Scribner's parlor," she stated instead.

Lord Sumner glanced from Augustine to Louise, his expression neutral. "I did not," he agreed.

"Oh dear. Why not?" Louise asked.

"Am I to understand Louise is now privy to our pursuit?" he asked Augustine. His tone seemed vaguely annoyed, but his expression remained impartial.

"I did not attempt to hide it from her," Augustine answered. "There seemed little point after you revealed your intent before my guests the other morning."

Lord Sumner's lips compressed for a moment, but then he answered, "That is only too true. I forget that for this once I *wish* my business to be a public matter."

Louise moved farther down the bench, patting the remaining space at the end. "Do sit down, Joseph, and tell us of your drive with Lady Christina."

He sat, half turned toward them, one arm casually resting on the back of the bench. "There is little enough to tell. We drove. We talked. Her father talked. It was all very pleasant, I suppose."

"But?" Augustine prompted, hearing a note of negation in his tone.

"But," he said with a frown, one perhaps aimed at an over-bold squirrel who dared to scamper over the toe of his highly polished hessians in pursuit of a chestnut. "I mean to say, there is little to object to in Lady Christina, yet I find I *do* object to her."

"Tell us why," Louise urged, nodding at Augustine as if to be sure her sister was listening.

"I cannot like to do so, for I know I will look petty in your eyes," Lord Sumner said. Despite his clear reluctance, he did not hesitate further though. "Yet my reasons are simple enough. I found Lady Christina's speech to be quite comfortable when we discussed elementary matters, such as the weather, the flowers, her latest stitchery, or the declining availability of worthwhile servants. Domestic matters, I would term them. But as soon as her father changed the subject to something outside the home realm, she became mute. I do not think it was bashfulness. I think she simply had nothing to say. No experience, perhaps."

He looked to both ladies, moving his shoulders in a small show of discomfort. "Of course, I scarce expected her to discuss the war, or join in a debate on parliamentary reform . . . but was I too far out of step to think she might have something to say of the rising cost of coffee? I would have expected either of you ladies to have an opinion as to the matter, but Lady Christina's only contribution to the discussion was to state that she usually preferred tea.

"All of which is well enough, I suppose, as she is young and not yet much exposed to the world. I could have seen my way past a lack of learning, only she then turned the conversation to a lengthy recitation of her friends' most recent pastimes. 'Miss Jones said this about Lord Smith,' and 'Ophelia Johnson wore an unseemly gown to Mister Gardener's ball,' and dozens of other *bon mots* mostly about people I do not know. Dreadfully dull stuff, that, and all the worse because I could not fathom why she thought I would be interested!"

"Perhaps she was wrought-up," Augustine offered.

"No, Lady Christina is always that way," Louise put in, nodding sympathetically at Lord Sumner. "She always has a dozen things to say about any one person."

"All of which might be forgiven and forgot—after all, if we married, we should eventually come to know the same people, and I might find such a recounting less tedious. And presumably, if it were a condition of nerves, Lady Christina's inclination to prattle on might decline with time, I should hope. And of course one would wish a wife who is also to be a ready-made mother to have a strong interest in the domestic arts. As I say, all might be tolerated except for one thing." Now he actually blushed, twin dull spots of color dusting his cheekbones. "It is her mannerisms," he blurted out, apparently abashed to have to list the lady's fatal shortcoming.

"Come now," Augustine said, squirming a trifle herself. She knew what it was to have to speak when the very idea of one's words went against one's sense of decorum. How many times had she been forced to speak plainly, even bluntly, to Christopher when that was the last thing she wished to do? When she found she could no longer accept his visits to her bed, had it not been the most difficult thing to tell him plainly why? But how else to inform him she feared the diseases his mistress might foster, than to say it in the most candid language?

"We all know you are a gentleman," she stated in a tone she hoped sounded logical and reasonable, "and that you cannot like to deprecate a lady. However, in this matter of marriage we must only be forthright, else we will achieve nothing of worth. Do go on, Lord Sumner."

He shook his head, once, but the action did not decline the logic of her words. "It is that she waves her hands about as she speaks! 'The weather is very fine today,'" he mimicked, making a sweeping sideway arc with his arm. "'Only listen to the birds calling in the trees,'" he continued, cupping a hand to his ear. He lowered his hand in disgust. "I cannot imagine why no one has thought to tell her she is not on the stage, and that it would greatly behoove her not to act as though she is. There is something terribly pretentious about all that waving and gesturing."

"She does gesture, you know," Louise agreed, nodding at Augustine. "I can see how it would quickly come to grate."

"So! Lady Christina is disqualified," Augustine said. She took her reticule from her wrist, spreading the drawstrings so that the top gaped open. "In her case, we can see there is no hope of applying the Second Indication of Love." She issued a resigned sigh.

Lord Sumner caught her eye. "You mean to give me another of those cards of yours, I warrant," he said dryly.

"I do." She checked the card to be certain it was the correct one, then handed it to him.

"Read it aloud," Louise urged. "I have forgot which dictate is number two."

"So you have been subjected to these cards as well?" Lord Sumner asked Louise.

"Indeed, and very helpful they were, too."

He made a guttural sound which may have implied either disagreement or disbelief, but then turned his attention to the card. " 'The Beloved's Charms Outweigh any Unfortunate Lapses in Demeanor,' " he read the words flatly, but then he nodded. "This certainly rules out Lady Christina. Her lapses prevent her from becoming someone I could tolerate beyond the length of one afternoon, and certainly there would be no hope of her 'charms' ever allowing her to become my beloved."

"I daresay so," Louise mused.

"Not that I seek a beloved," he warned her. "All I seek is a wife and a good mother for my son."

"Oh, surely—" Louise began.

"Surely I know exactly what I seek," he interrupted firmly, giving her a weighty stare.

"Oh . . . I . . . ," Louise flustered, obviously startled by his vehemence, her poise slipping as it always did when she perceived she had made a social blunder.

Augustine's foot itched as it had only two days before, and she wished it was her and not Louise who sat close enough to mar the shining surface of Lord Sumner's boot, for she might have given in to the impulse to kick him in his shins.

He surely sensed the aggravation of the two women staring down the bench at him, for he at once said, "My dear friend, Louise, I beg your pardon. My manners are not what they should be. I am afraid all this . . . business of marriage goes against my grain, leaving me short-tempered. Please accept my apology for speaking so harshly."

Louise brightened at once. "Of course I accept. I understand! Marriage is no small matter and must be approached, naturally, with some trepidation. Please, think no more on it."

"You are very kind."

Just then, Lord Sumner's carriage returned. "Ladies," he offered, standing at once, obviously gratified to change the subject. "Have you a carriage, or may I have the honor of escorting you home?"

"We walked, since the day was so fine," Augustine explained, also standing. "I believe I speak for Louise as well when I say we happily accept your offer."

"You do indeed," Louise assured her, the last to rise. "I sent my gig home after arriving at Augustine's, my lord, so may I request that I be taken directly to my home? My daughter's bedtime approaches, and this would save me from having to await my coach's return, or from having to borrow a gig and groom from Augustine. Besides, I do not like to be too late home. My daughter and I do enjoy a little coze before tucking her in, you see." Louise ducked her head, appealingly apologetic at what might be taken as a sign of indulging her child.

Lord Sumner graciously agreed, and in just a few minutes, Louise kissed her sister farewell and was handed down from the landau in front of her home. "Best wishes in your quest!" she said in parting to Lord Sumner, who nodded briefly and climbed back up into the carriage.

"Lady Wayfield's," he instructed the groom. As the open landau rolled forward, Lord Sumner made his seat on the rear-facing squabs, opposite the front-facing seat Augustine occupied, his gaze springing to the card she extended to him.

"Indication Number Three?" he asked wryly, reaching for it.

She nodded. "The second proved of no worth to us today, so I thought it might be best to give you another Indication to ponder."

"Give me all seven at once, and I promise to ponder them all with dutiful attention."

"I have never found that to be true. I insist upon one idea a day—well then, two," she corrected herself with a smile. "That is all a person ever truly can summon the energy to properly contemplate."

"My schoolmasters thought otherwise."

"And how many of the facts and figures they cudgeled into your head do you remember to this day? Only those you use continually. All the rest are lost, or I miss my guess."

"It is true," he conceded with a laugh. "I doubt I could conjugate a single Latin verb at this moment even if it were to save my life to do so."

"My point exactly. But a certain line from a poem that struck your fancy once, or the name of a battle that intrigued, or even a riddle that amused you, these we remember. Brevity serves us well, my lord, for retention. You will have all seven Indications, but not today."

He sat back, spreading his hands in a sign of surrender. "I yield to your greater wisdom."

"Read the card," she said, pursing her lips, but more to keep from smiling yet again than out of irritation.

" 'A Fool Will Twice Marry,' " he read.

"That is not what it says!"

He grinned at her. "It ought." She parted her lips to respond, but he lifted a hand in protest. "No! Do not scold me! I shall be serious a moment. In truth it says, 'You Desire to Spend Time in the Beloved's Company.' But that is too simple! And rather evident, I must say."

"Of course it is, but that does not make it any the less true. My lord, I have known persons who fancied themselves in love only to exhibit the greatest relief when the object of their affection leaves the room! Sometimes the obvious is never seen because we never think to look for it."

"Interesting theory," he said, looking away.

Did the words on the card make him think of Meribah? Did he recall times when he had wished for nothing so much as to be away from his wife's side? Surely so. Once Augustine had seen the discord between them, it had been evident to her searching eyes every time she had seen Lord and Lady Sumner together. A barrier had lain between them, one that was manifested in the absence of the idle touch, the missing smile of understanding, the disinclination to linger in one another's company. Augustine had known such lack, had also attempted to hide it behind polite words and expected courtesies, to never let society know of her private disillusionment. She marveled still that not everyone could see what was so obvious if one but took the time to look, to consider, but others seldom saw behind the facade, perhaps not wishing to know anything beyond surface conventions.

Perhaps all marriages, to one degree or another, resulted in facades. There was every reason to concede Augustine was the one out of step, the only one foolish enough to believe romantic love had any place in marriage. Perhaps the giddiness of courtship was all an illusion, never meant to be sustained over time. How could it? Who would want to live constantly in a world of thrills and fears, of hopes raised and dashed? How could passion coincide with the mundane nature of day-to-day life?

Was the marble statue she sought to gain, by assisting Lord Sumner, the only way romance could last, by being quite literally fixed in stone? Was love as much a delusion as was the Lady of Shallot, who never really existed, who was but a creation for the fevered minds of daydreamers? After all, it was not love of Christopher that drove her to work to gain *The Lady's Boat*, but a rather idle, silly wish to complete a garden. Just a garden. If the garden's completion was a testimonial to her deceased husband, it was made so not out of anything so grand as love.

However . . . had she not witnessed an on-going, satisfying love between some couples? Were there not pairs she had matched who looked yet upon one another with a warmth and regard still in their gaze? She had politely looked away more than once from an intercepted exchange of intimate glances between husband and wife, even some couples who had been married for years. She would swear she had witnessed lasting affection— No, call it by its true name: love. Their love might no longer be giddy, but it was strong and pure and real—and, even if it made her play the fool, Augustine would believe in it.

"What an amazing expression you have on your

face," Lord Sumner said, bringing her back from her wandering thoughts as he shifted on the bench so that he could stretch out his long legs. He crossed his arms, his pose lax but for the dancing light in his eyes that betrayed a keen interest. "Whatever are you thinking?"

Augustine blushed, vowing not to give him any further opportunity to disparage her romantic assertions. "Nothing of significance."

"Indeed?" He crossed one ankle over the other. "But it cannot be nothing that has brought that rather appealing set to your face. 'Defiant Angel,' I should call it. Quite lovely on you. I fancy Joan of Arc looked just that way. Still, as lovely a mien as it is, I must tell you it gives me pause. I almost shudder to ask, but I can only wonder if it bodes some new plan for my matrimonial ambitions?"

"Yes," she answered at once, glad for the excuse. She cast about in her mind for a hasty plan. "I have . . . er, I have decided. . . ." She frantically thought back on the afternoon, and inspiration struck. "I think you should list for me what sort of mannerisms you could tolerate."

He made a face. "Must I tolerate any?"

"Of course. Everyone has mannerisms," Augustine said, warming to her topic. "Some are merely simpler to indulge than others." She reached for the carriage strap to steady herself on the seat as they rounded a turn, but as soon as she could let go of it, she did, waving her hands about in what she expected must be an imitation of the rejected Lady Christina. "We already know you do not care for excessive gestures."

"You will cease doing that, if you please," Lord Sumner growled, but there was too much humor there for the growl to be truly forbidding.

Augustine complied, but only after giving an exaggerated, languid sigh as if she were utterly crushed to have her oversized motions banned. "But what of a lady's laugh?" she asked. "What would quickly vex you? A high, throaty laugh? A deep, resonating one? One that runs on too long?"

"Yes, yes, and yes."

"Come now, you must make some effort to assist me with this," Augustine reproved, but the admonition was, at best, light-hearted. It was, she thought, just the thing for their serious discussion to be lightened by banter . . . and she would not turn up her nose at the chance to tweak him, just a little, now it had presented itself. "What of a lady's laugh, Lord Sumner?"

"A lady's laugh?" He blew out a puff of air, lifting his hands in a gesture of defeat. "It is so difficult to tell! What might be offensive in one is charming in another."

"That is true, I suppose. Well, except in those cases where a laugh is such that it would annoy simply anyone," she mused. "But—"

"Laugh for me."

Augustine stared at him, and now she saw by the gleam in his eyes that he had no compunction about tweaking her in return.

"Make some laughing noises. I will tell you which grate and which do not," he said.

"Such folly!" she protested. "If you do not care to—"

"It makes perfect sense!" he said, and now he smiled outright.

The beast! He was aware his request nonplused her, and he was rather enjoying that fact.

"You make the sound," he went on, "and I will say whether it pleases me or not. Come now, my lady, you must not say me nay. If you can ask me to assist *you*, then I must be free to ask that you assist *me*," he insisted.

"Why is it I always suspect that, under the guise of

seeking my counsel, you are actually mocking me?" she grumbled, but his gaze remained steady and pressing, if unabashedly amused.

"I could say the same," he said.

Her mouth shaped to utter a protest, but honesty forced her lips together again. He made a good point. "Oh, very well then!" she agreed in a huff.

"Very well then," he returned.

She was hardly in the mood to give forth gales of laughter, so the first sound she essayed rather sounded like a crone's cackle. He gave her a steady look, not deigning to respond to the poor attempt. She cleared her throat, feeling as foolish as she no doubt appeared, and tried again.

One side of his upper lip drew up, his rejection clear.

"That was what I would call a 'girlish giggle,' " she explained, and when he shook his head, she joined him by also shaking her head in denial. "No, of course you would not care for it. Only the most empty-headed of fellows would find such an utterance appealing."

"I will take that as compliment," he said. He made a shooing motion in the air with his hand, urging her, "Go on."

She demonstrated for him a medley of laughs, from simple varieties of sound—a chortle, a snigger, a twitter—and leading on to every unusual sound she could think to utter. She gave a short, sharp bark; a long, rolling peel; an aria that went up and down in a way he declared to be "fruity and silly"; and then tried a few of honest intent. She called one of these a "behind the fan" laugh; another a "shy but encouraging" laugh; then "an intrigued" laugh; and a "matron's" laugh.

She thought of one last version, blushing and laughing at once at the exaggerated horror on his face. "I should have to call that last a horselaugh," she explained rather ruefully.

"Do that again and I shall have to cast you from my carriage, my lady!" Lord Sumner protested with a sideways grin. "I cannot have passersby imagining I pass my time with a charwoman."

"A charwoman!" she cried, her hands going to her hips in a gesture of mock offense, but underneath it she could not really be upset, for there was no denying it had been a particularly vulgar sound.

"Well, yes . . . but you did it very well," he assured her.

"Oh!" Augustine cried. "You insult me doubly!" But her anger was all pretense, and she laughed.

His grin lasted a moment more, but then some of his mirth gave way to a more earnest expression. "There, that laugh of yours—that is very pleasant. I would not mind such a laugh."

"Oh," she said, her hands still on her hips, but with all defiance fled from her bones. "But . . . my lord, how am I to find such a laugh as my own?" she said, attempting a light, self-jesting tone. "I have always thought my laugh to be particularly pleasant and individual."

He inclined his head in a single nod. "It is."

For a moment Augustine was utterly paralyzed by the thought that Joseph surely flirted with her . . . and that the experience was utterly delightful and welcome.

"And that way you have, that is one behavior I do not object to overmuch," he said, making a gesture toward her. "The way you put your arms like that, and put up your chin, and otherwise let me know I have stepped beyond the pale."

Augustine at once lowered her arms and her chin, quite possibly because she had very little strength left in them, no doubt due to the fact she only belatedly remembered to breathe.

No, she was mistaken, she told herself. This was not flirtation—or at least not meant directly for her,

Augustine. It was banter, the result of long habit, Joseph's way with women. His compliments carried no weight. Most certainly he was not wholly serious; she had only to see the growing glimmer in his eyes to know that.

"A show of defiance or disapproval can prove a useful thing in a wife . . . if it does not happen too often, of course," he explained, the grin spreading anew. "I could bear such mannerisms in a spouse."

"You could bear—! Oh, my lord, how delighted I am to have finally pleased you," Augustine blustered, the tone heightened by a rush of relief . . . or was it disappointment that gave her voice its edge? Nonsense! Even were she so foolish as to wish he might want to exercise his charm on her, there was no reason to believe *he* had any deep, ardent reason to do so. Their conflict was too long-standing, too deeply rooted, their mutual history too forbidding. Whyever would she think anything else? Foolish creature, to mistake badinage for attraction, even for a moment!

She made a play of waving her hand before her face as though it were a fan. She wished, in fact, she had brought one of her fans, that she might cool—or perhaps even hide—her too-warm cheeks from his gaze. "And how much may a lady use her fan in your presence, to be considered bearable that is?" she asked crisply, as if offering him a gibe were to somehow explain away her agitation.

"Well, certainly any more fanning than that would certainly cloy," he assured her.

Augustine allowed her hand to fall once again to her lap. "I see. How quickly may this lady move? Do you care for a quick-stepped girl who prances through garden paths, or for a languid lady only inclined to stately saunters?"

"Please tell me there exists something between the two?" he pleaded, hand to chest.

Her mouth quirked unexpectedly, but she ruthlessly smothered the laugh that bubbled to her lips. "And how many times may a lady bat her eyelashes during any one conversation before it disturbs you?"

"I feel generous," he declared, now with an expansive gesture of his hands. "I shall say six, no, seven times." He sat back, lifting a cautioning finger. "Eight is straight out though, I will have you know."

"Of course! But so many as seven? I fall behind." She batted her eyelashes several times in quick succession at him.

"Be careful, my lady, or I shall forget that you instruct me, and shall mistake your actions for flirtation," he teased.

"Never do so!" she declared, perhaps a little too shrilly, and could not think why she looked away from his gaze. She did not truly see a warmth reflected there, she had just told herself as much, and yet. . . .

Lord Sumner leaned forward. "Why, Lady Wayfield, I believe you are blushing."

Nine

"I never blush," Augustine denied roundly, regretting the lie as soon as it was out. "Or, if I do so now, it is because I have been forced to give a ridiculous laughing performance. Who would not blush to give such a display?"

Lord Sumner sat back once more, laughing lightly. "As you say."

He indulged in his own thoughts for a minute, giving Augustine time to gather her poise, even if he had not meant to do so. When he looked up again, he had cast aside his amusement for a more serious aspect. "But, come, we approach your home and therefore the end of what is in truth a useful conversation," he said quite reasonably. "I have a proposal. I will cease my teasing and say instead what you require to hear. I would not have you believing I have not given this matter of impending connubiality due consideration. It behooves you to know what manner of demeanor and temperament in a wife would serve me best. I have thought of some things, if you wish—?"

The look he gave her was quaintly anxious, and if Lord Sumner could be humble, this was the moment she was most inclined to believe him capable of such a trait. "Certainly," she said, and told herself her voice had lowered to invite any confidences he might wish to utter, not because he suddenly seemed even more charming in this vein of seriousness.

He turned on the seat, settling his back in a corner of the squabs, and brushing an invisible thread from his knee. "I wish . . . I would want to find a simple lady. Not a half-wit, that is not what I mean, of course, but a person who is unconcerned with extravagance or scattergood ways." He looked off into the distance, and Augustine could not say if he avoided looking at her because he wished to elude her regard, or because he sought to choose the right words to convey his meaning.

"It is not that I mean to pinch pennies when I say an uncomplicated lady would best suit, but rather that Marcus would be best served by a mama who more often stays at home than goes out to every social affair in the Town. She can dress as finely as she wishes, but, too, she should understand when it is time to be less than elegant, to sit on the floor and play jackstraws, to walk through the mud with bare . . . toes . . . ," he finished uncertainly, darting a glance at her.

It was not the manner of thing a gentleman said to a lady; to speak of bare anything was to offend her sensibilities—but in this case, 'bare toes' said far more than a dozen less direct words.

"I beg your pardon, my lady—" he began an apology.

"My lord," she assured him softly, "I refuse to find any words we need use in our discussions scandalous, if you will refuse to hold back that which best explains what you seek. Agreed?"

He nodded once, one corner of his mouth rising, perhaps reluctantly. "Since I am forever speaking too plainly, I deem your proposal most wise, particularly as you are forever pressing me on such subjects. So it is agreed." The serious moment was once again tinged with humor. "I shall be vulgar then, and painfully blunt. I shall denigrate other ladies freely within your hearing, quite unlike a gentlemen ought." The lift to his mouth angled upward and she caught a gleam of deviltry in his eyes. "And all the while, you will sit and quietly observe, and otherwise seem quite virtuous as I prove how base I can be."

"That sounds lovely," she assured him, batting her lashes anew.

"Charwoman!"

"Boor!" she countered, and laughed along with him, gratified to sense they had smoothed a path that they might follow in the next weeks. She would not go so far as to say they had repaired their one-time friendship, but perhaps each of them could cease with being prickly and doubtful and utterly uncertain of the other's intent.

At that moment, the carriage rocked to a stop before her home. One of her footmen came at once from the house, moving to place a block for the ease of the dismounting passengers. Lord Sumner opened the small door, and leaped down, turning back to offer his hand to Augustine.

"So, my Defiant Angel, have you learned enough from me to go forth and discover my ideal?" he teased, but there was no barb hidden behind the words.

"Perhaps," Augustine answered, accepting his hand down. As soon as she was free of the block, she took back her hand, and wondered why the little touch of exertion that came from exiting the carriage had caused her heart to beat so? She shook off the thought, and looked up at him. "I do have a notion as to where we might be well served to seek our gem tomorrow."

"And where is that?" he asked, crossing his hands behind his back, his eyebrows raised in expectation.

"The lending library."

Lord Sumner raised a hand to his forehead, groaning. "Dear me, did I say I was seeking a bluestocking?

If I did, I assure you it was merely an aberration of speech—"

"Tut, my lord! It is not only bluestockings who read, you know. Many ladies read. Many *unmarried* ladies, with time on their hands. . . ."

"Ah," he said, a dawning light of comprehension in his eyes.

"Ah, indeed," Augustine said with a smug nod of her head.

The following afternoon, Augustine smiled her acceptance of a cup of the tea provided for the customers at Hatchard's bookshop.

Lord Sumner was seated beside her. She glanced at him as she settled the cup of tea in the plate on the low table before her, only to see he made a discreet motion with his head. There was no mistaking he wished for Augustine to rise and join him, as he himself rose, mumbled something about searching for a particular book, and disappeared around a book-lined shelf. After a minute or more, Augustine made her excuses to the couple with whom they had been partaking of tea, and attempted to move discreetly in the direction Lord Sumner had taken.

She found him in a small alcove.

"Why are we taking tea with an old married couple?" he hissed at once when she joined him.

"Because they asked us to, and because I have a great fondness for Sir Terrence and Lady Dibbins," she answered calmly. "And they are hardly old. Or at least I hope they are not, for I am a year older than Lady Dibbins."

"Excuse me for not seeing how tea with this inestimable couple assists me in finding a wife," he said impatiently.

"What else are we to do here in this bookshop? Spring upon young ladies as they enter the door?" Augustine asked, nearly laughing at the image that leaped to mind.

His brows drew together. "No, of course not. But I cannot see how being engaged in idle chatter leaves me free for any other purpose either. Ought I not to wander about, accidentally dropping a book, that manner of thing?"

Augustine rolled her eyes. "Certainly, if you wish to be obvious."

"I do not care if I am obvious!"

"Hush, your voice grows loud."

"I would consider," he made a concerted effort to lower his voice, "issuing an advertisement in the *Times*, if such a thing would not only serve to repulse the most satisfactory candidates."

"You would do no such thing."

"No," he agreed, and it seemed he had to pause to master both his voice and his temper. "But it is a bit too late, you must admit, to care whether or not London has been made baldly aware of my search for a wife."

"Indeed. But there are more subtle ways of engaging ladies in conversation than casting books at their toes. A lady would not dare let you think her a hoyden by responding to such a transparent, tired ploy. Yet, if you are happily engaged in taking tea and conversation with others, then it is a simple thing to expand our circle and invite a young lady or two to join us. You see? Then, if she does not suit, it is easy enough to turn your attention to others of the gathering. No harm done, no insult offered, no toes broken by falling tomes. Simplicity itself!"

He took on an obstinate look—quite reminiscent of Marcus at times—but then he nodded agreement.

"Come back to the tea, and I think you will find that

Sir Terrence and his wife make for charming company between those times when we manage to entice wandering unmarrieds to join us," she said, taking his arm.

"Sir Terrence is a massive fellow, is he not?" Lord Sumner countered. "However did such a giant come to take the merest wisp for a wife?"

"That tale will have to wait. This is, in my humble experience, the busiest hour here at Hatchard's. Come, it is time to cast out our nets and see what we may catch."

Two hours of tea and conversation proved to include no less than eight ladies of unmarried status, who stayed and went at varying times, and all of whom found themselves sooner than later in conversation with Lord Sumner.

When the front door ceased to open every few minutes to admit another customer, and even Sir Terrence and his wife had made their *adieux,* a nod from Lord Sumner showed Augustine he was quite disposed to leave. He paid for a few books to be delivered to his home, which he amusingly grumbled he bought only to compensate the establishment for the price of all the tea he had drunk and now he was permeated with the vile brew, thank you very much, and then escorted Augustine out on to Piccadilly Street.

"Despite my misgivings, and a tendency to slosh, I must say that proved a pleasurable afternoon," he concluded, tipping his hat in salute to Augustine.

"I agree, but, too, it was vexing. I cannot tell you how many times I wished to ask you a question about any one lady, but of course it was impossible. We could scarce disappear around the shelving every other minute or so." Augustine adjusted the fit of her gloves, shaking her head over the last hour's frustration. "Ah well! So tell me now, did the day show you anyone who could bring forth your more tender emotions?"

"I inform you, again, that I am not seeking anyone to bring forth my more tender emotions. However, to answer the better question: no. There was no one."

Augustine allowed her shoulders to slump.

"I am sorry, but Miss Merriweather and Miss Jonas gave no indication of being of the temperament required for administering to children. And the others!" He did not bother to go on, instead giving an elegant *moué* of distaste.

Augustine straightened her shoulders. "I am afraid I have to agree. Miss Tompkins' lisp may be all that is fashionable, but it is also all that is exasperating. 'Weally, Ward Sumner, I simpwy adore wittle wambs!' "

"You exaggerate," Lord Sumner said on a laugh. "We never once mentioned sheep."

"Lady Harriet, bless her, can only be described as bird-witted. As to Elsbeth Killian's simper!"

He turned to her, beaming. "My dear Lady Wayfield! It is so kind of you to denigrate the ladies, saving me the effort. How can I thank you for taking on the task?" He took up both her hands as an earnest gallant might do, but his grin was anything but agreeable.

Augustine resisted the impulse to pull her hands free of his. She dare not, lest he note how disconcerted his touch suddenly made her—why, how ridiculous to have any other response than provocation at his teasing! What folly. It must be that they stood in the heart of St. James's and she was flustered to see several heads turn their way.

Augustine sniffed, putting her nose in the air. "Think nothing of it. I like to make my followers comfortable, so occasionally I must descend to their level." She stared off at nothing, taking on a martyred aspect. " 'Tis a burden, but one I hope I bear well."

Her hands were suddenly dropped, drawing her gaze back to Lord Sumner, who had one hand to his throat, one to his waistcoat, a pained expression on his face. "Pardon me," he said, his voice weak and thin, "but I suddenly feel quite ill."

"Oh, do stop!" Augustine cried, laughing despite her pique. "We are quite making a spectacle of ourselves. Only see how Lady Grishem stares from her landau."

Chuckling, Lord Sumner inclined his head in acknowledgment that their spoken raillery was at an end for the moment, but to Augustine's surprise he once again gathered up one of her hands, placing it on his sleeve. "So then, my lady of propriety, this seems to me to be a good time to tell me the tale of your friends, Sir Terrence and his charming, tiny wife," he said, as they began to stroll.

"Lady Dibbins truly is charming, is she not? They were one of the first couples I brought together."

" 'Brought together.' How quaint a phrase."

"Hush now or I will not tell you the story."

"And keep me awake wondering all night? Heaven forfend."

Augustine cast him a speaking glance, but continued nevertheless. "I will have you know that Sir Terrence and his lady wife are proof of the Fourth Indication of Love." She paused, reaching for where her reticule dangled from her wrist.

"I believe I am capable of remembering one sentence, my lady. You need not fetch a card for me," he chided her gently.

"Are you indeed? Then I shall assist you by speaking slowly." She smiled at his scowl. "Here then is my pearl of wisdom for the day: The Meek are Made Strong, the Mighty Made Gentle."

"And this dictum represents Sir Terrence and the charming Lady Dibbins? I can see where mighty enters into it, for Sir Terrence is a large man, and most jovial, but I would not call him gentled."

"That is because you did not know him before his marriage. He is a bear of a man in body, and was in habit once as well. He was a country fellow, rather misplaced in London, and his size frequented much unwelcome discourse. One round of fisticuffs led to another, and before long our Sir Terrence was said to be quick of temper and short of patience. His reputation spread, of course, and before long there was not a father in London who would allow his daughter to so much as a dance with the combative fellow he had become."

"Sir Terrence? I have difficulty imagining him in temper, but even more difficulty imagining why anyone could think they might better him in a fight."

"It was part of the sport, of course, to see how many fellows Sir Terrence could dispense with at any one time in an evening."

"Ah, I see! It was one against many."

Augustine nodded. "And he usually came out the victor. But one night he had taken one blow too many, and while attempting to walk home, fell unconscious in the road."

It was Lord Sumner's turn to nod. "And that is where Lady Dibbins found him, of course."

"Of course. Coming home from a ball, she insisted that her driver stop and that the man, Sir Terrence, be given medical care." Augustine sighed contentedly. "I daresay it was love at first sight. From that night forward Sarah, that is Lady Dibbins, would consider accepting no one else's offer but that of Sir Terrence. Naturally her father saw it differently."

"This is the part where you entered as matchmaker."

"It is. I listened to Sarah's glowing tale of how gentle and sweet and kind she had found the injured man in her carriage to be, for he had thanked her most politely and profusely, in language that had made her think him the most courtly gentleman. That impression lasted as he called upon her twice, and even after her papa brought word of Sir Terrence's reported character home. She was dismayed to learn how Sir Terrence spent his evenings, of course, but she was not shaken in her belief that he was at heart a good man.''

"And then you . . . ?" Lord Sumner prompted.

"All I did was insist they dance together when next they were in the same room, even though Sarah was shaking as a leaf in a high wind at the thought of disobeying her father's strict command that she was not to speak, let alone dance, with Sir Terrence. I had very little to do with what happened then, for it was in truth Sir Terrence's confession to her that he had indeed been acting a brutish beast in the city's pubs and coffee-houses, and that, if she would only look upon him in good favor as she had the night of his rescue, he would forever change and cease his belligerent ways at once. And he did! There was never another round of fisticuffs, not even with undue provocation.

"Lady Dibbins saw he had meant it and done it, all for her sake, and she defied her father, who was most appalled at the idea of bringing a huge, uncivilized country lad into his family. She insisted she would marry no other, and so in the end wed Sir Terrence. Happily, the family has since come to admire her choice of husband, but that is not the point of the tale. The point is that Sir Terrence was made gentle, and Lady Dibbins was made strong, to defy her father in that way, and all for the sake of love."

They stopped at the corner of the street, Augustine turning to beam at Lord Sumner as she basked in the remembered happy glow of the Dibbins' wedding day.

"Do cease at once," he murmured mildly, making a deliberate snuffling sound, "else I shall be forced to wipe a tear from my eye and ruin a perfectly good glove."

"Oh, you!" Augustine abruptly pulled her hand from his arm. "Men! You make sport of every tender sentiment. Not to mention you have spoilt my lovely story!"

"Have done, dear lady, I only meant a moment's sport," he said, his expression half mirth and half apology, so that she could not tell which was the greater."

"You may ridicule their love if you like, but it will not make it any less real."

"I never said it was not. You put words in my mouth, Lady Wayfield. I only meant to remind you that *my* happy ending is not meant to be quite so grand a passion as all that."

"Your real intention was to remind me that you do not believe in love at all," Augustine snapped.

Lord Sumner stared down at her, and she might have remained angry if his face had been an unfeeling mask, but it was not. Instead there was a question there. It reflected, she thought with a sharp pulling in of her breath as they stood there confronting each other, that he searched his very core for an answer to her accusation. There was no lack of feeling here in this man, but instead a hint of old pain and nagging uncertainties, of perhaps even fear. Was it a fear of the future? Of what a new wife might refute or prove to his heart? Was it a fear that the lack between him and Meribah would manifest itself again, no matter what manner of woman he took to wife?

He lowered his gaze, hiding any further revelations from Augustine's scrutiny. "You say I do not believe in love at all," he said slowly, quietly. "I . . ." Words failed him, or perhaps he chose not to finish his statement. Instead, he looked at her once more, and said in a careful, cool voice, "It does not matter if such love exists, not to a man who does not seek it." He turned away, lifting his hand, signaling to the watching driver of his carriage that he was ready to be taken up again.

She said nothing as they awaited the carriage and as he handed her up, knowing no mere words would change his conviction. Only time and care could do that; only the irrefutable proof of love itself. All the same, she could not keep herself from reaching out a hand to lay atop his where it rested on the edge of the landau. He glanced at her touch, but made no move to join her in the carriage, instead closing the landau's door.

"I will walk home, I think." He smiled tightly, pulling his hand free. "The air will serve to clear my head of fairy stories. These days, only Marcus has need of such tales."

"That is not true," Augustine whispered, but she spoke only to herself, for Lord Sumner had already moved away.

Ten

Sitting in Augustine's parlor the next morning, Lord Sumner appeared baffled. "A dog lead?" he repeated.

"Yes. Do you possess one?" Augustine asked, handing Marcus another block to add to the already teetering tower of blocks on the low parlor table before him.

"We have ten," Marcus chimed in, never taking his eyes from the tower. He carefully placed the block at the top of the stack.

Lord Sumner shook his head. "Well, perhaps not ten, but yes, we have some—"

"Then my plan can go forward. Go and fetch it, my lord, and one of your more attractive hounds, please."

"One of my hounds? I thought we were attempting to devise a new and clever way to summon yet more unwed ladies to my side?"

"Quite. Was not one of your requirements that your new lady should harbor a fondness for animals? I can think of no more direct way to test this attribute than to stroll about with one of your dogs on a lead, and see who finds the creature charming and who does not."

Lord Sumner tilted his head back against the chair in a gesture of reluctant resignation. "I would have it understood that I refuse to entangle anyone in the lead-string," he warned. "That would be even more trite than dropping books at their feet."

"I could not agree more. How hackneyed! I never proposed as much. But casually strolling with your favored pet—what could ever be found amiss with that? It will work splendidly, you will see." Augustine handed another block to Marcus. "I told you I but needed a moment to think this morning and I would have a new plan of attack," she congratulated herself.

"Now I know why you have made a matchmaker of yourself, my lady," he said. "It is clear you require a venting of your creative energies. I tremble to think what noisome little tasks your mind would conjure were it not bent to arranging matrimonial possibilities."

"Your thanks are as warmly received as they are offered." She gave him a deliberately acidic smile.

"I meant it as a tribute! Nelson ought to have had such knowing and crafty advisers."

"*That* was a rather knowing and crafty attempt at retraction, my lord, but you need not have bothered yourself. I had already taken your words as praise, howsoever faint. Now, will you procure that lead and hound, or must I do everything?"

He cast her a dark look.

"When you return, we will set out for a stroll together," she added.

"We cannot include Marcus," he said, standing.

"Papa!" the boy protested at once.

"Mrs. Rasmussen assures me Marcus is once again requiring a midday nap to compensate for a sudden increase in growth."

"I *loathe* naps," Marcus said emphatically, his tonal quality a higher-pitched reflection of his father's. He eyed his tower as if he were tempted to send its teetering height tumbling. Instead he put out his hand to receive another block.

"And so you will until you reach the age of thirty or

so, and then a daily nap will strike you as being a very excellent manner in which to spend your midday."

"Papa—!" Marcus began to protest again.

"No 'buts' or 'pleases,' not after we have spent all morning away from your studies so that you might sail your boat in Lady Wayfield's pond."

"It was a very little pond," Marcus pointed out. "It did not make me tired at all."

"And that is why you have been rubbing your eyes for the past fifteen minutes, is it? Because you are not in the least tired? Come, my lad." Lord Sumner stood, stretching out his hand. "Papa must walk the dog, you must rest, and then I will come and help you at your lessons later."

Marcus reluctantly got to his feet, knocking down the blocks with a clatter so that he could scoop them into the little painted wagon in which he had carried them over to Augustine's. Lord Sumner went down on one knee to assist in finding the various blocks that had tumbled to the rug, and Augustine retrieved the ones tangled in her skirt. The wagon loaded, Marcus took up the rope handle, and offered his other hand to his father without further fuss.

"I will return shortly," Lord Sumner assured Augustine.

"During my mathematics, Papa holds up his fingers so I may add my numbers above ten, you know," Marcus told her by way of a farewell, his small face gleaming in anticipation.

"How truly helpful," Augustine returned, unable to resist the sudden urge to reach out and ruffle the little boy's already mussed hair.

"G'bye," he said with a grin, lifting a chubby-fingered hand in farewell salute.

"Goodbye, Marcus." Augustine lifted her hand in return, and turned on the sofa to watch over its back as

the pair departed the room. She settled amongst the
sofa cushions, her chin resting where her arms crossed
on the sofa back, and issued a large sigh. Why had she
been denied the joy of having a child? Had it been some
manner of penitence for the sin of not loving her husband? Or was nature too wise to allow such a gift to
someone who had yet to prove she was capable of love?

Such were foolish notions, of course, for many unde-
serving persons, and many who shared no love between
them, had borne the fruits of their union. Only look
to Lord Sumner and his wife: they had been blessed
with Marcus, and if ever a couple had been, at best,
discordant, they were such a couple.

I could marry again, Augustine thought, just as she had
thought a thousand times before. Perhaps a new marriage with a different man would produce different results. She contemplated the notion at times. Many men
might wish to join her income to theirs; there would
be no shortage of volunteers. She could even select, say,
a widower, a man who had proven his ability to propa-
gate. . . . But, no, she would not marry just to be married, not even in hopes of bearing a child. Not again,
not having learned that marriage, for her, could never
be made bearable without love or true affection.

Augustine offered another sigh, and rose to go to her
chamber, wherein she changed from her kid slippers
to halfboots for walking outside.

Mosby found her as she descended the stairs to return
to the parlor. "Lord Sumner has returned," the butler
informed her, sounding nettled beneath his usual ve-
neer of serenity. "He claims you are expecting him."

"I am," Augustine said, pulling on her gloves.

"Very good, my lady. I have not placed him in the
front parlor, my lady. He has some manner of hound
at his side. I am pleased to report he did not wish to
bring the animal into my lady's hall."

Augustine smiled to herself, wondering for a brief moment what Mosby would make of children about the house if he so obviously disapproved of dogs. "Thank you, Mosby. I require my dove grey cloak and the matching bonnet, if you please."

Mosby bowed himself away to complete this task, and Augustine crossed to the entry. The door stood ajar, revealing Lord Sumner waiting without. One end of a leather lead was held in his gloved hand, the other end of the lead concluding in a leather harness fitted about the chest of a large, brindle-coated dog.

"I asked you to bring a dog, not a tiger," Augustine declared, staring at the large animal whose coat boasted charcoal grey and tawny stripes.

"This is Lewisham's Pride, although I call him simply Lewis," Lord Sumner introduced the narrow-headed, thickly-haunched animal.

"Lewis?" Augustine echoed as Mosby returned with her things. The butler assisted her in donning her cloak as she commented, "Such a small name for such a big beast."

"He is not a beast at all. He is a greyhound. I think him the most handsome of my lot, one who would best suit our purposes today."

"He certainly is a handsome fellow," Augustine conceded, offering her hand for the dog to sniff. The long, half-curved tail waved acceptance, and she was allowed to caress the animal's ears. "My goodness, fellow!" she said to the dog. "You are of a size for Sir Terrence." She stepped back, accepting her bonnet, tying the velvet ribbons under her chin. "But I do not think it would be wise to give his lead to *me*. He would have me at the run on the first pull."

"Not to worry. I will tend to him. He may be large, but he has always been well-mannered."

"I take it from the harness about his chest that he would be able to pull free of a more conventional lead?"

"Exactly. Having that narrow head over a thick neck allows him to simply back out of a throat collar. And he would, too, if he thought there were something interesting to chase after. He was born and bred to race, and was a winner, too. But at the age of five, he was all done in, and was going to be put down," Lord Sumner explained, reaching to stroke along the tall animal's spine. The dog leaned into his owner's leg in appreciation, forcing Lord Sumner to take a sideway step to regain his balance.

"So you told his trainers that he might have a home with you," Augustine supplied the end of the tale. "That was good of you."

"I confess to a certain fondness for dogs," Lord Sumner said, scratching the greyhound under the chin.

Three days ago, Augustine would have thought his statement only a casual comment, but now she looked at the way he stroked the dog's fur, and remembered the recent time a pack of the creatures had invaded her home. Lord Sumner had spoken firmly to them, expecting obedience, and she had thought him too harsh at the time. She had wondered if he knew how to be kind and forgiving to his little son.

She had taken the wrong impression then, she realized now. He was not a man of all severity and reproach, much as he chose to foster that impression. He might limit any showings of an easy, affable air, but for a certain few people he could be as agreeable and affectionate as any man. This was a man who had chosen the slavering but simple devotion of dogs to warm a heart made coldly infuriated by his unkind wife, rather than taking the comfort he could have found in a dozen other, less seemly, places. This was a man who sought to marry, that his son might be protected from an acrimonious grandpapa; a man who bestirred himself to walk next door to verify his child's welcome and well-being; a man who sullied the knee of his breeches to help that child retrieve blocks from the floor. Lord Sumner was capable of firmness, for Marcus' good of course, but any firmness was tempered tenfold by an inherent dedication to the boy's happiness. She knew that for a certainty now.

Augustine pretended at adjusting the ribbons of her bonnet, only to find her hands were not quite steady. Why this trembling, when all that had occurred was a simple revelation about her neighbor's truer nature?

Lord Sumner moved down the front steps, pulling on his dog's lead to bring the animal to his opposite side, looking up and offering his free arm to Augustine. She stepped down the stairs, placing her hand on his arm, pleased to note how a few quick breaths had caused her hands to steady once more.

Joseph glanced down the length of Cleveland Street. "Which way do we wander then?" he asked Lady Way-field.

"Bloomsbury Square, I think," she suggested.

At their first steps, Lewis leaned against his harness. Joseph checked the dog with a brief tug at the lead, and the hound fell contentedly into step, nose twitching as he scented the air.

If only humans could mirror how a dog took knowledge from the scents wafted on the wind, for then Joseph might have some sense of what had made Lady Wayfield's eyes grow so round and her expression so astounded. For a moment she had quite lost her poise, and if she had not at once struggled to disguise that loss from him, he would have questioned her directly. Had he said something to bring forth a painful memory? Or did she perhaps recall another walk with another man—Lord Wayfield, or perhaps a suitor?

Did Lady Wayfield have suitors?

Hanged if I know, Joseph thought with a frown. It could be these outings on his behalf took the comely widow away from an admirer . . . or even a lover. How astonishing that he had not considered the possibility before now!

"My dear lady, I have just thought that perhaps this was not the most auspicious time to embark on a new venture on my behalf. If you had other plans for the afternoon, we could certainly choose another time—"

"What is this? Do not tell me you are loathe to put forth a new offensive?" Lady Wayfield admonished.

"No, not at all. It is just that I thought perhaps *you* might have a more pressing occasion at which you would prefer to spend your time—"

"Stuff! I should have said as much were that the case," she assured him, giving him a curious glance. "After all, I have a statue to earn, do you remember? Or could it be that you are attempting to withdraw your offer to assist me in acquiring *The Lady's Boat?*"

"Never a bit!"

"Good. I thought perhaps your pull via the Foreign Office was proving not to be sufficient to persuade the Italian gentleman to await my offer?"

"It is quite sufficient," he said, allowing a cross tone to sneak into his words.

"Then, enough putting off what must be accomplished."

He accepted her dictate, if not the dismissive manner in which it was delivered.

"Allow me to explain how best to employ Lewis should we come near a likely candidate," she told him, apparently oblivious to his growing ill humor. "Ah! There is Miss Donnabelle Brown now, with her own pup in tow. She is an appealing lady, with clear and intelligent speech. Not stuffy, no, and the sort to be comfortable with children, I believe. Pray tell, Lewis will not bite or attack another dog, will he?"

"Only if provoked."

"Hmm, I certainly hope you are right. Too late to worry the matter now! You must allow him to venture close to Miss Brown's pup. It is only natural that once the dogs have noted each other, so must the owners. I shall make the introductions."

They sauntered closer to where Miss Brown walked her far smaller terrier, all the while Lady Wayfield scolding in a quiet voice to the dog, "Lewis, look there! Over there, boy," but Lewis remained fascinated with the movement of a bird overhead, heedless of the other approaching dog. He scented the air, his perked ears dropping as the bird settled out of sight on a branch. The dog lowered his head, snuffling about the walk, then came to a complete stop to inspect a patch of grass at the foot of a plane tree.

Joseph glanced up from his uncooperative dog, and found in mild surprise that, despite Lewis' lack, Miss Brown indeed observed him. However, no sooner had their eyes met than did she look away at once, in a manner that suggested a deliberate and polite blindness such as people walking their dogs in the park must cultivate. Joseph turned back to his dog, not the slightest surprised to find that Lewis had taken the opportunity to relieve himself against the tree.

"Lewis!" Lady Wayfield hissed, only to earn a wag of his tail from the mutt.

Joseph bit down hard on his lower lip, but it was almost not enough to keep the laughter from escaping him. "Bad dog," he tried to say, but the sound was garbled and he had to go back to biting his lip.

"That was most untimely," Lady Wayfield told the dog when he chose to return to the walk.

"Most," Joseph managed to agree.

"And only look, Miss Brown has quite been taken up by her carriage. We have missed our chance to impress her."

"On the contrary, I am certain we have made an impression on her," Joseph said, and then he simply had to laugh.

"Oh, stop! What schoolboy humor, honestly!" Lady Wayfield scolded, but there was no real sting in her words. She allowed Joseph a moment to compose himself, then insisted they move on to greener grass.

Joseph watched with interest as Lady Wayfield bypassed the widowed Lady Pitshanger ("Too set in her ways, and unlikely to be gracious to children"), and as she sighed with relief when Miss Russell turned the corner away from them ("Far too meek for you, my lord"). Miss Evergard and Miss Fetterson were similarly dismissed, as well as Lady Brockbury ("Too old! She is surely closer to fifty than thirty!" Joseph stated almost before Lady Wayfield could speak to reject the woman herself), and a decree of "Insufferable!" was all that Miss Williston earned.

They had a brief conversation with one Miss Harnhorst, due not to Lady Wayfield's recommendation but the fact that Lewis abruptly stood stiff, staring fixedly at Miss Harnhorst's corgi, Lewis' muscles quivering in anticipation of a good chase. Miss Harnhorst's announcement that she found Lewis' fixed attention "horrid and frightening" quickly put paid to that discourse.

"You *are* frightening, I suppose," Lord Sumner informed his dog as they strolled on, "but you are most certainly not horrid."

Lewis promptly disproved this by spotting a mouse in

the shrubberies and yanking Lord Sumner nearly from his feet as he set out in pursuit.

Joseph recovered his stance and pulled on the lead, but the dog was too engrossed in pursuing the crazily darting mouse to pay much heed. Lady Wayfield leaped back with a forgivable squeal when the bedeviled rodent dashed directly before her toes. Joseph tugged even harder, bringing the dog briefly under control. Control was but an illusion, however, for Lewis lunged forward anew. The dog gave a grunt against the restraint of the harness but still managed nearly to snatch up the mouse with a snap of his jaws. The tiny creature fled the opposite direction, into the bushes. Lewis followed him, bringing Joseph into the branches as well.

"I take back my words," Joseph muttered from between clenched teeth, kicking aside the snagging branches and dragging the animal free of the bushes.

"Oh, he caught the mouse!" Lady Wayfield cried in dismay, pointing at the tail sticking out of the dog's mouth.

Lewis, for his part, wagged his tail and lowered his head, dropping the creature between his paws, at once using one paw to pin it anew. The dog looked up, evidently pleased to show his hunting prowess, but before he could make a meal of his catch, Lord Sumner summarily caught him by the back of the harness, pulling the dog away from its prize. Lewis tried to lunge after the stunned, motionless mouse, but was caught short. He gave a frantic bark, the sound of which caused the mouse to miraculously spring back to life, making a crooked but rapid retreat under the bushes.

Joseph stood, breathing heavily as though to match Lewis' forlorn panting, and returned his gaze to Lady Wayfield, who stood with her hands on her hips, looking rather vexed. "Lewis is usually quite well-behaved," he said, and even to himself the comment seemed feeble. "He is only following his nature."

"My lord," Lady Wayfield said, and he was gratified to note she was not tapping her foot as her tone implied she might wish to do, "this cannot go on. You are discouraging anyone from approaching us."

"I!" he exclaimed, sputtering with affront. He pointed an accusing finger at the dog. "I am merely the victim here."

"Blaming the dog will not alter the fact we waste our time if no ladies will dare to come near. Now, tell Lewis to heel," she spoke with firm command.

Joseph glared at her, then said sharply, "Lewis! Heel!"

Lewis gave one last short bark of disappointment that he was to be denied the mouse, then feeling Lord Sumner release his hold on the harness, docilely moved into the heel position next to his master.

Now Joseph stared at the dog.

"You surely knew that racing dogs are taught such commands?" she asked mildly. "My papa explained to me that the handlers must be able to keep order in the pens. 'Heel' means they are to—"

"I know what it means!" Joseph growled.

"Honestly, my lord, you ought to learn to restrain that tone of impatience that comes into your voice. It can be most off-putting."

Joseph made a deliberate effort to unclench his teeth, and took a deep breath. "Quite right," he said calmly, although it was a struggle. "My regrets if I seemed at all harsh with you."

"Apology accepted. Now, we shall have no more difficulty if you will but keep the dog on a shorter lead. And brush yourself off," she instructed him, moving to dash at where bits of twig and leaf clung to his coat and waistcoat.

"Thank you. No, I shall do it, thank you," he said brusquely, stepping back from her to dust off his

breeches as well. He made a show of it, but not so much
to tidy his appearance as to escape her touch. Not that
he was angry at her, even though he had been incensed
with the situation but a moment earlier; no, that was not
it. It was not even that she was being kind—she was not,
she was being wholly irksome. It was not that he responded to the age-old stimulus of standing just a shade
too near one of her gender. It was, somehow, the very
fact that it was *her* touch that disconcerted him.

This reluctance to allow her hands idle access to his
person stemmed no doubt, he thought, from the full
knowledge that she was dictatorial, obstinate, and un-
deniably intrusive in her guise as matchmaker. He was
quite right to want to keep her at arm's length, to stay
her from thinking she might have some claim on him
once this business was behind them. It was only correct
and proper that she not assist him in ordering his appearance; such was far too familiar an act for mere business acquaintances.

The lead snapped tight as Lewis went stiff again, his
racer's body poised, his keen vision steadied on a sight
across the street.

"Miss Daniels," Lady Wayfield said, announcing with
seeming satisfaction the name of the lady across the way.
It was, however, certainly the caramel-spotted white greyhound at her side that had captured Lewis' attention.

"We are, I presume, going to cross the street?" Joseph
said.

"We are. Miss Daniels is a cheerful sort, well worth
cultivating."

Miss Daniels, lacking classical beauty but possessing a
nonetheless lively and appealing countenance, met them
cordially. She introduced her companion, Miss Clarkston,
an apparently older cousin who was not loathe to stand
and converse. The two dogs circled and wagged their tails
and made their own introductions to one another.

"This is Nanette," Miss Daniels named her pet, reaching down to pat the dog on the head, and getting Lewis' head thrust under her hand as well for her trouble.

"This is Lewisham's Pride, or Lewis if you prefer," Joseph said, pulling the lead closer to his side, for Lewis seemed to think the pat he had received meant he was free to misbehave. The dog tugged at the lead, leaning down on his front legs almost as if he bowed, when in truth it was an invitation to Nanette to play. At her lack of response, Lewis gave a few, sharp barks.

"Nanette scarcely ever barks," Miss Daniels noted, looking momentarily startled.

"It is unusual in the breed," Joseph agreed, wondering why in heaven's name, of all his dogs, he had chosen to bring this miscreant?

"He is so playful," Miss Daniels said, but she did not sound forbidding. "That shows he is a well-contented animal. Does he get to run much? I find Nanette is so much the healthier and happier if she runs several times a day."

"Indeed. My houndsman would quite agree with you, Miss Daniels," Joseph said.

Out of the corner of his eye he saw Lady Wayfield move to the cousin, Miss Clarkston, pulling her a little aside by asking if she was the talented lady who had made the lace of her dress' collar? Joseph did not physically acknowledge Lady Wayfield's ploy to leave him in close conversation with Miss Daniels, but he almost smiled to see it. He turned his attention back to Miss Daniels, nodding at her expectant gaze. She seemed gratified, which was a great relief since he could not say what she had been speaking of other than it had something to do with the nature of a greyhound's delicate coat.

She is pleasant, he thought as they talked on. Not loud, not gauche, not haughty. She proved with her statements that she had an intellect, one that was perhaps not quite keen, but wide enough in scope as to keep from boring a fellow after ten minutes. She had a very pretty smile, her best feature certainly, and she tolerated Lewis, despite his continued attempts at misbehavior. For the moment at least, she would do.

"Miss Daniels, would you do me the honor of agreeing to walk out with me tomorrow afternoon? With the dogs, of course?" he asked, taking the plunge.

It was only then that Lady Wayfield turned back to him, looking pleased. Miss Clarkston appeared gratified as well, beaming permission at her young cousin.

"How delightful. I would enjoy that very much," Miss Daniels said, blushing.

It was rather agreeable, Joseph thought to himself, to see that the lady was flattered by his attention . . . unlike Lady Wayfield, who was disposed to correcting his comportment rather than admiring it.

They made their farewells for the day, Joseph agreeing to meet the ladies at the northernmost bench in Bloomsbury Square tomorrow at three. Lewis strained at his lead, slavishly devoted to the idea of following Nanette home—that is, until a falling leaf caught the whole of his attention.

"I will situate myself elsewhere in the green tomorrow," Lady Wayfield told him, falling into step beside him. "In case the walk with Miss Daniels does not go well, we cannot afford to waste time. So I will be at hand to be of assistance in such a case, although you have no need of my company otherwise."

"You mean I am to be free of my nanny?" he asked, and was glad to see she accepted the quip in the light manner it had been meant to be taken.

"Miss Daniels might be the one," she said, and he could almost see her preening in satisfaction at the day's work, even though her tone had grown soft, thoughtful.

"For tomorrow's outing I will bring Marcus," he informed her.

"You did not tell Miss Daniels as much—oh! I see! That was quite deliberate. You wish to see how she responds to your son when she is not expecting his company."

He nodded. "Should she show any indifference or dislike for Marcus, there is little possibility of his being perturbed by it, as he will be far more interested in Lewis' antics than those of any adult. Marcus will have an outing with his papa, and I will hopefully see an honest reaction from Miss Daniels." He gave Lady Wayfield a sideways glance. "This is the place where you tell me how prodigiously clever I am."

"You are prodigiously clever—"

"Thank you."

"—although it was *my* idea to speak with Miss Daniels. So I suppose that makes *me* the prodigiously clever one."

"There is no gainsaying you, is there, Lady Wayfield?" he said on a sigh that just managed to transcend a laugh.

"I will concede that both of us need be clever if we are to find you a wife in, what say you, a little more than five weeks now?"

"Five weeks," he muttered, but it was of tomorrow that he thought. How strange it felt to think of going about the business of courting Miss Daniels, and stranger yet that it seemed somehow peculiar to do so without Lady Wayfield's steady, assessing gaze fixed upon him. How curious that in a matter of a few days, he had gone from being wholly unused to her company, to expecting her to be there as he stuck his reluctant toe into the treacherous tide of matrimonial waters.

Oh yes, he thought, *I must indeed be thinking of marriage*—for what other objective causes an otherwise sane and worldly man to act even more foolish and addlepated than Lewis?

Eleven

At a little after two the next afternoon, Joseph mounted the stairs in search of Marcus, only to stop at the window of the narrow landing halfway up to the bedchamber story in his townhouse. His gaze was drawn to the movement in the house beyond, to the dim outline of a person behind the glass of the window opposite. The outline most probably belonged to Lady Wayfield—Augustine—because it was her bedchamber window. Her writing desk sat before that window; there was no silhouette of her unless she sat just there, right before the window, but he had seen her there many times. Yes, it was Augustine sitting there—he knew by the way she smoothed the hair at her nape as she sat thinking.

He hesitated, not shifting to one side to obscure his presence behind the window curtain, but also not moving to capture her attention. What did she work on? Was it a letter to her mama? Or to a friend? A lover? Or could it be nothing more than a list of items her servants were to purchase from the grocer? Did she list the names of possible women for him to meet?

He shifted his weight from one foot to the other, wondering who occupied her thoughts when she was not matchmaking. What had ever impelled her to marry Lord Wayfield? Had Lord Wayfield been rather dull and uninspired, as Joseph looked back on the man now, or had he only seemed that way next to his spirited wife?

Joseph shook his head at his fanciful thoughts, but all the same it was with a sense of reluctance that he turned past the newel post to mount the remaining stairs. It was time to gather Marcus, to venture on to Bloomsbury Square and Miss Daniels.

By the time he walked out his front door with a freshly scrubbed and combed Marcus on one hand and a harnessed Lewis on the other, Joseph was in time only to see the retreating back of Lady Wayfield's coach. She was already on her way to her solitary bench in the square.

The sight of her grey and black coach inspired a glance at his pocketwatch, and although he was not running late, he did not resist a sudden feeling of esprit that struck him as he turned to walk with his son and dog back to the mews. Perhaps his search was over already. Perhaps Miss Daniels would prove to be the sort who could value a little boy who had not been born to her. He saw at once that his landau and team stood readied, declared so by the groom even as Joseph approached.

Lewis' lead—this time a long one, as Joseph anticipated letting the animal run on the lawns, if possible—was tied to the rear. Lewis relished what this meant, even though he consistently outpaced the horses as the carriage moved forward, ending by running beneath the carriage itself, no doubt with tongue happily lolling. Marcus was quietly delighted, shifting from one side of the landau to the other to peer at the parade of people and vehicles on the streets as their carriage rolled the short distance to the square.

The groom pulled the horses to a halt not more than thirty feet from where Miss Daniels and her cousin sat on the allotted bench. Joseph lifted a hand in greeting before jumping down from the carriage, turning to lift Marcus down as well, and then the two of them saw to untying Lewis.

Miss Daniels' greyhound wagged her long, thin tail in greeting as the threesome approached, and the two ladies stood.

"Miss Daniels, Miss Clarkston, I would like to introduce you to my son, Marcus. Marcus, this is Miss Daniels and Miss Clarkston."

Marcus gave a dutiful if unrefined bow and murmured, "How d'you do?" but his attention was truly already given over to Nanette. "May I pet him?"

"You have a son," Miss Daniels said, her eyes wide. "Of course, I suppose I knew that." She blinked. "What a handsome boy."

"May I pet him?" Marcus repeated, his hand already stretched forth.

"Her. It is a 'her.' Yes, you may," Miss Daniels said.

Joseph did not watch his son—unless mistreated, greyhounds were not given to snapping—instead observing Miss Daniels. There was no denying she had been momentarily confounded by Marcus' presence, but since she had not expected his attendance that was not to be wondered at.

"What is her name?" Marcus asked, nose to nose with the dog, who licked his face.

"We certainly have fine weather for a stroll, my lord," Miss Daniels said to Joseph.

Joseph just managed to keep his eyebrows from lifting—perhaps Miss Daniels had not heard Marcus' question. "The dog's name is Nanette," he explained to his son, then said to Miss Daniels, "Yes. I believe the weather means to hold fair for a while."

"Can I hold her lead?" Marcus asked Miss Daniels.

Miss Daniels looked at him, but it was to Joseph she spoke. "Shall we proceed?"

They strolled the perimeter of the garden, under the tall, summer-green trees and in the shade of the lovely terraced homes of the square. Joseph tried, he truly tried, to forgive Miss Daniels for her inattention to Marcus. After all, many people thought children should not speak unless first spoken to. She might have been concerned such a small boy could not control her large dog. And she was most probably flustered by the arranged meeting today, a sensation he admitted had been induced even to a certain degree in himself. But when she made no effort to include Marcus in any conversation beyond one token "Do you like dogs?," any other charms she might possess became no more engaging than the dust of the path their steps disturbed.

Marcus, fortunately, was as heedless of the lack as Joseph could have hoped, more than content to find himself the playmate of two large hounds. He talked with, sang to, and mostly unsuccessfully played "keep away" with them, grinning whenever they stole a stick from him or each other.

They met a betrothed couple with whom Miss Daniels was familiar, and introductions were made all around . . . all except for Marcus. Well, that was not quite right: she had not introduced the dogs either, Joseph noted sourly. He could wish to shake his head at the speculative glances the couple gave him and Miss Daniels, but of course he would not. Just as he would not ever ask to walk with Miss Daniels again. There was no question of that. The only question pending was how soon he might bow himself free of her company.

Marcus, as it happened, provided the impetus needed. "Lady Auggie!" he cried, having spied their neighbor. He abandoned the otherwise fascinating dogs to dash inside the iron railings of the square's garden to where Lady Wayfield sat reading on a bench.

She looked up, smiling and immediately putting aside

her book. "Master Marcus!" she greeted him, extending a hand to him.

He grabbed her hand and collided into her skirts, making her laugh rather breathlessly. "My dear fellow, whatever has put those stars in your eyes?"

"Look, Lady Auggie. That lady has a greyhound, just like Papa's, only white."

"Oh, I see," she said, looking up at Joseph as he stepped nearer to the bench. She nodded to him, and there must have been some conclusion as to Miss Daniels' suitability writ on his face, for Lady Wayfield reared back ever so slightly, and one corner of her mouth turned down momentarily. She checked the expression, and then greeted the two ladies who wandered slowly in tow. "Miss Daniels. Miss Clarkston."

"Lady Wayfield," Miss Daniels returned, as did her companion.

"What good fortune this is to encounter my good neighbor this way," Joseph said, knowing it sounded too theatrical but unable to playact any better than that. "I have meant to speak to you, Lady Wayfield, about the . . . er, the fence that adjoins our properties. Might I stroll home with you as we discuss the matter?"

"Certainly," Lady Wayfield returned smoothly, proving herself the superior actor. She stood and picked up her book, then offered a hand to Marcus. "Come, my little friend. Shall we see if you can find the way home without my telling you?"

Marcus' agreement was a whoop—a wholly uncharacteristic sound that caused Joseph to lift his eyebrows in wonderment at the carefree noise.

He made his excuses to the ladies, not lingering once Marcus had taken his farewell of Nanette. He noted the boy made no effort to say good-bye to the ladies, and could not bring himself to insist on better manners.

They returned north across the lawn, Lewis' lead extended full out, giving the dog the chance to run and dance about Marcus. Beyond the wrought iron railings Joseph spotted his carriage just returning from walking the horses, so he lifted a hand until he saw his groom's nod of acknowledgment.

"Watch me, Auggie! Watch Lewis!" Marcus cried to Lady Wayfield, already back at his game of stick with the dog.

Lady Wayfield applauded the dog's theft of the stick from behind Marcus' back, and laughed when Lewis dashed away with the prize at a speed the little boy could only try, wholly inadequately, to emulate.

Her hands still clasped together from applauding, Lady Wayfield turned to Joseph, and for the first time he could remember in years showed an uncertainty in her manner. "I can see Miss Daniels disappointed you."

Joseph crossed his hands behind his back and nodded. "She disregarded Marcus, more than once. More than I could forgive for youth, or uneasiness, or for any other reason," he explained, keeping his voice low so that it would not carry to Marcus. He shrugged. "I know I am the boy's father, and partial to his company, but Miss Daniels chose to ignore his every word, and I found that unacceptable."

"Surely not every word?" Lady Wayfield echoed, her brow creased with what looked to be worry or agitation.

"Nearly every word."

"Well, Miss Daniels has certainly failed at the Second and Third Indications of Love," she said, her lips compressing.

He blinked rapidly, thinking a moment to recall the references. "Ah yes. Something about charms outweighing lapses in demeanor, I believe your card said. And for number three, I was to experience a desire to remain in the lady's company, which is obviously not so."

She nodded. "She is definitely not the woman we seek." She opened her reticule. "Here then."

She handed him a list—could this be the very list he had seen her making at her writing table this morning? The thought filled him with a strange kind of warmth, perhaps a belated embarrassment at having spied upon her.

" 'Miss Delia Plumhouse, Southampton Row. Miss Bernice Wyatt, Theobold's Road. Lady Fulholt-Simons, Russell Square'," he read aloud. He lowered the list, which contained a dozen more names, thinking he'd had the right of it earlier today: she had made a list of likely ladies for him. "I presume," he said, not sure whether to smile or scowl, "that you intend for us to call upon these addresses and hope the ladies will receive us?"

"Precisely. With Lewis in tow, you see. Each of these ladies is an admirer of the species, and you will quite impress them with his presence." She put a hand on his sleeve. "I am sorry about Miss Daniels. I had no idea. I hope Marcus took no offense, my lord?"

"Oh, no, happily," he said, and wondered why her use of his title seemed oddly distancing. She had not called him Joseph in years, so why did he find himself of a sudden wishing she might address him as such? To lessen the tension that must inevitably exist between two estranged persons who must suddenly work together? Naturally that, and perhaps to make it all seem a little less artificial. And how was it that her touch had seemed too intimate earlier, but now seemed befitting and even welcome? He even put his own hand over hers—only to have her pull her hand away at once. He lowered his hands, crossing them behind his back again.

"I am pleased to learn he was not upset. There was no lasting harm done then, other than a loss of time otherwise well-spent. Lady Fulholt-Simons, I must say, would certainly have better sensibilities about children, as she has three of her own. The oldest is twelve, I believe, a girl."

Joseph glanced at the list before tucking it in his pocket. "Russell Square is near at hand," he pointed in the general direction with a nod of his head, "so we would be well-served to take the opportunity to see if the lady is at home to receive us. That is, if you are inclined to continue on with me? I am acquainted with a few of the ladies on your list, and so do not require an introduction to be admitted at those houses. Shall I return you home?"

"What if no one is receiving, and what of the ladies whose acquaintance you have yet to make? No, I think I ought to be at hand to assist and for consultations," she said with a solid logic.

A moment later, however, the confidence slid aside. She looked down, as if she needed to watch her steps, and there was a diffidence in the way she moved. "I must say it disturbs me that I went so far wrong with Miss Daniels, my lord." She brought a finger to her chin, pondering this fact with a hint of distress writ in the creasing of her brow.

"She is not an intimate of yours. How were you to know how she might behave around children? Or perhaps it was Marcus himself who caused her not to shine. He can be a quiet child, and could unnerve someone who—"

"Nonsense!" The distress had fled, replaced by disdain, clearly targeted at the missing Miss Daniels. "I heard him laughing clear across the gardens myself. He was behaving as any child might, and not being a bother at all. The fault lies with Miss Daniels, not Marcus," she stated firmly.

A glow of gratification at this echo of his own opinion filled him, causing his shoulders to relax.

"But how can we avoid such situations in future?" she wondered aloud, stretching out a hand to Marcus as they came to the iron railings. Marcus took the offered hand, and they moved out on to the street. Joseph crossed to inform his groom that they had decided to walk home later and that the man was free to return the horses to their stalls for the day.

"I hope you do not mind all this walking?" Joseph inquired as he returned to Lady Wayfield's side.

"Never a bit. It gives me time to think. In fact I have been pondering, my lord, if perhaps *my* criteria as to what manner of woman would make a worthy mother is a far cry from what others, particularly *you* of course, would consider appropriate. Perhaps it would be wise to have you describe a good mother to me."

"But how would I know, Lady Wayfield?" he said, knowing any bitterness in his tone was only a shadow of an old, deep hurt. "To speak plainly, my mama was most things I do *not* want, so how am I to know and judge what constitutes a good mother?"

"Ah," she said, but there was no censure in the sound, only a kind of regret.

"I only know whoever this woman is to be, she will be one who is capable of genuine tolerance of Marcus, and will be mindful of his feelings. Does that make a good mother, Lady Wayfield?"

"Yes, among other things, indeed it does, my lord."

"Joseph," he said, then felt color flood his face, for he had not intended to offer the suggestion of familiarity. It was too late to take back the proposition, however, so he clarified, "Please feel free to call me Joseph, as once you were wont to do. Working so closely together, it seems foolish to be so formal. . . ." His words trailed away.

"And you must call me Augustine, of course," she said, her face strangely blank except for a widening of her eyes.

"Delighted," he murmured, but in his head he said her name several times, trying the weight of it after these six years, finding it would sit well enough on his tongue.

"Yes. Ah . . . as to selecting the attributes of a good mother," Augustine hurried on, apparently eager to get past the moment. "You have already listed two things you would care to find in a mama, those being tolerance and attentiveness of a child's sentiments. So let us play a game of opposites. I will mention those things I think would *not* be desired, and you must tell me a kind of opposite, and whether or not it is a consideration for you."

The suggestion could serve to smooth any lingering awkwardness, so Joseph nodded agreement. "As you wish."

"Good. What word comes to mind when I say vanity?" she offered.

Joseph thought a moment. "Modesty."

"I see, yes. But come, this is not a mere parlor game. You must feel free to expand on your thoughts," she chided gently.

"Well . . . I suppose I mean a woman who is unpretentious. Someone who can take pride in her appearance without insisting others admire her as well." He felt his jaw tighten, as it so often did when he remembered Meribah—and with such a word as vanity he could not help but think of her. "This woman should hopefully be someone who does not require constant courting and flattery."

Augustine nodded, but Joseph sensed she had not learned anything new or revealing from his reply. She went on, saying, "Selfishness?"

"The opposite would be generosity, of course. I mean to say, more generous with her attention than with money or goods." He stooped to retrieve the stick neglected by Lewis when the dog spotted a crack in the roadway's edge that evidently required investigation. "You know what I mean to say. The kind of someone able to enjoy simple pleasures." He threw the stick, reigniting Lewis' interest in it.

She nodded, but then there was a slight hesitation before she went on. "Dishonesty?" she asked with seeming reluctance, as if she sensed she might be thrusting barbs into old wounds.

"I look for someone who understands the nature of a promise," he said, not looking at her, and not quite able to keep a bitter edge out of his voice.

She ducked her head. "Someone who is harsh?" Her voice was reduced to hushed tones.

"Harsh, eh?" Joseph repeated, watching Marcus give a triumphant grin when he reached the stick before the greyhound—by luck of being nearer to where it landed—and shook his head, remembering the unintentional harshness his own father had too often shown him, and his mother's too-frequent indifference. "Marcus' mama must be anything but harsh," was all he said in answer.

Augustine did not press him to expand. Instead she seemed to shake off the subject, briskly saying, "That is enough. I find I am not too far mistaken in the lady for which we seek. We have had the right plans, even if the results have been failure so far. It is a matter of staying the course."

"Do you think so?"

"Do not tell me you begin to doubt our eventual success?" Augustine teased gently.

"There are moments when I doubt everything about

this venture," he returned dryly, only speaking the truth.

"Well, have heart! Even as I say, it is only a matter of staying the course," she assured him firmly.

Even to her own ears, Augustine sounded less certain three hours later. It was with a decidedly dejected nod of her head that she agreed Lord Sumner should hire a coach to take them up and return them home.

"I admit to being wholly fatigued," she said once she was settled on the coach's padded seat.

"How could you not be?" Joseph returned, tucking a drowsy Marcus against his side. "A dozen homes in three hours? And nearly all of them receiving?"

"It was grueling."

"It most certainly was. Have I mentioned I am quite beginning to take an aversion to tea?"

Augustine laughed faintly.

"All the same, it would have been worth it if I had found a lady to court."

"If only you had! But I understand. No one struck me as at all suitable. Lady Fulholt-Simons may have a touch with children, but I saw no evidence of that. Her daughter was a nervous little thing, was she not? And the two boys! Scamps at best!"

"Miss Plumhouse certainly admired Lewis, but I am afraid she was not nearly so impressed with myself," Joseph pointed out.

Augustine sighed, unable to argue the point, and felt half-inclined to close her eyes in imitation of Marcus. Instead she reached into her reticule, pulling out a card to hand across to Joseph. He accepted it without banter or protest—a sure sign he was weary as well, she thought.

"Indication number five?" he asked. At her single

nod, he read aloud, " 'Like to like.' " He lowered the card to gaze across the coach's interior at her, a question in his eyes.

"It means common interests are often what draws two seemingly disparate people to one another. There are only so many hours that can be spent with one's children or friends and acquaintances. There comes a time when a man and wife simply must share a room, a conversation. No, do not look so disbelieving of my methods, my dear Doubting Thomas! A woman who shares your interests is also more likely to be the kind of woman you seek for her other attributes."

"So you presume."

"Yes, it is but a presumption, but I have managed to bring a few couples together, have I not? You have long since admitted it. And have you a better thought?" she demanded with mock hauteur.

"No. Between us, you are the one who ever has another thought of how to go about this ghastly business."

"That is certainly the oddest compliment I have ever received. Ghastly, indeed!"

Now it was his turn to give a faint laugh. Marcus stirred at his side, so Joseph gathered the boy into his arms, cradling him in his lap. Marcus settled at once, his pudgy five-year-old hands relaxed in total sleepy trust against his father's chest. A thickness like unshed tears suddenly blocked Augustine's throat, and she had to look away for a moment. There was something about the picture of father and son that caused an unexpected wash of emotion to course through her.

"Augustine," his use of her name drew her gaze back to his, and somehow let her push aside the obstruction in her throat. "How do you propose we test out the fifth Indication of Love?" he asked.

She physically startled, the action having everything to do with his use of the word we. She prayed the slanting autumn light of the early evening sun coming through the coach windows hid the flush of color spreading across her cheeks. How could it be that she should be given an innocent statement and take from it a reason to ponder what she might have in common with this man across the space from her? They *had* nothing in common, surely. And he never meant the word "we" the way she had at first heard it.

"I . . . ," she floundered, striving to remember the question as he had asked it. "I . . . yes, well. What to do? I . . . ," she looked to him helplessly, at a loss.

Joseph shifted Marcus in his arms, giving her an expectant gaze. "How are we to seek those ladies with things in common with myself?" he urged, as if he had deduced she had lost her way in their conversation.

Desperation proved an aid, making words tumble rapidly from her lips. "Ah yes! Like to like, even as I say. We are seeking a woman who can be a willing, loving mother to Marcus, so we ought go where such ladies gather."

He gave her a curious glance, then made a face. "Among the dowagers at parties?"

"That would do as well, but I was thinking of a pamphlet I saw at Hatchard's."

"A pamphlet?" Now he was openly distrustful. "Pamphlets are printed in order to lecture a person about how his sins are chipping away at his hopes for an eternal reward, or else to educate the populace. Educating the populace is a deadly dull affair, let me assure you, particularly lectures where ladies are allowed, no offense."

"Perhaps, but this lecture is entitled, let me think . . . something like 'Healthful Living and Well-Being in Children,' or such as that. It sounds to me to be just the place to find ladies who are concerned with providing good and uplifting households for children."

"To find wives and governesses, you mean!"

"Oh, no, I assure you, the young ladies attend these lectures, for their mamas approve. Short of Almack's, what better place to view a widower's potential? I feel sure it would prove a most useful affair. It is at five o'clock in the evening tomorrow."

He made another face, but then looked down at the child in his arms, steadying the boy as the carriage rolled to a stop before Augustine's home. When he looked up again, it was to nod. "As much as it pains me to think how dull the evening no doubt will prove, we will do it."

There was that word again: we. A simple, blameless word, unlikely to make the heart leap, and yet that is exactly how it made Augustine's respond.

As she waited for the coach door to be opened and the step to be put down, she thought, *why do I suddenly and desperately wish I had never said I would go with him to the lecture tomorrow?* Surely the first answer that came to mind was not the proper one. Why should she know a sharp distaste at the thought of watching him meet his future wife there? That was the very point of going, to find the woman they sought! But . . . perhaps it was only her good sense speaking to her: she might prove a hindrance rather than a help, her presence at his side keeping him occupied out of politeness when he ought to be circling the room, talking to other ladies. . . . Or somehow she might interfere without meaning to, causing the important connection not to occur as it ought.

Joseph was a man grown; he could certainly go to the lecture on his own. After all, only he could know the right woman when he met her. Augustine's presence at an event where she was as unlikely to know the parties as was he, really, served no purpose. *I should tell him I just recalled other plans,* she thought as one of her own footmen came from the house to hand her down,

Joseph's arms of course being occupied with the sleeping Marcus.

She did not declare any prior plans, however, instead only murmuring a farewell.

"Good evening, Augustine. And thank you," Joseph said quietly.

Augustine descended from the carriage, struck speechless by this rather uncharacteristic murmur of thanks from the usually gruff—if not quite uncivil— Lord Sumner. She moved up the stairs to her front door, half-convinced her feet did not touch the stones below her shoes.

Goose! she scolded herself, *what sudden fancy allows you to think you could float on air?* Indeed, why did she feel as light-hearted and daft as a moonling? All that had passed between them was a simple word of gratitude.

She glanced back at the carriage, gaining one last glimpse of Joseph before the footman closed the door, but a glimpse of his hand raised in farewell, a smile for her on his lips, was all she needed to set her blood to pounding loudly against her eardrums. That pounding had nothing to do with the thought that she might be near to earning the coveted statue of *The Lady's Boat*, nothing whatever.

When Mosby opened her front door to her and offered a greeting at her return, Augustine found her head was too filled with a nameless emotional whirlwind to give any reply beyond a nod of her head. She went directly to the stairs, hurrying, nearly running, up to her bedchamber. She closed the door behind her and gave a sigh of relief, but the sound was short-lived. Gazing about the familiar, quiet confines, it struck her that her bedchamber might be a refuge from the world and the disturbing people who inhabited it, but it was also a lonely place, sadly and too-long unoccupied by anyone but herself.

She crossed to ring the bellpull, needing someone, anyone, even just her maid or Cook, to help her fill the solitary space. She needed bustling and voices to keep her from thoughts of how a bedchamber ought to be filled with love and laughter, desire and contentment . . . of how it ought to be shared with a man.

A vision of a dark-haired, light-eyed man sprang into her mind, but she forced it away, tried to think of a dozen attractive men she knew. She tried, but failed. The simple truth was other men might be more handsome, but other men did not make her pulse race as it did, even now, even though the man who flooded her thoughts was absent from her side.

Perhaps if she allowed herself to think her disturbing thoughts freely, then she might arrive at some manner of conclusion, some restfulness of spirit? Perhaps she should not fight against herself, but allow her troubled reflections to run their course?

Yet, even after the maid arrived to break her solitude, to fill her ears with easy prattle, even after she had taken a tray in her room, and then settled in bed with a book, even then her thoughts circled round and round, and she found no answers that she wanted to hear.

Twelve

The next afternoon, Augustine nibbled the seam on the forefinger of her glove. The time—twenty minutes before five—was well known to her, so it was witless to look once again to the clock on the mantelpiece, but look she did.

"It only takes ten minutes to reach the lecture hall, you realize," Louise observed, glancing up at her sister. "Joseph is not yet late." She sipped from her teacup and turned the page of another fashion plate periodical. "Oh, this pink striped one is charming!"

"I suppose I dressed too soon," Augustine murmured, more to herself than to Louise. "I know it is not fashionable to be ready when a gentlemen calls, but . . ." She let her words trail away, having no "but" to add to her statement. She pressed her forehead to the cool texture of the wall next to the window, trying not to think the thought that once again raised its unwelcome head. It was no good, however, for she had already realized she was dressed and ready to go because she was looking forward to the evening. No, not the evening itself, not the lecture, but to sharing it with Joseph.

I am acting foolishly, she thought. *I am behaving as witlessly as any who has fallen in—* She abruptly cut off the thought, her breath catching in her lungs. "No," she whispered aloud, the sound nearly a moan. "No, do not say the word. Do not even think it! I *cannot* have done such an irrational thing!"

"What is that, my dear?" Louise asked idly, her attention fixed on the pages before her.

"Nothing," Augustine murmured, making sure her back was to her sister before she pressed chilled hands to cheeks flooded with warmth. Thankfully, Louise accepted the reply, and Augustine was left to peer out the window.

She shivered, at once both too warm and too cold, all of which had nothing to do with the temperature of the room. *Go on then,* she thought intensely to herself, *muster all the denials you want . . .* but she knew the insights gained from her restless night, followed by an anxious day, proved otherwise. She could not even whisper the words that floated upward from her heart to her tongue, but that did not keep them from echoing in her head: "I have come to admire Joseph. To crave his friendship."

Be honest, an internal voice reprimanded. There was another word waiting just out of sight, a frightening word, one that was a disastrous avowal threatening to take shape. She did her best, again, to thrust it aside ruthlessly, knowing if it were allowed to take on form she would no longer be able to deny it.

"You are restive this afternoon," Louise noted, bothering to glance up from the periodical for a moment. "You used to pace . . . when you were married to . . ." She let her words trail away.

"I am not pacing," Augustine pointed out crossly.

"Might as well be."

"I am bored." It was not truly a lie, but it was not all the truth either.

Louise's reply to that was to put aside the teacup she had been holding, and stand with a wry smile. "I choose not to be insulted by that declaration. All the same, I find I am ready to leave. Do let me know if any of these fashion plates pleases you, and I will try to resist having my dressmaker copy it. You know I live in dread of one day being at a ball, and looking over to see we are wearing much the same dress. It was awkward enough when Edwina Locklyle chose to don the exact same pomona green velvet as I, but I assure you I could never abide it happening with my prettier sister!"

"Prettier, pish!" Augustine scoffed, momentarily diverted from her silent struggle. "You were ever the family beauty."

Louise cocked her head to one side, a fond smile shaping her mouth. "Not tonight. You appear so well in that rich blue you are wearing. You were meant to be clothed in any of the jewel-like colors. I was never so glad as when I saw you leave behind your widow's weeds."

"Black was not a happy color for me."

"No, nor were the white and pastels of a young lady. Just think, at least your marriage to Christopher allowed you to move into the brighter tones—we have that much to thank him for."

Augustine smiled faintly, turning back to glance out the window.

"Come, kiss me farewell then, Sister. Melissa will be done with her afternoon nap and wanting me."

"Of course," Augustine said, crossing to give Louise a kiss on the cheek.

Louise kissed her back, and looked her in the eye. "Truly, Augustine, you look very fetching tonight. Do not be too surprised if, even as we hope for Joseph, you also encounter someone worthy of your regard tonight."

"I cannot see that happening," Augustine answered quietly.

She returned to the window once Louise had gone, and wondered yet again if she would actually go to the lecture. She had changed her mind a hundred times.

She would go, to revel in their triumph, if triumph

were to be theirs tonight. *She would not go, would plead a case of the megrims.*

She must go, to assist him, for she had said she would. *She must not go, so as not to stand in the way of any possibilities.*

He had sought her out that she could aid him in an area where he lacked skills. *But truthfully he never lacked skills, only entree to a wide enough sweep of faces.* He was not the first man to be perplexed by the intricacies of discovery and courtship, and who should wonder at that with callous Meribah having been his wife?

Perhaps the evening could best be handled by sending Joseph a note that informed him of an intention to arrive at the lecture on her own. *No, it was foolishness to be neighbors and yet not share the drive.*

Of course, her inner debates were all nonsense, she knew, surrendering to the truth at last. She rested her forehead against the curled fists she raised, her eyes closing as though to hide from pain. She may well have learned the art of denial during her marriage, but she had not mastered it. Try as she might to hide from the truth, it had found her, pressed at her, made her think the thoughts she had tried to keep at bay.

She knew why she stood gaping out her window like the merest chit, why she could not bring herself to decide whether she wished to be in Joseph's company this night or not. Somehow, the admiration she confessed for the man had grown into something more, something exhilarating and uncontrollable.

The arrogant lord had transformed in her eyes, his arrogance now seen for the self-protecting weapon it was. His sternness had reshaped itself into caring concern for his child, for maintaining the sanctity of his home. His insistence on having his hounds kept wherever he traveled had been revealed to her not as a pomposity, but a preference formed from affection. His cutting wit had turned to shared mirth, any residual real sting turned only in on himself. Even his insistence that he had no need, no desire, to adore a new bride was only a reflection of a deep-seated dread of being cruelly wounded by love again.

Love—there! she had said the word to herself. The word danced through her mind, causing every nerve to tickle and tingle . . . but, too, for each breathtaking tremor there was an answering sharp sting in the vicinity of her heart.

That word, love, so small and yet so weighty, was replete with the demands and delight of friendship, but, too, it held an even deeper, searing reality, a split promise. The emotion the world called love could be the harbinger of either the greatest joy or the darkest despair . . . but the direction fate might take was not Augustine's to decide. That privilege, whether to love in return, to accept the love she reluctantly, achingly acknowledged she wished to offer, belonged to another . . . to Joseph.

And that was why she had dressed to drive out with him tonight, because the impractical part of her wished, no demanded to be with the man who had somehow sneaked past the guards she had mounted around her battered heart.

She did not even try to fool herself, however, into thinking that any show of deep affection on her part would be returned. Her heart was capable of pounding too loudly in her ears, of thrilling at a compliment, of swelling in joy at the sight of him, but it was surely not capable of mending the bruises that had long since taught her the folly of attempting to bestow affection where it was not welcome. She could not simply ignore reality: Joseph wanted her to find him a wife, not to become that wife.

How many times had she been made aware that not

all was mended between them? How could she ignore the truth he had presented to her a half-dozen times, and yet hope for the impossible, for friendship to grow, to bloom into love?

She could not.

"I love him," she whispered, just once, just to put it behind her, as she knew she must. She could laugh, almost, for she had proven her own point to herself, that love could and did exist. Not the brief lust she had once known for the man she had wrongly taken as husband, but love, the unfeigned wish for another's happiness and well-being even above and beyond one's own contentment. She knew this quickening in the heart was real, as surely as she knew how to breathe, for this force, this searing fire, she now acknowledged was powerful and pure . . . as it would have to be to give her the strength to find for Joseph that which he sought: a wife who was not herself.

"How ironic," Augustine murmured, too overcome to allow any bitterness in the words. "Once I did not love but longed to do so, but now that love has found me, I wish it had not."

She lowered her hands and straightened her spine, turning to sit on the nearest settee, breathing deeply, striving to find a shred of composure. She must collect herself, for despite these potent, shattering admissions, she at last decided she would not decline Joseph's company tonight. For perhaps tonight would be the last they would be required, allowed, to spend together; perhaps tonight he would find his future bride, and after that he would have no need of his neighbor's company.

Even in the midst of her indecision, Augustine had dressed with care, knowing that if she chose to go tonight, she wanted him to see her, perhaps for him to carry a memory of her at her best. She reached to smooth the rich azure-blue overskirt of her dress, knowing the gold-shot threads woven into the fabric glimmered every time she moved, catching even her eye when she had looked in her mirror. Her bodice was of the same rich material, with small, puffed sleeves, the cut trim, the neckline not too low, but just right to be flattering. The underskirt was made of many flounces of tulle, seeming to fall from the deeper, richer blue of the overskirt, each flounce a shade paler than the one above it, until the last flounce that just brushed the floor was so pale a blue as to be almost white. White kid slippers covered her feet, and she had allowed a gold-set sapphire bob earring at each lobe, although she did not wear either the necklace or the bracelet that went with the set. She was too grandly dressed as it was, just to go to a lecture.

All the same, Augustine looked with regret at the dark blue cloak that rested on a chair, awaiting Joseph's arrival, for this night she did not wish to cover the most beautiful gown she owned, not even for the length of the drive. But the cool of an autumn evening would not allow otherwise, even should she be so bold as to venture out without a cover.

"Whether or not the hall is terribly chilled, I vow I will take you off the minute I arrive," she informed the cloak. No diva of the stage would do any less if she thought it might be her last performance.

The sound of a carriage moving up the drive between their two properties foretold of Joseph's approach before the knocker could announce his arrival at her front door. Augustine waited for Mosby to come and announce Joseph, and for the man himself to be shown into the parlor. It was then that her heart began a slow, heavy thudding in her chest, not wholly unexpected. When that organ leaped with pleasure at the sight of him, resplendent in dove grey and a snowy white stock, she realized the sharp stab that accompanied her heart's dance must surely be only a precursor to a pain that would be, must be hers when he decided upon another.

She took up her cloak, lowering her glance to the carpet as she greeted him, "Joseph."

"Augustine."

There was something in the way he said it . . . no, be honest, it was the very sound of her name on his lips that caught at her, that made her fight to keep a tremor from coursing her spine.

"You look lovely tonight."

"Thank you." She lost the battle to control the tremor, but hoped he did not notice as she handed him the cloak. She turned her back to him, that he might place it about her shoulders. Their close proximity only created a second tremor, however; one doubled by the brief touch of his hands on her shoulders.

It was too late to declare an unwillingness to go tonight, much as she experienced a temptation to utter as much, so she made up her mind to be unobtrusive and as quietly helpful as possible, but in any other way remain distant from him. She would pray, for all the wrong reasons, that they were successful in their search tonight.

"I do hope this is one of those affairs where we are first served wine and biscuits," Joseph said as they rode to the lecture. "Besides bribing the populace into staying, it would give us time to meet and chat with the ladies. After all, we cannot depend on anyone choosing to stay afterward, especially if the lecturer drones on for hours."

"That would be well," she agreed, pressing her hands into her skirts that he might not see how her fingers trembled. Silently she vowed to attach herself to any available group, to leave him free to course the room without her.

The carriage halted before the church that served as a lecture hall for the night. As Joseph handed Augustine down, he pointed to a mounted slate. "It is even as you warned me, for the entire title of our lecture tonight is 'An Examination of Matters Regarding the Rightful and Healthful Rearing of Children.' Gadzooks, madam, I must be a desperate man to agree to be edified as well as bored."

"Perhaps not edified, for I do not expect you to pay heed to the lecture. You do perceive a conversation can be quietly had with a little discretion, do you not, even at a function such as this?"

"And glares, too."

Augustine shook her head, pulling forth a smile, and moved into the church as he held the door for her. Another slate provided the direction of the lecture, and since the particular murmur of a voice at lecture was already carrying from the room ahead, they slipped in the single door and found seats at the back at once.

Augustine settled in the chair as she saw that a matron was indeed already addressing the assembly—so much for a bribery of refreshments! She reached to unbutton her cloak, only belatedly gazing about at the gathering at large. "Do see," she leaned over to whisper to Joseph, "everyone else in attendance is a female!"

He make a choked sound, causing her to look up at him in alarm, only to realize he was doing his best to stifle a bout of laughter. She frowned, then followed his gaze around the room. "Oh, no," she cried, the sound louder than it ought to be. "Everyone here is . . . !" Words failed her, and she felt her jaw working soundlessly.

"Oh, yes!" he said, his voice barely under control. "Every one of these ladies is with child!" He stood abruptly, making another smothered sound of mirth. "Excuse me," he just managed to mutter to the nearest ladies, and then he was out the door.

Augustine rose almost as swiftly, flushing scarlet again. A quick, desperate glance around the room did not immediately reveal any familiar faces, but these were not mere shopgirls or maids, but proper wives, churchwomen, the quality of their apparel revealed that. Oh, how would it look that she had come here tonight! With Joseph in tow! Oh, no, surely anyone would see it was all a mistake . . . ! There would be no one, surely, to spread rumors of . . . !

Augustine fled.

She found him outside the church's entry, doubled over in mirth. "I . . . I think . . . I saw my true love in there . . . !" he gasped out, only to be lost again to gales of laughter.

"Fie!" she said, but then of a sudden she was laughing, too.

"I say, they all looked . . . looked the motherly type to me!" he crowed.

Augustine could not answer that, too given over to laughter to do more than add a whoop in appreciation of his wit. She had to lean against the wall to keep from doubling over as did he, and her stomach started to hurt from the effect of such hilarity. Finally she managed to gasp out, "Oh, Joseph! I am so sorry. I had no idea—"

He waved away her apology, slowly straightening, chuckles still racking him.

Her own humor abated, slowly evolving into a wide smile. How good it was to laugh, to ignore her heavy heart, to come close to being able to put her newfound emotions behind her. How good it was to see Joseph laugh like this, unrestrained, unwary.

"You!" he said, wiping at his mouth and then revealing a grin. "You owe me a vast favor for that little mistake!"

"I owe you nothing," she retorted. "*I* am the one who will suffer for my error. There will be a dozen rumors concerning me flying about tomorrow!"

"And a dozen church ladies on your doorstep, wondering if you have sinned!"

"Wondering whom I sinned with!" she returned, and just as quickly wished she had not, for the implication of his involvement was only too clear. She felt her shoulders tense, as if ready to take on the weight of his dismay and disapproval.

Fortunately the observation only made Joseph chortle again. "By jingo, my dearest, what will we name the child?"

"Beast, after his father," she suggested crisply, her shoulders relaxing once more.

"If that is to be the case, I favor Toad myself."

"Done!" She grinned anew, deliberately making sure the slant of her mouth was only faintly tilted by the ache that whipped through her.

"Not to worry though, my dear Augustine," he said with a dismissive movement of his hand and a couple of last chuckles. "I doubt there is a soul in London who would be willing to wager so much as a groat on the likelihood of any child of mine, er, making its debut in your home."

Her grin faltered. Was making love to her so impossible to imagine? Sharing a home, a child, with her? It seemed it was, and although she knew he never meant to sound callous, his statement cut her to her core, mortally wounding her dream almost before it was born.

She managed to affect a kind of humor during the brief return ride home. At his insistence, Augustine vowed on her honor that she would not take him to any further lectures.

"But what do we tomorrow? Or are you weary? Shall we have a day free of the chase?" he asked sincerely, even if he continued to grin across the carriage at her.

"Time is too short," she reminded him. She shrugged, to hide a sigh of resignation that she must trudge on, must ignore the leanings of her heart, must help him find another to fill his house, his life. "Let me think on it. I will have a plan by tomorrow noon, at the latest. I will send you a missive. Is that acceptable?"

"Once I would have said yes with no qualms, but after this evening's incident . . . !" he teased. "No, no, do not frown at me so. I assure you, I wait with bated breath to learn what our next scheme will be."

He set her down before her home, as always not asking if she would mind walking the short distance from the mews to her home but assuming it was his duty to see she need not.

Mosby opened her front door as Joseph's words "our next scheme" played in her mind. She particularly mulled over the new word just added to the vocabulary that grew between them: our. It was just a little word, nothing to catch the ear normally, but now so forlorn. Our.

She made a point of shying entirely away from the ludicrous thought of any child-bearing rumors that might spring to life come the morrow. It was, naturally, ridiculous to fear anyone would believe for two minutes that she and Joseph would ever have a child together. Everyone knew they had scarcely been civil to one another for years. Yes, he was only too right, she had nothing to fear in that regard. She was ridiculous to allow her thoughts to linger, even for a moment, on any rumors that she might be carrying Joseph's child.

Almost as ridiculous as lying in bed, sleep elusive, tears flowing. When sleep did come at long last, it cruelly brought with it visions of giggling dark-haired babies.

"Louise, you must help me!" Augustine cried the next morning even before she was all the way into her sister's receiving room.

Louise rose to greet her, instantly looking anxious. "Augustine, my dearest, whatever has occurred?"

Augustine pulled off her bonnet, shaking her head.

"I am sorry, I did not mean to alarm you. It is merely that I require your advice."

"Advice," Louise repeated, looking relieved. "From me? That makes for a change. Come, sit down. I shall ring for tea."

"Please," Augustine said, taking the offered seat as Louise crossed to the bellpull. When Louise returned to her side, Augustine said at once, "It is Lord Sumner. Joseph," she amended.

Louise lifted her brows at the use of his first name, and Augustine attempted to ignore the hint that her sister had noticed the new intimacy.

"I have promised that by this afternoon I shall have conceived a new contrivance by which he might meet new females. But I cannot think of a thing! There is no point in going to the various routs and balls, for all the same ladies attend them, and he has already rejected their number!"

"So many? Already? Could it be Joseph does not really wish to marry?" Louise asked.

Augustine pondered this, almost wishing her sister could be right. "No," she said, her mouth turning down. "No, I believe he truly has decided to marry—it would solve so many difficulties for him. Although it is entirely true that I do not think he *wishes* to wed, he *is* committed to completing the act."

"If only you felt the same way."

Augustine stared, feeling even more flustered than when she had hastened into the room.

"About marrying again. I mean to say, being committed to the idea. Christopher was a great bore, and ever neglectful."

"He did not neglect me . . . well, not at first," Augustine protested faintly.

"Yes, he did! Even on your wedding day he spent more time tipping his cup with his fellows than at your side. I vow, from the moment you said you would accept his suit, he never gave you more than the merest of attentions. Good heavens, Augustine, do not tell me you thought your marriage a *customary* one?" Now it was Louise's turn to stare.

"I . . . but you never said . . . no one ever said. . . . Of course I thought it was customary!" Augustine cried. But although she protested, she knew Louise was entirely correct—and it had taken only one day of acknowledging her feelings for Joseph for Augustine to know it.

"Oh, Augustine! All this time I have been holding your hand and telling you you would recover from your marriage, and you were thinking your life with Christopher had been in the usual way of things? You, the matchmaker? How could you expect so little from marriage?" Louise reproached gently.

"I expected more," Augustine said, her toes and fingers starting to tingle as if waking from numbness. "Louise, I expected so much more. I have seen so much more! I thought . . . thought the problem lay with me. Christopher was happy"—Louise made a scoffing sound—"and it was I who would not, could not love him."

"My dearest, dearest goose!" Louise said fondly, although there was a sisterly ache in her gaze. "How *could* you have loved such a cold, uncaring man?"

Augustine stared down at the gloves yet on her hands, trying to steady her whirling emotions. How, indeed, could she have loved Christopher, or even thought she ought?

"It was the romantic in me," she exclaimed bitterly. "You always told me I was a romantic fool, and I suppose I had to prove it by . . ." Her words trailed off.

Louise would not leave the statement unfinished however. "By marrying an unlovable man."

"I always thought he was decent, and, later, that someone . . . else might have loved him."

"Someone just as shallow and distant, if such a love is possible," Louise said firmly.

"Some loves are not possible," Augustine agreed quietly.

The tea tray arrived at that moment, and after Louise had poured for them, Augustine lifted her teacup with shaking hands. She had come seeking advice, and found instead a revelation that made sense of her past. Christopher had not been a good husband! It was one thing to feel in her heart that her husband could have been a better man to her, and another to find the world believed it as well. A weight, one she had been aware of but had long since got used to, lifted from her shoulders, and suddenly her hands no longer shook.

"Louise, you are a treasure. I only wish you might have shared your wisdom with me a trifle sooner!"

"But you are the matchmaker! I thought you saw something in Christopher the rest of us missed," Louise protested.

"I daresay I saw less," Augustine said tartly. She lifted her chin, and shook her head, putting the past behind her for the moment. "But this is not why I came, not to talk of me. As I said, I must somehow compose a scheme to advance Joseph's situation."

Louise put a finger to her chin, and the two sisters sat, thinking silently for well over a minute.

"All the usual comes to mind," Louise said at last. "I can only think of various invitations Andrew and I have received. Balls, dinner parties, musicales . . . but all with much the same people. As you say, we need something new. . . ."

"Precisely. But what?" Augustine sank back against the cushions in frustration.

"I have a thought!" Louise cried, sitting forward.

"One of the invitations we received was to attend Lord Bromleigh's foxhunt in High Wycombe, two days hence. I had said we would come, but then I thought Melissa might be coming down with the sniffles. As it turns out, she is quite well, and Andrew has said she will be happily cared for by Nanny, and that we should go to the hunt."

"Foxhunt? I know autumn is beginning to show her colors, but it is not a trifle early for a foxhunt?"

"His invitation said he would have a fox there and readied. Do you suppose there are people who know how to find foxes when needed?" Louise asked, momentarily diverted.

"I suppose."

"No matter. The important matter is that simply *everyone* has agreed to attend! The invitation calls the hunt a stopping place for those leaving London for the year, and I know at least two families who meant to visit for the hunt. Of course Lord Bromleigh means to bring in all his neighbors as well, so there will be many faces, hopefully new ones, to ponder."

Augustine said nothing, considering the idea.

"Lord Bromleigh would have no objection to two more attendees, I feel sure. His country estate is drafty and crumbling in places, but it is also fitted with dozens of chambers. And it is so close to London, that even should it fall short of your needs, you could easily return to Town the next day! Oh, what do you think?"

"I must admit the idea holds promise. I should not care to be an uninvited guest however."

"He invited my family, of which you are a part," Louise argued, smiling encouragement.

"And Joseph?"

"Joseph can be charming if he chooses, and he will so choose out of good manners if nothing else. Our

host will be pleased to have him at the table delighting
the other guests, I make sure."

"Louise—"

"Have you a better thought?"

"No." Augustine pulled one of the settee cushions
into her arms, hugging it in consternation at the
thought of traveling over a distance in a carriage with
Joseph. How much of an actress was she? If he spent
too much time at her side would she be able to keep
him from suspecting her true feelings? Would too long
a silence or just the wrong word reveal all to his gaze?

"You have to admit I have had a clever idea," Louise
prompted.

"I admit it. And I certainly have no other scheme to
offer Joseph."

"Splendid! Now, I hope you do not mean to hurry
away?"

"No. I will send Joseph a note from here." Augustine
put the pillow aside, her tone brightening as a thought
occurred to her. "In fact, Louise, I should like to stay
so that you may assist me." She stood, crossing to her
sister's secretary, wherein she knew she would locate
paper and ink.

"Assist you?"

"With making a list of any available females you believe
might be attending this foxhunt. When I have a list of
names, perhaps I will be able to arrange for certain parties to drive together, all the way to High Wycombe."

"Oh, yes, I see! Joseph is to be placed among the
ladies."

"If I can arrange it. It would serve very nicely for
compelling the parties into conversation, do you not
think, and long before they ever reach the hunt. Proximity being nine-tenths of attraction, of course."

"Pish, Augustine, you do not believe that! You cannot

after your marriage—" Louise cut herself off abruptly, obviously not wanting to reopen that wound.

Augustine bent her head to the task of writing the note to Joseph, not bothering to deny her sister's words, for they were only the truth. Of all people, Augustine could not believe there was any magic in mere proximity. *No,* she thought, *it requires a particular and unpredictable enchantment of the heart*—an enchantment Joseph obviously did not experience when he looked at her, Augustine.

Louise surely thought it sad her older sister had never been touched by love's magic—how much sadder would she find it if she knew Augustine had known that touch, only to have it remain outside her grasp?

Augustine signed the note, and rose to summon a footman by way of the bellpull. As soon as he left with the missive in hand, Augustine returned to the secretary, picked up the quill and pulled out a fresh sheet of paper. "Now," she said, "A list of possible attendees, if you please."

In half an hour she and Louise had assembled a list of ladies, three of whom Augustine declared must be persuaded to ride to High Wycombe with Joseph. "Only think," she said to Louise, pleased that her voice did not break or waver, "one of these may be Joseph's next wife."

"I am sure any of these ladies would prove to be pleasant company, and perhaps even appeal to Joseph," Louise said, leaning over Augustine's shoulder to glance at the list. "So I cannot imagine what there is to make you scowl so, Augustine."

Augustine did not reply, since she could not deny she had been scowling, and because she would not burden Louise with the awful weight of her secret.

Thirteen

Joseph turned from shaking hands in greeting with his host, Lord Bromleigh, just as Augustine, Louise, and Louise's husband, Viscount Ruchert, descended Bromleigh's sweeping staircase. They had obviously just freshened themselves after their drive from London. It was not Viscount and Viscountess Ruchert he noted however, but Augustine's tidy figure in her gown of Forester's green. The dress' accoutrements were simple, being only small sleeves shaped of delicate silver lace, a belt of braided silver threads just below her shapely bosom, and a silver comb that held her chestnut hair secured in a manner that allowed a tumble of curls from the knot crowning her head. Yet for all its simplicity, the effect was striking, almost as fetching as the gold-shot blue gown she had worn to the lecture.

The memory of the lecture had him smiling broadly as he crossed to the ladies. He supposed, too, from the sense of pleasure he experienced that he was relieved to be greeted by familiar faces on his arrival to Bromleigh's estate, the carriage he had ridden in being one of the last of this morning's party to arrive.

"Louise. Augustine," he greeted them, sweeping them a bow as they curtsied and returned his greetings. He offered a second bow to Louise's husband. "Ruchert, a pleasure to see you again."

"My pleasure entirely, Sumner," Lord Ruchert replied with a nod and a smile. "I understand you are soon to be assigned abroad?"

"Indeed, too soon," Joseph answered.

"Somewhere far from the fighting, I hope?"

"So I am assured."

Lord Ruchert nodded. "Have you seen that Foxy Tredlemeyer is here?"

"Lord Sumner has only just arrived," Louise explained to her husband.

"Ah! I see. I only mention it because the fellow just informed me that he means to forgo the hunt! Can you conceive it? Foxy Tredlemeyer passing by the chance to ride to the hounds? Says the lady he drove down with, Miss Monmark—"

"Moncraft," Louise corrected.

"Yes, Moncraft. Foxy says Miss Moncraft does not care for the sport, and so he has agreed to forebear from it when they are together. Remarkable!"

"Ah!" Louise cried. "I daresay that sounds very like proof of Augustine's first Indication of Love, to give up something for the sake of another."

All eyes turned to Augustine, who flustered a moment, then agreed in a quiet voice, "I daresay it does."

"Do please excuse me, my good fellow," Ruchert said to Joseph, lifting a hand to acknowledge someone across the room. "I see the party I agreed to play a round of cards with is awaiting me."

"Of course," Joseph excused him. Lord Ruchert bowed to the ladies before moving to join his tablemates.

In his absence a momentary silence fell, in which Augustine remained uncharacteristically quiet, while Louise leaned toward Joseph, putting a hand on his arm. "Do say that once you have shaken the dust of the road from your heels, you will find a moment to tell us of your day's drive. We are eager to know if any good things have come of your travels."

"You need not wait so long as that, my dears," he said, at last drawing Augustine's gaze. "You, madam," he said in a direct but quiet voice to her, "will never put me unprotected in a carriage with three half-learnt witlings again."

Instead of the laugh he had meant to engender, she responded by lowering her eyelids, obscuring her reaction—did she hide mirth or some other sentiment?—and he knew a prick of disappointment when she did not immediately speak up and put him in his place.

Was it his imagination, or did she hold herself aloof in a way she never had before? This morning when all the travelers had met before adjourning to their various carriages, he had noticed an odd coolness about her, which he had attributed to a distaste for morning travel. Now he wondered if he had been too quick to dismiss her distanced demeanor, for it lingered still, despite the long morning's drive from London. Had her travel companions been as fatuous as the three ladies with which he had driven down? Was she tired?

Of course, it would not be difficult to believe he had taken up too much of her time, had kept her from tasks or enjoyments in which she would rather be engaged. And now here they were, committed to at least two days removed from London, and all for his benefit alone. Although Augustine was too polite to let any resentment show overtly, he could not help but think something troubled her. That something might just be a weariness with his cause . . . or his person.

"You do not reply!" he teased. "What, do you no longer care to know my reasonings for rejection, or have rejections become a habit for us all?" He smiled, hoping she would accept the comment in jest. "How

cruel of you not to inquire as to the whys and where-
fores of my journey's discomforts."

"Discomfort, sir?" Her speech was yet oddly formal,
lacking warmth perhaps, but there was something of
her usual raillery in it. "Was Miss Redding's carriage
not to your liking then? It looked a fine vehicle, but if
the springs were not all they should be . . . ?"

"It was not the vehicle, but the company, and you
know perfectly well that was what I meant," he said
more sternly than the comment warranted.

Fortunately, Louise missed the moment of dishar-
mony, for her attention had been captured by a passing
acquaintance, with whom she exchanged greetings and
eager tales of how she was finding motherhood.

For her part, Augustine merely looked down her nose
at Joseph.

He experienced a mounting irritation with her, stung
that she did not reap the humor he had sown, and that
her own humor seemed at best stifled and forced.

"Augustine!" he began to remonstrate, but at the
sound of her name, a shadow raced across her face,
making her appear for the briefest moment to be in
pain, stealing from him the reprimand he had meant
to utter. "Is something amiss?" he said instead, all irritation erased in a flash, spontaneously reaching out a
hand to take her elbow.

"Of course not," she said, even as she took a small
step back, away from his touch.

"Augustine?" he said again, but this time it was a
question, and even he could hear the puzzlement—
rather sounding like hurt—in his voice.

She looked away. "I am sorry. I suffer from the megrims," she mumbled to the empty air beside her.

"My dear lady! All that travel has proven a burden,"
he declared at once, now feeling all the worse; not only
did he keep her from her own life, but on his account

she suffered from the trials of travel. "Please allow me to call a maid to your side, to see that you—"

"No, no!" she interrupted him, glancing at her sister briefly. "Louise can see to me." Louise turned back to them at hearing her name. "Please, I will be fine. I simply require a . . . a chair, and perhaps a glass of water."

"Of course!" He took her hand and placed it on his sleeve, ignoring the faint protest she offered. He led her from Bromleigh's entry hall and into the nearest parlor, Louise trailing and clucking with concern.

"Here is your chair," he said, handing Augustine into a gilt-legged seat. "I shall obtain some water at once."

"No!" she said, putting up a hand to touch his sleeve again. "Please, my lord—"

"Joseph," he corrected her, stopping at her touch and staring into eyes he now saw were glistening, as though with fever or unshed tears.

"Joseph. Please, you are here to meet new faces, not to tend to my needs. Louise, you will serve as nursemaid to me for a moment or two until I recover, will you not?" At Louise's assurance, Augustine looked back up at Joseph. "Please. I do not wish to keep you from your aim."

Joseph looked to Louise, who lifted her shoulders ever so slightly as if to say she was as surprised as anyone to find her sister made ill by the drive, but, too, that she was not overly concerned.

He nodded his acceptance of Augustine's request, and then left the room, to find a servant to show him to his chamber, that he might remove the mark of travel as a gentlemen ought.

When he returned, arrayed in fresh attire, his Hessian boots restored by a footman to a spotless shine, he found Augustine still with that distanced air about her, but much recovered from her earlier spell. She smiled at him at once (even if it was a shallow smile), and bid him sit and tell his tale of his travels with the three ladies (even if the invitation lacked a show of real eagerness.)

"But take care to keep your tale brief, that you should not linger too long with us ancient matrons," Augustine told him, the comment seeming more her usual self. "I spy many young lovelies here who require your attention."

He took the offered seat. "None more lovely than yourselves," he said, causing Louise to laugh, and receiving a slight smile from Augustine. "Let me only ask, ladies, if *you* have ever had the misfortune to ride for miles with three ladies just free of the schoolroom? My head rings yet with their chatter and their squeals—"

He got no further in his recitation, however, for at that moment their host's daughter made a grand entrance into the large parlor where the guests had gathered. All eyes turned to her, including Joseph's.

"My heavens," Louise said faintly. "I had no idea Lord Bromleigh's daughter was old enough to leave the schoolroom. What a beautiful girl!"

Joseph could not argue the point. The young lady in question, introduced as Miss Dorianne Ousby, only daughter to Lord Bromleigh, was a stunning vision of coal-black hair and naturally reddened lips. She wore a yellow gown so pale as to almost be ivory, the hue somehow making her light skin glow golden under its pure white perfection.

"She is lovely," Augustine said at Joseph's side, but the look on her face was uncertain when he glanced at her.

"But she is also very young, perhaps not even quite eighteen," he said, finishing Augustine's unspoken comment.

"Yet, she has lived in the country and so must have

a sense of how to run a household." Augustine seemed to warm to her subject. "Lady Bromleigh surely saw to the girl's education before she passed away. When was that, Louise?"

"No more than two years ago," Louise supplied.

"So, if anything, the womanly burdens have no doubt already settled on Miss Ousby's shoulders, young though they may be. We must not dismiss her merely on the grounds of youth. You should go at once and be presented to her. Louise can do the honors," Augustine said, although he could not say that she spoke with any true enthusiasm. "Come, you have met with a dozen eighteen-year-olds in recent days. Now is your chance to meet a beautiful one."

Joseph rose to his feet, smothering a sigh. "I am here to meet any likely lady, am I not?" he agreed, offering his arm to Louise. He lingered a moment, waiting for Augustine to solicit a promise to return and tell her the rest of his tale concerning the journey down, but no such behest was forthcoming. There was nothing for it but to go and meet the beautiful, painfully young Miss Ousby.

She, for one, did not eschew his company once they were introduced, batting long lashes at him over mahogany-colored eyes. In fact, her eager attention went a long way toward assuaging the chafing Joseph had felt ever since he had said "good morning" to Augustine hours ago.

"I must say I do not see much that is motherly in Miss Ousby," Augustine said sourly to Louise.

Louise handed the glass of ratafia she had gone to fetch to her sister, spreading the skirt of her ballgown as she resumed her seat to watch the evening's dancing. "Perhaps Joseph should have brought Marcus, to test the ladies' reactions to the boy," Louise suggested. "Not at this dance, of course, but tomorrow after the hunt, perhaps. I never thought to suggest the idea to him."

"Joseph would not care to see Marcus' feelings hurt, not after the debacle with the intolerant Miss Daniels. I think he means to rely on his own judgment in future."

"Well, that is wise, I suppose. Perhaps that is why he is spending so much time at Miss Ousby's side, do you think?" Louise gazed at Joseph, who stood at Miss Ousby's side, holding the lady's glass for her while she was busy bidding farewell to some neighbors who obviously meant to return home before the hour grew too late.

"He has certainly been attentive to her," Augustine agreed, her voice sounding hollow.

"He has," Louise mused, her head on one side. "The three he rode down with appear to be utterly put out with her for capturing his attention, do they not?"

Augustine nodded, having noted the pouting lips and beckoning eyes of the Misses Burnham, Oliphant, and Tunnell herself. "Perhaps he stays at Miss Ousby's side to avoid having to be at theirs," she suggested, allowing a hint of a smile.

Louise laughed lightly. "Perhaps, but I tend to believe her exquisite face may have more to do with having captured Joseph's attention than a lack of charms on the part of the other young ladies. Miss Ousby rivals any woman in the room," Louise contended, missing the tartly amused glance Augustine sent her way at the unintended insult. "Her hair is even darker than his, and so thick and beautiful! I could wish to trade my average brown for a head of hair such as hers."

"Your hair is not average brown," Augustine protested. "It is quite lovely, the color of tea with cream in it."

"Thank you for making the description sound a compliment, even if I could wish it were your rich chestnut or Miss Ousby's sable coils instead of something so ordinary as tea-colored!"

Augustine gave a disdaining sniff. "I would suppose your coloring can support a wider variety of hues in your gowns than Miss Ousby's ever could," Augustine replied, glancing to where Miss Ousby laughed brightly at something Joseph had said.

"True. Such a striking color must be limiting in that regard. But you must admit with her form she would look well in a riding habit," Louise sighed. "She is of the hunting set, I believe. That is all the talk among the group who seem to be her intimates. See? That tall fellow who is such a goose as to walk about with a riding crop tucked under his arm? He is in a fever for tomorrow's hunt, for that is all he spoke of when he led me out for the fourth set. He nearly struck my cheek with that crop, I will have you know. Anyway, near all the talk I have heard all evening has been of hunting. They seem mad for it."

"Yes, well, we *are* here for a foxhunt," Augustine said logically.

"Only too true. I understand Miss Ousby means to ride out with the gentlemen tomorrow, as do a few of the other ladies. I shan't ride. I know so little of the sport. Will you ride out, Augustine?"

"Me? I never have. No, I have no plans to do so." That was one more method for staying out of Joseph's path. Let him and Miss Ousby, and any of the other dozen unmarried women present who cast him hopeful glances, ride out together unhampered by Augustine's presence.

"Do you think Joseph will wish to return to London after the foxhunt?" she asked hopefully, finding a previously unsuspected desire to be home, away from fox-hunts and all that went with them.

"That would depend on whether or not he has had a chance to talk with all the ladies."

Augustine gazed across the room, seeing Joseph take Miss Ousby's hand on his sleeve in preparation of assembling for a second dance with the young lady. "It may take him quite some while to talk to *all* the ladies if he continues to concentrate on just one," she grumbled.

Joseph felt Augustine's gaze on him the next morning, even as he slipped from the dining hall out to the garden with Miss Ousby on his arm. The hair on the back of his neck stood up, for no reason he could explain, no more than he could explain the faint sense of fault that assailed him. Fault? For what? Miss Ousby had offered to show him the hunters they would ride an hour from now, and if he took that offer as a sign that the young lady would not take some flirtation—perhaps even a stolen kiss—amiss, then where was the fault in that?

Miss Ousby had a quick, clever mind, he had decided shortly after being presented to her. She was witty, and gay, and certainly beautiful. There could be worse fates in this world than seeing such a comely face of a morning . . . but, no, he did not really feel that way. Meribah had been a beauty, and still he had scorned to share his morning meal, any meal he need not, with her. What, then, of Miss Ousby's temperament? She seemed pleasant, and she was obviously flattered by his attention, so perhaps she was not so vain as one might expect in a beauty. She did not seem to take his regard for granted, and if she was a trifle coy with him, that was ordinary enough behavior between the genders.

He was pleased to go with her to see the hunters—perhaps to procure that kiss she seemed to promise, but more to see how she was with the beasts. Animals and children were different coins, but a tolerance of one bode well for tolerance of the other.

"Do you like to hunt?" she asked as he pushed open the stable door for her.

" Sometimes," Joseph answered, just before a groom leaped to attention from the bed of hay in which he had been half dozing.

"Bring your carriage around, sir? Miss?" the lad asked at once.

"No, Lonny, we are here to feed some sugar to the hunters," Miss Ousby said. "We have no wish to disturb the staff. Go about your duties."

Here was another show of the girl's intellect, for she had managed to say nothing untoward, yet still told the lad to mind his own business and keep himself scarce. Joseph would have been tempted to add that the stalls, to judge by their scent, required a good mucking out, but it was not his place to order the business of Lord Bromleigh's stables.

"This way," Miss Ousby said to Joseph, leading the way down the long corridor to the boxes where the horses were housed. "This is Brutus," she introduced the bay that turned in his box to stick out his large handsome head at her.

"Hopefully not a fitting name," Joseph said, pulling from his pocket the cloth they had brought along, filled with bits of sugar broken from a loaf on the breakfast table.

They fed the lumps to Brutus and a few of the other horses that snuffled out their interest in the treat, and Joseph had to admit he was not wholly immune to the artful way Miss Ousby cast eyes at him around a horse's nose or across its withers. It was not unlike a peeking game he might play with Marcus, only this version was charged with an invitation that had nothing to do with a tickle and a wrestle afterward. Or perhaps, he laughed silently to himself, it did.

The sugar gone, there seemed no excuse to linger. Miss Ousby moved as if to exit the stable, but then abruptly turned and pressed her back against the wooden door of a box, her lower lip caught in her teeth. She half-lowered her gaze, looking quite appealing, her posture overtly expectant. Joseph wondered if she had meant to stop before a neglected stall door whose wood had clearly been nibbled by some unhappy resident, as if to use the door's poor condition in contrast to her own dark-headed beauty—or perhaps she failed at all to realize she had placed the distressed wood at her back. No matter. He would have been a fool to not take the opportunity offered, and a heel to ignore her invitation.

It did not concern him that the lady had been kissed in such a place or manner at least once before, for this was obviously a practiced flirtation she cast his way. In fact, he would be glad to avoid a too-chaste woman, one inclined to shrink and cringe from the intimacies of living in the same house, of sharing a bedchamber. He moved before her, putting a hand on either side of her, playing the game as if he were the one doing the seducing. She did not cavil at the last moment, earning even more regard in his eyes, as he pressed his mouth to hers.

She had not been kissed too many times, he thought, smiling down at her as he pulled his lips from hers. Their kiss had been a simple thing, modest and far less world-wise than the girl pretended at being. It would seem she was innocent in more intimate matters, yet, happily, not afraid to learn. The lady's list of attractions grew by the moment. She smiled back at him, looking belatedly demur.

"Have you anything else to show me?" he asked, broadening his smile when her eyes opened wide and she said, "Sir?"

"The hounds, Miss Ousby. Are we to visit the hounds of the hunt?" It was an excuse to remain relatively secluded with her, of course, but it also served to show she was not unduly flustered by teasing. Indeed, she struck him without rancor on his shirtfront, and led the way out. There was perhaps an exaggerated sway in her steps for his viewing benefit, but Joseph saw no reason to complain. She led him to another, far smaller building where the hounds were kept, a wooden fence providing a small run area for the pack of fifteen or more.

Joseph greeted the dogs with soft calls as the creatures barked and squirmed to come close to the visitors at the fence. He made a face, his own nose wrinkling in distaste as he extended his hand to be sniffed by a succession of wet dog noses. If the stables had needed a mucking out, the dog run was well-past requiring a mere simple cleaning. "Surely this is not the extent of their running area?"

"Oh, but it is," Miss Ousby stated. She did not follow his suit by extending her hand, instead standing back from the fence a pace, her own nose wrinkled in distaste. Joseph could not really blame her, for the dogs were muddied and the air thick with unwelcome scents. "Why do you ask, Joseph?"

"I am curious as to why are they kept in this way, so they must sully their own quarters. Why are they not given the run of the fields?" he asked, utterly perplexed.

"They frighten away too much game if they are allowed out."

"Perhaps in the immediate area, but I would think—"

"And Papa does not care for their soil everywhere."

"Well, yes, of course," Joseph said, and then spied the area where the dogs were fed. The wooden trough of table scraps had been turned over, and it was clearly not the first time it had happened, with no sweeping-up in-between. The dogs' water was supplied only via a large muddy puddle, the results of which were to be seen by the untidy coats of the dogs pressing against the fence.

"Deuce take it, Miss Ousby, why is there no trough for the dogs' water?" he asked in rising ire.

"A trough—?" she repeated, appearing startled by his tone. "Why, I believe Papa said that it tips constantly and runs out. The stable lads were spending all their time fetching water, whereas this pond holds the water for a day or so."

"But why not affix the troughs in some way so they would not tip?" he asked, attempting to moderate his tone.

Miss Ousby gazed at him, and lifted her shoulders in a delicate shrug. "Well, yes, I suppose that could be done."

Joseph stared at her. "Could be?"

"One of the lads could," Miss Ousby said, looking perplexed. She then looked at the run, and her forehead smoothed. "It is rather untidy, is it not? Papa will have to order it cleaned. I had never really thought much about it. They are Papa's dogs, after all."

Joseph stepped back from his mounting outrage, slightly mollified by her words. "Order that it be *kept* clean, and the troughs secured, you mean to say."

"Yes, of course."

"Well then," he said, relaxing the set of his jaw. "That is fine."

"What is fine?" came a familiar voice.

Joseph turned. "Lady Wayfield," he acknowledged

her, using her title as was only proper in mixed company. She sauntered toward them, a roughly dressed man and Lord Bromleigh in her wake. Her eyebrows were lifted to indicate the pending question.

"The dogs," he explained, pointing to the run. "They need to be put in order."

"Indeed they do, Lord Sumner," Lord Bromleigh said. "Curtis here," he indicated the roughly dressed man, who had a dozen or more leather leads looped over his arm, "is Master of Hounds, come to get 'em for the chase."

Curtis tugged at the brim of his hat, murmured, "m'lord," and stepped to a gate in the fence. The dogs recognized what was to come, and were seemingly happy to participate, tails wagging enthusiastically as the leads were attached to their collars.

Joseph moved away, as though to escape the baying and yipping chorus the dogs had raised, and Augustine followed, walking slowly at his side back toward the house. He buried his hands deep in his pockets.

"You appear vexed," she said in a low voice, one that would not carry.

"When I said things needed to be put in order I was not referring to the hunt," Joseph replied, just as quietly.

Augustine glanced back to the run, her expression making it clear she instantly took his meaning.

"I will not say anything, though, until I can say it in private to Bromleigh. Surely he did not realize . . . ," Joseph's murmurs faded away, and he doubted his features were unclouded.

Miss Ousby stepped away from her father, cutting a path to intercept with theirs. She put out her hand. "Come along, Lord Sumner," she trilled. "The hunt begins!"

The only polite thing to do was to offer his arm as a rest for her outstretched hand.

"We must talk after the hunt," Joseph said *sotto voce* to Augustine, who nodded her head just before he crossed to escort Miss Ousby.

Joseph frowned from his saddle as the caged fox was released mere feet from the snapping jaws of the hounds. The dogs were scarcely held in check long enough for the smaller creature to bolt across the nearest field, let alone come anywhere close to the salvation of the small wood in the distance. There was nothing sporting about this chase, Joseph thought grimly, giving his horse some rein but not bothering to put his heel to his mount as the field of riders moved after the frantically dashing fox and baying hounds.

Joseph made an effort to stay near Miss Ousby, at least for a brief while, to observe her. He dropped back in short order, however, only faintly disappointed when Miss Dorianne Ousby proved she was just as indifferent to how she pulled at her horse's mouth and wielded her riding crop as she was to the living conditions of her papa's hounds. Joseph could not truly say he was surprised.

Long before he heard the calls that signaled the fox had been run to ground, he had already turned back. He rode toward what was from a distance only a brightly colored skirt, but which he guessed to be one of the rich gowns such as Augustine would sport. His guess proved correct, so that after Joseph had turned the hunter over to a groom, with instructions and a handful of coins to guarantee the stalls be properly cleared and fresh straw put down, he crossed to where she stood directing a group of servants.

"The run is being cleaned!" he noted. "You have put the servants to the task." He took up both her hands, offering a squeeze of appreciation.

"I suppose it is very rude of me, but I thought it ruder still to keep the hounds in such a manner," she said with a brief smile. She took back her hands, smoothing the ends of the fringed shawl draped about her shoulders. "I spoke to Lord Bromleigh, and he was amenable to the cleaning. He does not mean to be negligent, I think, but with his wife deceased I believe he is often overwhelmed at managing all the demands of his estate."

"And at a loss on managing his daughter as well."

Augustine angled a gaze up at him. "I surmise the attraction between you two had suffered. Does she not appreciate dogs?"

He shrugged. "She appreciates them too little to note their uncomfortable circumstances."

"So much for my conjecture that the young lady would have been trained up to know how to run a household. And so much for the sixth Indication of Love."

"Which is?"

"A similar humor."

"Your Indications grow simpler as we go along."

"Simpler to state, more difficult to find."

"Explain," he asked, brushing back the tails of his coat to put his hands in his pockets.

She shrugged. "Nearly everyone has a sense of what is amusing. No two think the same, never exactly. The trick is to find someone to whom you need not always explain your jests, or that you were only funning. Someone who laughs with you far more often than she scratches her head and looks perplexed."

"I have not tested Miss Ousby's humor. Indeed, I have not discovered if she possesses the capacity."

"If you have not seen it already, then there is no commonality there for you to discover."

"I see, and I agree."

"Ah well. There are other ladies here. Let us turn our attention to them." She did not seem unduly discouraged to learn of the loss of yet another matchmaking candidate.

"Must we?" Joseph said with a sigh. He moved to the fence, pulling his hands from his pockets to lean against the fence top with his weight on his forearms, his hands folded together. "The thing of it is, Augustine, I do not wish to turn my attention, to make any efforts. I grow weary of this game."

"It is no game, Joseph."

He sighed again. "I know. Certainly not as it pertains to Marcus. I just wish it was done and over. Miss Ousby is quick-witted, and often charming, and she and I seemed to have much in common if you put aside the matter of humor. I thought, for a brief while, this was the lady, I am done with looking. I was relieved." He shook his head. "But I can hardly ignore the fact the lady possesses a certain callousness, can I?"

"Of course not. And you should not."

He turned to her, one elbow planted on the fence in a casual pose that belied the dissatisfaction in his voice. "What am I doing wrong, Augustine? I do not think I am being too particular, but perhaps I am. I could almost wish I looked for love, as you think I ought, or at least simple attraction, for I vow that might be easier to find than the sensible, kind, caring lady I seek."

"There you go again, thinking you cannot have both," she said, smiling ever so slightly.

He smiled too, and shook his head. "You are ever the dreamer, my dear lady."

"Yes," she agreed, and he could swear something wistful crept into the single word.

"What say you to returning to London, now? Without delay? Without staying on another night here?" he offered at once, and was rewarded by a brightening of her expression, which at once faded.

"But we should stay, to see these other ladies—"

"I have seen them. I am not captivated."

"But the people I drove down with, Mr. Davidson and his sister—"

"Hang 'em! And my threesome of giggling girls with 'em. They can manage a drive without our company," he said with a dismissive wave of his hand.

"Joseph!" She gave an exasperated laugh.

"They are all of Bromleigh and his daughter's ilk anyway."

"Well, not all, for Louise and Andrew would remain, I imagine."

"They being the exception. But come. Surely there is someone in London you are longing to see, to return to?"

He did not miss the faint shake of her head, and that the suggestion of returning to London did not cause any particular eagerness to come into her attitude. Perhaps there was no one special in her life after all . . . it was not kind in him to feel cheered at the thought, but it was good to think he did not keep her from missing another's company.

"Come, Augustine, there is nothing here to intrigue us. That is, not unless you feel tempted to stay and marry Bromleigh, to set his house in order?" He made his eyebrows dance, teasing her. Even though he funned, he watched her face, looking to see if this tack brought an interested gleam into her eye. Lord Bromleigh might not be too poor a matrimonial catch, not for a lady wise enough to reshape the management of his household and undoubtedly the man himself.

"How soon can the carriage be made ready?" was her reply.

He laughed. "Twenty minutes."

"I shall be ready in fifteen."

He laughed again as Augustine crossed the yard to see to the packing of her belongings, and experienced a very real gratification that she did not wish to stay. This feeling was no doubt relief at escaping the speculative glances Miss Ousby threw his way as she rode into the yard, returning from the hunt. And, he admitted silently, perhaps in just a small measure, in knowing that he would be sharing his carriage, not with three silly flirting females, but with the sensible, kind, and caring Augustine.

Even as he thought the words, he realized they were the very ones he had used to describe to her what he sought in a wife.

Fourteen

Marry Augustine? Joseph thought, as he had thought a dozen times before as they traveled together from High Wycombe back to London. Even as the carriage wheels rolled down Oxford Street, just a few short blocks from home, the question occurred to him again. And why not marry her?

Well for one, he thought with a grim amusement, *she has to want to marry you.* She had not chosen to renew their association, or even if she had to a small degree done so, it had been only to gain the marble so keenly missing from her garden, and for no other reason. The last two days had surely proven she was weary of his company—even if she seemed content, even happy, to return to London alone with him in his carriage.

Yes, the lady sitting across from him was sensible, kind, and caring. Even more, she was discerning, tasteful, graceful, quick to smile, and gentle. *And beautiful,* he added, not even comparing her to Miss Ousby, for the latter's behavior had lost for him any aspect of beauty. *And Augustine is by all appearances fond of Marcus.*

This last revelation rocked him in his seat, making the impossible seem possible. Only see how far they had come in a handful of days! They had moved from alienation and enmity, to a show of tolerance and even something bordering on friendliness. Was it so impossible to imagine tolerance and friendliness being turned into a contract of marriage?

If only he could see past the gently impartial smile she had borne all during their drive, the cultivated chatter, even past the pensive light that seemed to have settled in her eyes. Did she sense his revelation? Did she fear he would speak, that she would have to refuse an offer? Would she further decline to assist him any longer? Suddenly he realized how difficult it would be to swallow her rejection, or to lose her pleasant company.

Doubts weighted his tongue, making his prattle more idle and stilted than her own.

The carriage rolled to a stop before her home. Joseph opened the door and leaped down, offering Augustine his hand. The groom moved to pull her valise from the boot as she descended, and she nodded to Joseph. "Thank you, Joseph. I was more than ready to leave that place," she said.

"As was I." He did not release her hand. "Augustine—"

"Joseph!" interrupted a stentorian voice, one he recognized as belonging to his father even before he looked up to see it was indeed his papa, mounted and approaching them across the cobbled road. Joseph did not know what he had meant to say to Augustine, but the opportunity was lost now anyway. "I have these two days been attempting to see you!" Papa announced, sounding irritated.

"I was away from London. Papa, I believe you know Lady Wayfield—?"

"Certainly I do. For years." His tipped his hat to Augustine, but he did not bother himself to dismount. "Lady Wayfield."

"Lord Tinsley." She curtsied in greeting.

His father dismissed her with a nod of the head, turning his attention once more to Joseph. "I am given to understand you are to travel abroad in a matter of weeks."

Joseph stiffened, inclining his head just once in acknowledgment.

"I should preferred to have been informed of this development by you, not to hear it at my club," his father said. "Especially as I am to have Marcus under my feet while you are gone."

"Indeed you are not, sir," Joseph said, his voice level even as it was firm. "Marcus will be cared for at my home."

"Eh? You cannot mean to leave my grandson for months on end in the care of mere servants!" Papa's horse put back its ears, perhaps in response to his stern tone.

"No, sir. In point of fact I mean to marry before I leave. I am only surprised the gossipmongers did not inform you of that fact as well. I have made no secret of my intention," Joseph said, mentally stepping back to await the outcry this announcement would surely bring. His expectations were not disappointed.

"Marry? With nary a single word of it to me? A second marriage, you say? To whom?" His gaze narrowed on Augustine. "Is this the one?"

"Certainly not!" Augustine cried, her cheeks staining pink.

"Well, and I am glad to hear it! A man should look farther afield than the house next door."

"If he is indeed a man, he will look where he chooses," Joseph said from between tight lips.

"Hmmph!" replied his father. "I see no reason to stay and be growled at. You will do as you please, I know, but recall I expect you to keep in mind the consequence of our family name." He did not await a reply, pulling his horse's head around and putting his heels to its sides. The horse trotted down the street, hooves ringing against the cobbles.

Joseph searched for the words to make an apology, but found his father's effrontery had left him speechless. His father might as well have said Augustine was beneath them, beyond considering. In what way could Papa object to Augustine when he had never objected to Meribah, the liar, cheat, and cuckolder? The insult was inexcusable.

"He holds me in too high a regard," Augustine said dryly.

His gaze connected with hers, and he saw with relief that the encounter held no lasting sting for her.

"Augustine, please accept my apologies! The man . . . he . . . he *amazes* me at times! I do not think he completely realizes how his words can wound—!"

"Do not consider it. After all, it was a learning experience, for now I know how to please him: all I have to do is find you a wife other than myself," she said.

That was it then, the end of any consideration he should put toward marrying Augustine. If her hasty denial to his father that she could be his intended had not been enough to snuff the thought, then surely her dismissive humor eliminated it as ever being a possibility. It was clear the thought of marrying him had not occurred to her, or at least had never thrived for so little as a moment in her mind. But if the notion were planted . . . if she were to give it serious consideration . . . was a marriage between them too completely impossible . . . ? Or was he just as big a fool as his father thought him to be?

"You are very kind to be so tolerant—"

She waved away his words, just as a small streak in blue came running from the house. "Papa!" cried Marcus as Joseph stooped to scoop the boy up in his arms, while two small arms encircled his neck in a fierce hug.

"I saw your carriage from the window," Marcus explained his presence.

"Dear boy, I was only gone overnight," Joseph said, hugging the boy back. "The way you are squeezing me I should think it had been a month!" He gave a tentative laugh, even as he experienced a tendril of trepidation at the idea of the weeks he would spend far removed from his son—weeks in which Marcus would have no one to hold him like this.

The boy twisted in his arms, lunging toward Augustine, who just managed to keep him from toppling to the ground. "Lady Auggie," he greeted her, planting a noisy kiss on her cheek.

"Marcus," she said in return, half-laughing as the wiggly fellow lunged back into his papa's arms.

Joseph smiled in return, and then a thought struck him. There was a way of testing new waters, of building a bridge over the seemingly impassable river that separated the two of them.

"Augustine?" he asked over the boy's shoulder, stopping her from turning to stroll up her short front walk.

"Yes?"

"If we do not find a wife for me before I must leave . . . I mean to say, of course we will, but just in case . . . would you be so kind as to take Marcus into your care while I am away? I could pay the expense of *The Lady's Boat* and the cost of shipping it from Italy in exchange for this onerous duty—"

She turned away before he could finish, and was stiffly silent for a moment.

"But, no matter, forget I asked—" he blustered, startled by her reaction.

She spoke, but not to him, only over her shoulder in his general direction. "Of course," she said, her voice sounding thick. "I would gladly take Marcus into my home." She paused long enough to take a deep breath, then went on, "But not for what I might earn, my lord, but rather out of friendship. I will pay for the marble myself, if you please." She took two steps, stopping again abruptly. "And please keep in mind that we are coming closer to finding someone who will suit as your wife, for you must admit Miss Ousby was a near thing. We *will* find you a wife, my lord. I vow it."

Joseph was left standing alone on the road, the vehemence of her last words ringing in his ears. He could almost sigh in relief to know that Marcus would be cared for regardless of his own fickle behavior in this matter of marriage, and yet he frowned, utterly perplexed as to how he had offended Augustine, and utterly unable to think how to go about apologizing for the insult he had obviously and unknowingly offered her.

Two evenings later, as they arrived at Lady Poscombe's masked ball, Augustine vowed not to allow any lingering resentment to show. In fact, she would even claim there was a kind of agitated eagerness in the set of her shoulders as she and Joseph stalked through the throng of attendees at the masquerade. Both she and he had both worn simple black dominoes, a guise she had chosen by dint of being unable to summon any enthusiasm for compiling a more elaborate costume. There was a bounty of colorful and unusual costumes around them, however, and they had timed their arrival in order to search out new faces, for midnight was past and all the masks had been doffed.

She would find him the wife he coveted, even though it would mean Marcus' care would not fall to her. She had vowed it, and she would do it, and would ignore the fact her determination felt very like a penance.

Never mind that Joseph had insulted her by offering her payment to care for Marcus. Augustine only regretted she had been unable to hide her anger from him—for how was poor Joseph to know that he had prostituted their friendship with the offer? Indeed, did he even call the connection they had a friendship? It would seem not, for otherwise why would he have felt the need to bribe her to perform this favor for him? No, *friends* exchanged favors; members of a retinue performed services, for pay. He had made it abundantly clear into which camp she belonged.

She halted, her attention caught by a particular lady across the room.

"What do you see?" Joseph asked.

"Not what, but whom."

He followed her gaze, a moment later shrugging. "I do not see anyone new or unusual. Who makes your nose twitch that way?"

"My nose does not twitch," she denied. "Do you see the lady dressed as a Moorish dancer?" There was a movement of the crowd, revealing a woman dressed in a profusion of brightly colored fabrics. The unpretty lady gave a spin for the benefit of the group with whom she spoke, ending with her arms lifted exaggeratedly in the air.

"Lady Christina," he identified her after only a moment's glance. "Still gesturing away, I see."

"Do not be severe, Joseph," Augustine said, then smiled. "I see an opportunity here—no, not for you! For Lord Walkins."

"Walkins! That plaguey fellow! Whatever could you want with him?"

"*I* want nothing with him, but did you know he adores the theater?"

"The theater?" Joseph echoed, looking confused.

"Yes, indeed. Everything about it. The costumes, the music, the dancing, the plays, everything."

Joseph spread his hands, silently asking for further enlightenment.

"But surely you realize Lady Christina is of like mind? Why else would she be given over to her dramatic gestures as she is?"

"I imagined it was because she is an earl's daughter, and so no one ever hazarded to tell her how silly she appears."

"Nonsense. Her nanny would have told her, if no one else! No, it is because she has a love for dramatics as well. Please excuse me while I go to introduce the two of them."

Augustine crossed the room, telling herself she was pleased to turn her attention to someone other than Joseph. This is what she needed, to get back to the way things had been before he had returned to her life and consumed all her time . . . all her thoughts. Besides, if she were busy with other needy souls, she need not expend so much energy on avoiding looking into his lightest-blue eyes, would not have to constantly pretend an indifference to his presence at her side.

Augustine could not say there were instant sparks between Lady Christina and Lord Walkins, but she left them once they had agreed to share the next dance together. She did not turn back to where she had left Joseph, making good on her inner promises to not forever be at his side, and so was taken aback when he appeared not twenty feet before her. He was unaware of her, however, for one Miss Harpshaw was on his arm, flagrantly making eyes at him, and another lady, the widowed Mrs. Totbury, was sharing a smile with him at something he had said. Mrs. Totbury rapped his shoulder lightly with her fan, obviously having just surrendered him to Miss Harpshaw.

It seemed Joseph required Augustine's assistance as matchmaker less and less these days, she thought on a sigh, knowing it was exactly what she had been working toward but disliking the sensation of being cut loose all the same.

Augustine moved through the room, looking for new faces, but also sneaking glimpses of Joseph as he passed through the movements of the dance he shared with Miss Harpshaw. It was not to be wondered at that Mrs. Totbury, and Miss Harpshaw, or a dozen other ladies, sought him out, flirted with him, strove to catch his eye and hopefully his regard. Even if it were not known throughout the city that he was actively seeking a wife, they would flock to his side all the same. Such was his appeal, with the sardonic manner he adopted attracting rather than repulsing. At long last Augustine understood why Louise had always refrained from parting company with him, had refused to surrender his clever if sometimes biting commentary. Her shy sister had somehow seen past the exterior gruffness to his more deeply hidden and very real charm.

So the patron outgrows the matchmaker, she noted silently to herself. Had he ever truly required her assistance? Perhaps a trifle, for her reputation as an arranger of marriages had certainly taken his search to a prominent and visible position. And even now, a glance at the indifference he tried to mask for Miss Harpshaw proved he had failed once again to find the lady he sought. He attracted but was not himself drawn to anyone.

He had no lasting need of Augustine, but, by jingo! it would be she who found him the perfect lady. That would be her small compensation when all was done and settled, that it had been she who had secured his happiness. A contented union for him had been her original goal when he had first dared her to accept his charge, and it was only her misfortune that she had ever allowed her heart to stray beyond the confines of that goal.

Still, when Joseph's good friend Mr. Prescott stopped

at her side, informing her in a quiet aside that a be-trothal was just about to be announced, her heavy heart was constrained from enjoying the satisfaction the words would normally have brought her.

"It is between Foxy Tredlemeyer and Miss Moncraft," Mr. Prescott explained. "Joseph told me how you paired the two of them, and now they are to wed. You must be delighted to have proven your talent yet again, and in such short order! I understand they have known each other an age, but only have felt the agreeable barb of Cupid's arrow in the past two weeks or so."

Augustine glanced at the two young people who were accepting best wishes and a profusion of hand-shaking, and sighed. Whatever platitude she meant to utter froze on her lips, and instead she asked, "Who is that woman?"

Mr. Prescott looked toward the young couple as well. "Do you mean the stately lady just now talking with Foxy? The one dressed as a goose girl?"

"I do indeed. I have never seen her before."

"That does not surprise me, as she is just returned from the Americas. Her name is Mrs. Gavarny."

"Oh. *Mrs.* Gavarny?" Augustine said in disappoint-ment. There was something about the woman that caught one's eye: the statuesque way she held herself; the manner in which she made a goose girl costume work in utter contrast to what she surely was out of the garb; the sensible but attractive style of her hair, which she wore in a soft caramel-colored chignon. These, and the fact she was clearly no young miss just newly on the town, but a more experienced woman of perhaps thirty. She was most attractive, not in any silly, frilly way, but perhaps in part because of her impeccable carriage and ready smile.

"I understand her husband left her some land in America. She has been there in recent months for some reason, to make a home there perhaps . . . but I believe someone told me she has decided to sell the land, after all, and abide in England."

"Her husband *left* her the land? That would mean she is widowed?"

"Oh yes. Sorry, did I not say that? She is obviously out of mourning, so he must be at least a year gone. I do not remember Gavarny, but then they might have lived abroad."

"Hmm," Augustine answered absent mindedly, and wondered for a moment if perhaps her nose *did* twitch after all, as Joseph had accused, for there was something about this woman that resonated with her. "You have been presented to her?"

"Only just tonight."

"Excellent. You may perform the introductions for me," Augustine informed him, taking up the arm he belatedly lifted to match her touch.

"Certainly, Lady Wayfield, if it pleases you," he agreed.

"It does. And hopefully it will please Joseph to make her acquaintance as well," Augustine said, sounding confident even to herself.

She only hoped any wistfulness that accompanied her confidence went unnoted by Mr. Prescott.

"I found a blue one!" Marcus said four days later, popping up from among the long wild grasses in which he searched. He held his prize, a cornflower, aloft, and grinned at Augustine.

"How very pretty, and how lucky that it waited all summer into autumn before it bloomed for us," Augustine replied, reaching to accept it from his hand. "We must put it in the very front of the crown we shall weave for you."

Marcus dove down amongst the green and browning grasses again, and Augustine pretended at searching for wildflowers as well. In truth, she sneaked glances toward where Joseph and Mrs. Gavarny—the woman had bid them all call her Eudora—sat upon the picnic blanket, caught up in conversation. This was Eudora's fourth outing with Joseph in as many days, and it seemed to be advancing as well as the other three had done.

The woman was perfect. She was absolutely the type of person Joseph had said he sought. She was gracious, and literate, and befittingly gay at times, while being just as equally capable of a correct and somber mien when appropriate. She loved to play the harpsichord, had an attractive singing voice, played cards well, and danced beautifully. She spoke French and Italian, and had interesting stories to tell of her time, a year and a half, spent in America. She went to church every Sunday, and the way she sometimes brushed back a wisp of hair was charming rather than an annoying habit. Her laugh was that of a gentlewoman, not too high, not too full. Her sense of style was irreproachable, and the fact she did not follow the very latest mode spoke to a sensible management of her funds, that she was perhaps not willing to cast her coin about for every little new fribble. She had a head well-shaped to sport a hat, looking especially well in the brushed high crown hat she had worn today.

After yesterday's ride in the park, Joseph had commented to Augustine how Eudora was gentle with her horse's mouth, his tone reflecting satisfaction even as he had said it, and from that moment on Augustine suspected he would find nothing to object to in Eudora Gavarny.

The woman had explained to him that she had been married five years before her husband died of a fever two years ago. She had traveled to America, thinking to make a home there on land not entailed for her husband's heir, but found she missed England too much. She had returned not even a month since, living once again in her father's home.

She had no children from her marriage . . . and instead of experiencing a commonality with the woman over that fact, Augustine had waited for Marcus' appearance at the picnic today to bring forth the woman's one flaw: an intolerance of children. Only, it had not happened that way. Instead of reacting to Marcus with dismay or dislike, Eudora had in short order coaxed the boy on to her lap during the drive out of Town producing a boiled treat as a temptation that even shy Marcus could not forbear. She had chatted with him easily, drawing a few brief replies, and it had been Eudora who suggested she would weave him a crown of wildflowers if he would but find them for her.

The woman was even markedly attentive to Joseph's dogs, insisting when she met them earlier today that they not jump up on her skirts, but otherwise petting them and throwing sticks for the relentlessly demanding Lewisham's Pride, even as she did now for the two water spaniels that had accompanied the picnickers for the day.

Augustine glanced at Eudora, who reposed on the shade-doppled blanket they had spread for their picnic. The woman sat elegantly half-reclining, balanced on one wrist, just the very tips of her shoes peeking from beneath the full lie of her skirts. She could dance among the changing seasonal leaves of the trees and not look out of place, for her rich russet gown with yellow military-style frogs and epaulets was an ode to autumn. She appeared cool and elegant and pleasing to the eye, and the smiles she occasionally sent Joseph's way were formed of white teeth beneath well-shaped lips.

Perhaps her conversation was as captivating as her appearance, for Joseph was stretched out on the blanket, occasionally laughing lightly at something she said.

Augustine gazed down at herself, suddenly and acutely aware of the dust of the field on the hem of her gown, the errant blades of grass and fading flower petals clinging to her embroidered muslin overskirt, and her fingertips stained a yellow-green from where they had reached to snap the flowers' stems. She was aware of the beads of perspiration just under the brim of her bonnet, brought into being by the warm sun that defied the calendar's declaration that the weather ought turn colder. She was too warm and untidy—the antithesis of a cool and composed Mrs. Gavarny.

A little hand reached up, leveling a flower before Augustine's vision. "Oh, Marcus, I see you found some more."

He nodded, putting up both hands. "May I have them?" he asked. "So Mrs. Galarny can make me a crown?"

"Gavarny," Augustine corrected softly, turning over the posy of wildflowers he and she had gathered.

"Galarny," Marcus repeated with a nod.

Augustine smiled slightly, and watched as Marcus scampered through the tall grass, returning to the picnic blanket. Her smile faded, and she thought how this was the only advantage, if it could be deemed an advantage, she yet retained over Mrs. Gavarny: that Marcus called her "Lady Auggie" in a show of familiarity and trust.

But how long would it be before Marcus was calling Eudora Gavarny "Mama"? Or was four days too soon to form such a conjecture?

There had not been one word of rejection from Joseph, not in four days. He had first taken a stroll around the Serpentine in Hyde Park with the lady, after which he had informed Augustine that he and Mrs. Gavarny were to attend the opera the next night. Augustine had not seen him the day after the opera, the day he had ridden in the park with the lady, not until he had returned home.

He had caught her looking out her chamber window, he just inside the long windows of the first staircase in his home. Their eyes had met across the wide distance; she had felt as much as seen his regard. When he lifted his hand in salute and then gave an exaggerated single nod of his head, she had known he had seen her behind the glass of her window. She had nodded in return, ignoring the squeezing pain in her chest, trying to ignore the implicit signal of acceptance . . . not of her, but of another woman.

And here Augustine was today, invited on the picnic they had arranged, ostensibly to review the lady's charm for herself. She supposed she was, after a fashion, looked to for a nod of approval. Where a young man would bring his chosen bride home to meet his parents, instead it was to Augustine that Joseph brought his, seeking her blessing.

The marriage banns must be read and posted for three weeks, Augustine reviewed to herself, not allowing the corners of her mouth to turn down. There was just barely enough time to post the banns before Joseph's anticipated leave-taking, and that only if he dare ask Eudora for her hand in the next day or two. Of course, they could always be married under a Special License, which would be costly, but with Joseph's connections it would also be far from impossible. Surely the Foreign Office held some sway with the Archbishop of Canterbury even if Joseph himself for some reason did not—although the archbishop would have no reason to refuse, especially as both parties were old enough to know what they were about.

Augustine walked slowly toward the group on the picnic blanket, unknotting her hands from where they had been agitatedly crushing the fabric of her skirt. She looked up to see Joseph with Marcus clinging to his back, the little boy waving an imaginary crop. Father and son laughed together, and Marcus was jiggled and galloped about, laughing aloud in an unrestrained manner that was a delightful departure from his sometimes subdued manner.

Augustine's heart squeezed anew in pain. How happy they both looked. How Marcus had blossomed in recent days! How satisfied his father appeared, even as he turned his head to say something to Eudora, whose response set him to laughing as Marcus urged his horse back into action.

Augustine twisted her lips to one side, as if the motion could draw back the unwanted moisture that momentarily clouded her vision.

So, Joseph will have his blessing from me then, she thought with an anguish she could keep from her face but not from her thoughts. She would give her sanction of the alliance today. Today, to be done with it, to end her obligation to him, to leave his side. Eudora would take her place as his confidante—no, be honest, Eudora would transcend it, would become so much more as Joseph's wife and Marcus' mother.

Augustine blinked back tears as she came within steps of the blanket, absolutely determined not to allow a single glimmer of her feelings to be seen or suspected. A deep breath steadied her, only to be caught in her throat when her gaze met that of Eudora, watching Augustine from her seat on the blanket. They stared, each unmoving, the moment brief and yet oddly extended, and Augustine realized with a body-shaking certainty that her caution came too late, her secret stood revealed.

Eudora continued to stare into Augustine's eyes, even as Joseph and Marcus capered about them, still playing their game. Understanding flashed from gaze to gaze, and Augustine longed to shake her head, to deny the truth the other woman had seen, but could not bring herself to lie so blatantly.

She would have to talk with Eudora, later, would have

to explain that she understood she was not to be a part of Joseph's life, that she would never indicate to him what Eudora had so unfortunately seen for herself.

But then Eudora smiled. It was a slow, uniquely feminine smile, one of triumph laced so liberally with malicious conquest, with contempt, that Augustine gasped aloud.

"Augustine?" Joseph ceased his horseplay, turning to her. "What is wrong? Were you stung by something?"

Augustine looked to him, and back to Eudora, finding in that flash of a moment that all sign of what she had witnessed was erased from the woman's face. Joseph could not possibly have seen it. But she had seen it, and it had been cruel and selfish and possessive, and she could not dismiss it as anything else.

"Stung?" she echoed, leveling her gaze one last time with Eudora's. "Yes," she said slowly, then with rising conviction, "Yes, I believe I was stung indeed."

"Perhaps we should leave, Joseph," Eudora suggested calmly, even sweetly. "We would not wish for any further injuries."

"Indeed not," Joseph said, looking to Augustine with a show of concern. He lowered Marcus from his back to the ground, and reached to touch Augustine's arm. "Are sure you are all right?"

"Yes," she said, even though it was far from the truth.

Joseph turned to indicate to the two servants waiting beneath a nearby tree that it was time to pack up for a return home, and so missed the ever so brief dismissing curl of Eudora's upper lip at Augustine.

Augustine did not miss it, however, and could think of little else as they drove home together. She had plenty of time to consider her thoughts, for Eudora entertained Joseph the entire way, capturing almost the whole of his attention. Once or twice he looked to Augustine, his brow furrowed, supposedly by a residual concern for the sting she had received, but then he would be drawn back into conversation by Eudora.

Marcus grew sleepy with the rumbling of the carriage wheels over the rutted road, but refused to put his head on Eudora's lap as she suggested, claiming the seat was "already crowded with Papa and Mrs. Galarny." He chose to snuggle into Augustine's lap instead, and she was grateful to have the tousled curls to draw her gaze downward, that she might not have to politely gaze upon Eudora's easy conversation with Joseph.

When the carriage pulled before Augustine's home, she waited until Joseph climbed down, giving her more room to maneuver and slip her skirts from under the now sleeping Marcus. She kissed her fingertips, not caring if Eudora saw and caring even less what the woman made of the deed, and pressed the kiss to the little boy's cheek.

Joseph offered his hand to help her from the carriage, and startled her a little when he did not release it once she had negotiated the step down. Instead he caught up her other hand, and pulled her toward him, his lips descending. His mouth caught her own off-center, part mouth, part cheek. The caress tingled instantly, making her catch her breath and stare mutely up at him.

He stared in return, and it seemed he wished to say something. His mouth worked a moment, but then he dipped his head once more, this time to put his mouth near her ear. "So you must tell me," he said for her alone. "I have been thinking . . . wondering . . . is she the one?"

"Oh, Joseph, I do not know. . . ." Her voice trailed away as she thought how to explain what she had seen. But he did not wait for her to find the words. "I must say you have done what seemed impossible. You have found an excellent woman, in only a few weeks. It seems I can but thank you and call you the jewel you are."

He stepped back, looking down at her, smiling ever so

slightly, although she might have said the smile did not reach his eyes. "You have done well by me," he said quietly.

For Augustine the fine autumn day suddenly turned bleakly cold. "Are you sure . . . she is all she should be?" she asked, her voice unsteady.

"Of course," he said brusquely, glancing toward the carriage for a moment. "She is everything Meribah was not. How could I possibly do better?"

How was Augustine to answer that? Was she to tell him she had seen a look—nothing more—and on that basis felt the woman was utterly wrong for him? Tell him that they had both, again, failed in judging a lady's true worth? All from a mere glance, a tiny turning up of a lip?

"Joseph—"

"Farewell, Lady Wayfield," Eudora trilled from inside the carriage, fluttering a handkerchief in the direction of the open carriage door. "Come along, Joseph, we do not want the evening air chilling Marcus, now do we?"

"No, of course not," he said to Eudora, releasing Augustine's hands. To her he said, "Again, thank you. I will let you know everything about *The Lady's Boat* as soon as I lay hands on the information. If I cannot complete the transaction myself before I leave, you may rest assured that my aide at the Foreign Office will see that all transpires as per my instructions, never fear."

He hesitated a moment longer, then suddenly leaned forward, planting another kiss on the opposite corner of her mouth. "Good-bye, Augustine."

She did not answer, for she could not. Her throat was too thickly blocked by dismay and unshed tears.

The sensation did not pass until exhaustion finally found her, many hours later, desolate and alone in her bed.

Fifteen

"No, I am afraid you cannot stay downstairs," Joseph explained four nights later to Marcus, who watched with keen interest as Wickers, Joseph's valet, secured a freshly knotted cravat with one of Joseph's gold studs. "Except for a brief appearance before our guests, you will have to be in the nursery with Nanny Rasmussen."

"Why?" Marcus asked, as he picked up another stud, this one holding a sparkling emerald, which he proceeded to secure on the front of his shirt along with four others of varying hues he had already acquired. "I like to play cards, too."

"I know you do, my lad, but tonight is just grown-ups. You and I will have a game tomorrow, but tonight is a gathering just for ladies and gentlemen."

"Nanny says I behave like a most proper little gentleman," Marcus asserted.

"And so you are. But you understand what I meant, Marcus," Joseph said, shaking his head in denial of the boy remaining below with his elders. Wickers stepped back, giving the circumspect nod that meant he considered his master properly adorned. Joseph gave one last tug to the lay of his waistcoat, and then pointed to his son's shirt. "We will have all of those studs returned now, if you please."

Marcus accepted this with equanimity, and did not

protest when his father reached to assist him in removing them. Joseph eyed his son's bent head, and thought of how the child had grown in confidence in the past few months. He would ever be a quiet child, choosing his merrier moments, and would never be continually boisterous as some boys were, but a quiet nature was not the same thing as a meek one. Surely this new poise his young son exhibited in budding degrees was the direct result of spending time in the company of women, women whose gentle touch, soft voice, and ready smiles encouraged the child. Eudora . . . and Augustine.

In truth, it was almost wholly Augustine who had lain the foundation upon which Eudora now built a connection. It was Augustine who'd had the patience to draw out a shy child, in a fuller way than Nanny, or even Joseph, could manage. It was a natural gift, this way Augustine had with children.

And I have been so fortunate as to meet two women possessed of such a gift, Joseph thought, only to frown. There was . . . something . . . it was impossible to put a name to it, but something that niggled at him regarding Eudora, some aspect incongruous with the easy flow of her company. She had been nothing but wonderful, and yet. . . .

Of course, it was entirely possible the something was the lingering feelings for Augustine that burned in the center of his chest, morning and night. He still asked himself a dozen times a day "why not marry Augustine?," only to always answer "how?"

He had been right to thank Augustine for finding him Eudora, had been right to let her think he was on the brink of asking the other woman to marry him.

Augustine had seemed . . . what? Uncertain? Or had she merely stepped back, allowing him to choose his own path, as a good matchmaker ought to do?

Joseph shook his head, feeling more befuddled with

each new day that passed since he had implied to Augustine that he would marry Eudora.

"Marcus," he said.

The boy looked up for a moment from where his fingers worked to remove the final stud. "Papa?"

"Tell me what you like about Mrs. Gavarny."

Marcus was silent a moment, concentrating on working the metal free of his shirt. After a moment he glanced up and shrugged.

"Oh, never mind then," Joseph said, reaching to ruffle the boy's hair, knowing the question was too broad, too unfair to ask of such a young child. "Are you ready to go below and greet our guests?" he substituted, holding out a hand to Marcus.

Marcus delivered the last stud into Wickers' outstretched hand, accepting his father's grasp in turn. "Will Lady Auggie be here tonight?" he asked hopefully.

"No. She said she did not have a head for cards," Joseph replied, experiencing yet another flash of doubt, even as he had when first he had received Augustine's missive crying off from attending tonight's card party. Years ago she had possessed a head for cards—he knew, for she had sometimes been partnered with him. The excuse was an obvious pretext—and it was very unlike Augustine to deal in pretexts. Perhaps it was this that nagged at him, a minor mystery that served to bedevil him in moments of repose.

Moments of repose, such as the picnic just a few days ago. One moment he had been laughing, enjoying Eudora's company, her witty *bon mots,* and the next he had looked to Augustine and found the casual laughter fading from his throat. There had been something in the way Augustine walked, slowly and at a distance, looking sadly isolated in that field of tall grasses, something in that lowered chin that tugged at him.

That pull was the result of their coming to an ending,

of course. He had known even then that the sense of
loss he experienced was a natural one. Say what you
will, he and Augustine had repaired a broken friendship in the past few weeks, by dint of an intense con-
federation built out of time and mutual purpose. The
living thing that was friendship had put down roots.

Joseph remembered, too, her dusty skirt and stained
fingers, her endearing disarray as she entertained his
child, and felt a ghost of a smile turn up his lips as he
descended the stairs. Marcus held his hand, reminding
his father of how the child had also held Augustine's
hand in this same trustful way.

His butler informed him that several callers had already arrived for the evening's entertainment, and that
they had been shown to the library, a room that was
warmer than the front parlor and more inducive to sitting of an evening, Joseph maintained. He nodded to
his butler, and said to Marcus, "You may play with my
ivory chessmen for five minutes after you have made your
bows, and then it is to be upstairs for you, my boy. No
arguments."

Marcus readily agreed, his eyes alight with the promise that he would be allowed to maneuver the intricately
carved chess pieces about.

Joseph stepped into the library, seeing at once that
Eudora was one of the early arrivals, was in fact acting
the part of hostess for him, pouring out the tea and
coffee his staff had provided the guests. It was good of
her to perform the duty, if mildly . . . presumptuous.
But then, perhaps she had every reason to presume, for
he had been just skirting offering a proposal for three
days now. He knew *she* knew what words had lingered
a dozen times just behind his closed lips, for she did
not shy from offering him a direct, telling gaze and
occasional silences he supposed were provided in case
he felt a need to fill them with an offer. It was almost

a game, both of them knowing what was coming, but neither speaking directly of it.

Well, he certainly could not propose at the moment— but perhaps she would stay after the other guests had left? Should he whisper as much near her ear, or wait to see if she provided the opportunity herself? Somehow, the latter seemed preferable, and he kept his suggestion unwhispered.

The evening ought to have been all that was pleasant, but there was something strangely hollow to it, he considered half an hour later. The laughter seemed less ready, less easy, less . . . real, although he could not say why. The conversation was full of court gossip and the usual serving of *bon mots,* but for all that it was clever, it seemed flat. Even the wine in his glass seemed less than a vintage year, but he did not put his glass aside, instead carrying it about, taking just enough sips to afford him a reason to return to the wine tray several times. For at the wine tray he was able to look out the parlor window, across the way to his neighbor's house. He did not know what he sought when he looked out into the dark night beyond the glass, but his person and his thoughts ever strayed there, until such time as Eudora called him back to see to his guests' needs.

Augustine stayed far back from her chamber window, knowing she could scarce be seen if she was a foot or two distant from the pane. Her shadow might be noted if she moved, but standing still as she was, she had the advantage of being able to see out without being seen herself. She was spying—call it what it was—and was shocked by her own cheek at standing there, doing just that. But the house next door had been filled with lights and laughter all evening, and had inexorably drawn her eye.

She waited to see if the final carriage would leave with its owner, Eudora Gavarny, in it, or whether it would return home empty, leaving the woman behind in Joseph's home. Augustine was no innocent, she knew that women and men sometimes chose to act upon impulse, to spend their nights together without benefit of a clergyman's blessing. Joseph might even be thinking it could serve him well to learn if Eudora was as compatible in that regard as she apparently was in all others.

Even if the lady did not stay the night, however, it was abundantly clear that Joseph would marry her if nothing—or no one—moved to intervene.

Augustine closed her eyes, stabbed to her core by the mockery of love she had twice brought into his life, once with Meribah, and now with Eudora. Or was Euroda a more practiced actress? If Joseph married her, would it be years rather than months before he learned the lady's true nature?

Or did Eudora aim her malice only at other females? Was the cunning displayed and intended only for those who conceivably threatened Eudora's status? What Augustine saw as a scheming possessiveness might be perceived by Joseph as an understandable display of feminine jealousy.

And perhaps it was. Perhaps Augustine had read too much into Eudora's superior smile, her conceited curl of the lip.

No. She had been no more mistaken in Eudora's quelling arrogance than the other woman had been in seeing that Augustine was in love with Joseph.

And yet if Augustine went to him, attempted to describe the other woman's two-faced nature, what had Joseph ever seen in Eudora's behavior to make him believe it? He had said Eudora was everything Meribah had not been; he had thanked Augustine for pairing him with the woman. How could she go to him and say she had twice made the same error of mistaking surface for substance?

How could she not?

Why had she proven as inapt at fulfilling the needs of Joseph's heart as she had been with her own?

"Perhaps I ought to investigate buying a different home," Augustine muttered to herself, her jaw tight with indecision. Revelations or no, marriage or no, how could the neighbors go on in future? Perhaps she could take a home in Manchester Square, or Portman Square—somewhere a far walk from here. Or perhaps she ought to remove to Manningstone Hall in Kent. After all, soon she would have *The Lady's Boat* to install there . . . as if that mattered in any way whatever.

She was so sunk in dissatisfaction at either thought, she nearly didn't catch the sudden rectangle of light spilling from the house across the way. Her heart spun and tripped when she saw the light came from Joseph's open front door and that Eudora was being led out on his arm.

Eudora was dressed in a velvet gown, the muted candlelight coming from the open door turning the fabric Augustine knew to be palest blue into a shimmering silver. Her bonnet was tied beneath her chin in a matching silvery bow, gloves were on her hands, and there was something in the way Joseph led the woman forward that gave the appearance of a leave-taking. The notion, to no particular avail, cheered Augustine.

Joseph handed Eudora into her carriage, not sketching a kiss over her hand as he might have done, and bowed himself away. He moved into the house, closing the door behind himself, and then the door on the side of the house opened, and out came Marcus. He was garbed only in his night clothes, seemingly oblivious to the night's chill, something held in his hand.

Augustine flew to her window, throwing open the

sash, prepared to cry out to the boy to keep free of the carriage wheels, only Eudora's groom had yet to mount his box and so also beheld the newcomer.

"Master Marcus?" the groom inquired, obviously having met the lad before. His voice carried easily up to Augustine's ears.

"I want to show Mrs. Galarny my crown." Marcus held aloft the fading remains of the flower crown woven for him at the picnic. "It has got all dried up," he informed the groom.

"As you please," the groom answered with a nod, opening the carriage door and lowering the step for the boy. "Master Marcus to see you, ma'am," he told Eudora.

"Spriggs?" came Eudora's voice, obviously speaking to the groom. "Why do you—?" Her question was interrupted when Marcus thrust the crown toward her.

Augustine missed the interim conversation, for it took place within the muffling confines of the carriage.

She almost turned away from the scene, sick at heart. It would seem Marcus would soon have no need for a neighbor's praise, an afternoon's venture into bread-making, or a tolerant smile that told him he might stack blocks on the table if he chose—not when all that and more would soon be available to him in his own home. Even if Eudora were willing to allow Marcus to continue to call upon Augustine, could Augustine bear the continuing contact, the inevitable moments of encountering Joseph, a Joseph married to another woman?

Her question was thrust aside as Marcus came from the carriage with a scowl fixed upon his face. "I never meant to!" he cried. Eudora must have said something, for Marcus repeated in a howl, "I never meant to!"

Eudora leaned through the open door. "Go back in the house!" she said sternly to him.

"I will!" Marcus declared, and cast the flowered crown on to the ground, turning his back on it and the carriage.

His little shoulders heaved in outrage, yet it was only when he unintentionally looked up and caught sight of Augustine leaning from her window that he burst into noisy tears. "Lady Auggie," he said, or something weepy that sounded very like it, and ran toward her door.

Augustine's gaze locked on Eudora's, in spite of the distance and the dark, and she did nothing to hide her contempt before she withdrew from the window.

She ran down the stairs, knowing Mosby would have long since secured the doors for the night. As soon as she had the door open and had bent down to the boy, he pitched into her arms, sobbing with his face pressed into her shoulder. "I . . . did . . . did not . . . mean to!" he hiccoughed through his tears.

"There, there, Marcus. Calm yourself, sweeting. You can tell me in a minute," she soothed, standing with him in her arms. She patted his back and rocked him gently. "There, there, dear boy."

It was in such a posture that Eudora came through the open door and found them, and close behind her followed Joseph.

"What is the matter?" he demanded at once, reaching for the boy, who went easily upon hearing his father's voice, his sobs renewing. Joseph stroked the boy's heaving back, but it was to Augustine that he looked for the answer to his question. "I heard a cry, and I thought it was Marcus—" He glanced down at the boy now curled in his arms, plainly perplexed to find his child not home in bed.

"He came out to show Mrs. Gavarny how the flowers in his crown had dried," Augustine explained. She refused to call the woman Eudora any longer, for such a familiarity was shared by friends, and Eudora Gavarny was no friend of hers.

"Was he hurt?" Joseph asked anxiously, attempting to level the boy back for an inspection, only to have small arms cling tenaciously to his neck. "Are you hurt?" he asked of Marcus.

"His feelings are," Augustine supplied.

Marcus' only reply was to hide his face against his father's coat.

"I am afraid it was I who hurt his feelings," Eudora said, her lashes fluttering as though to blink back tears. "I told him he must not be out in the chill night air in naught but his night clothes. I think he must have taken my surprised words as a reproach." She reached out a hand as if to pat the boy, but Marcus saw the motion and squirmed away in his father's arms, his face screwed up for another bout of tears.

"Marcus dear, do calm down and say you understand," Eudora urged.

Augustine narrowed her gaze, fighting back words of denunciation. What did she know anyway? Nothing more than what she suspected, that this woman was Meribah all over again. Her proof was inadequate at best, and it was not difficult to think Eudora could twist them to seem like some manner of spite or rivalry on Augustine's part. If she opened her lips to tell Joseph how she saw this woman, she did so risking he would have no reason to believe her, would not want to hear that a second woman had fooled them both, not with his pending need to leave the country so close at hand. How could Augustine blame him if he refused to listen to aught but what his own ears had told him, to choose to draw only upon his own experience of the woman? Was she a fool to cast away his friendship on the grounds of a suspicion?

No matter, for she would be a greater fool yet to lose their friendship by keeping a terrible truth from him. She was and would remain his friend, whether he claimed her as such or not—and a friend must speak.

"Joseph." There must have been something solemn

to her tone, for all eyes turned to her, even Marcus'. "I do not know all that was said, but I do know Mrs. Gavarny upset Marcus very much, and it was not just by insisting he return to the house."

"I never meant to step on her dress!" Marcus wailed. With all of the belligerence a five-year-old could muster he declared to Eudora, "I am *not* a horrible, nasty little boy!"

"Marcus, darling, what are you saying? Of course you are not! I never said—"

"You did, too! Papa," Marcus cried, lower lip so pouted as to make his speech difficult to comprehend, "I am *not* a horrible, nasty little boy, am I?"

Joseph shook his head, staring into his son's face.

"Joseph, I—" Eudora began, but when Joseph looked to her, she ceased to speak, instead drawing in a sharp breath. She lowered her gaze, one hand creeping up to spread across her breast, as if she had taken a mortal wound there. "I . . . I did say as much," she confessed in a very soft voice. "I admit it. It was horrible of me. He stepped on the hem of this gown, my best blue velvet, and would not move when I asked—"

"Did too!" Marcus declared.

"Well, that is neither here nor there. The fact is I spoke too harshly, and I am sorry for it. I suppose I am tired. This week . . . it has been wonderful, but, too, tiring . . . ," her voice trailed away, followed by a tentative smile.

Joseph scowled, not repressively so, but rather in a considering manner.

"I apologize, of course," Eudora said. She squared her shoulders. "Marcus, you are a very nice little boy. Do say you will accept my apology?" Again she reached out a hand, touching the sleeve of Marcus' night shift.

Marcus frowned terribly, turning his face away in refusal. Eudora withdrew her hand.

"Marcus," Joseph warned gently, "it is ungentle

manly not to accept an apology." However, he did not attempt to force the boy to turn about.

Marcus said nothing, maintaining his silent refusal.

"Thank you for your apology," Joseph accepted in his stead.

"Thank you for understanding," Eudora said at once, a tentative smile fleeting across her features.

These manners were all very pretty, Augustine thought to herself, but to her ear they lacked the ring of authenticity.

"Good night then, Eudora," Joseph said, nodding at the woman. He set Marcus down, and moved to hold the door of Eudora's carriage.

"Good night, Joseph. Truly, I am sorry—" Eudora began, but then she gave a strangled shriek as Marcus jumped forward, firmly planting his small, dusty foot on the hem of her gown.

"Marcus!" Joseph roared, springing to pick up the boy, but he was too late, for Eudora had already yanked the fabric from under Marcus' foot, unbalancing the lad. Marcus fell with an audible thump, his backside striking the dirt at their feet.

Augustine and Joseph lunged for the boy at once, nearly colliding heads. She saw with relief that Marcus did not cry, and so could not be much hurt. Joseph stood the boy up, dusted him off, and then picked him up.

"Marcus, you must apologize to the lady," Joseph said in a tone that refused all argument.

"I am sorry," Marcus said with his chin tucked under but a defiant gleam in his eye as he glared at Eudora.

"You must not do that ever again," Eudora said to the boy. "It was very ill-mannered of you."

"No more so than your action, Mrs. Gavarny!" Augustine declared hotly.

Eudora gave her a cool glance, but it was to Joseph she said, "I am ready to go home now."

"She will do the very same again, and worse, I would wager," Augustine announced to Joseph.

He gazed at Augustine, his head turned a little to one side, like a dog that hears a distant whistle. "You have reason to believe that?" he asked quietly.

Eudora raised her hand to her temple, as a lady might do in hopes of holding back sudden tears. "What have I done wrong?" she wailed. "Joseph, why do you let this . . . this person attack me? I have done little, except to protect my property. But you cannot think I was at fault in any way in this . . . this incident." She lowered her gaze, only to raise it again in a beseeching manner. "This dress is special to me. I bought the fabric the day Mr. Gavarny passed to his reward. I had it made into this dress on the anniversary of . . . of his. . . ." She seemed unable to say more, and reached into her reticule for a kerchief to press against her mouth.

"But it is only a dress, Mrs. Gavarny. It scarcely compares with a child's feelings—"

"Augustine," Joseph interrupted, raising the hand that had been stroking Marcus' back once again. He spoke to Augustine, but it was to Eudora he looked. That woman returned his sky-blue gaze, which was fixed on her, level and unblinking, and then a tremor of shock coursed over Eudora's face.

"Enough," Joseph said, at last looking to Augustine. "We must allow Eudora to return home, and Marcus to get to bed."

"But there is—" Augustine tried to protest.

"Enough," he said again, not harshly. The man she had once thought of as arrogant gave no sign of that now, for all that he spoke in a voice that suggested he was not to be opposed in this matter. There was no haughtiness, no dismissal even, just a quiet assurance that the threeway conversation was at an end.

Augustine parted her lips to argue, only to decide he

was right. Mrs. Gavarny should go, and Marcus ought to be tucked into bed, but then! Then Augustine would say her piece, and he would be made to listen. He would have to hear her out, even though it would no doubt cost her his friendship.

Just a few weeks ago she had vowed to find him a wife, but tonight she vowed to do her best to see that any wife of his was not the woman she now handed up into the coach.

When the carriage rolled forward, Joseph turned to Augustine, the sleepily drooping Marcus snuggling on his shoulder.

"He must be half-frozen," Augustine said, moving to chafe a bare little foot between her hands.

"I never minded the cold when I was little," Joseph said. "He will do fine. But you are correct, he needs to go inside."

"Yes. Then, Joseph, I must speak to you—"

"I thought you might."

"It shows?" She summoned a brief smile.

"Yes. You have never been short of things to tell me, not since we began our little enterprise. I recognized the symptoms, you see, of yet another oration."

She fought to keep her mouth from quirking downward, from letting any hurt show in her gaze where it met his, so near. "I am sorry. I never meant to be a boor."

"Did I say you had been a boor?" he asked, shaking his head, and there was something in the way he said it, in the steady way he inspected her features that told her he had only meant to gently tease. "Augustine, allow me to get Marcus settled, and then I will come to hear what you have to say. Tonight, if that is not too inconvenient?"

"Tonight," she readily agreed. "My parlor."

He nodded, and turned, murmuring some words of comfort or endearment to Marcus, leaving Augustine alone wishing he had murmured such words to her.

Sixteen

"Lady Ruchert?" Augustine echoed not five minutes later to Mosby. "She is here? At this hour?"

"Yes, madam."

"Show her in, of course," Augustine said, even though a midnight visit with her sister was the last thing she required before Joseph arrived. She needed time to gather her thoughts, to be able to make a cogent statement to him, to convince him of that which she was herself convinced. There was time yet to find another woman, a far better woman for him. Augustine had brought her attribute cards from her chamber for that very purpose, spreading them on the table in her front parlor, reviewing them repeatedly as if she could find the perfect woman's name spelled out among them somehow. She would talk to Joseph, have him expand on his requirements. . . .

Louise floated in, charming in a gown of green striped silk, with the slightly rumpled appearance and good humor of someone fresh from a party, a fact she soon verified. "I danced the evening away, as I have not done since Andrew and I were first married. It was such fun, I find I am in high spirits and not ready to return home, even though Andrew has gone off with his fellows. We were celebrating, you see. Do you wish to know why?" Louise asked in the breezy manner of someone who has thoroughly enjoyed their evening.

"Certainly, my dear, although it might have to wait for the morning, as Joseph is due to arrive at any moment—"

"Joseph! At near midnight! Augustine, I daresay you would be better served to ask me to stay than to try and chase me away, if you have a mind to retain your reputation," Louise cried, although she appeared far less scandalized than she tried to sound.

"He is my neighbor," Augustine said, making the word sound as dry and uninteresting as stale toast, but Louise was not to be dissuaded. "We are going to talk about . . . about ending our association. He has found his bride, you see."

Louise sat up. "Mrs. Gavarny?"

"Exactly."

"Mrs. Gavarny?" Louise repeated, pulling a face. "I cannot like her."

"Truly?" Augustine asked in some surprise, pleased in an entirely unchristian manner to hear her own sentiment echoed. "Whyever not?"

"She is too perfect."

Augustine sighed, slumping back against her sofa cushions in a posture very like Louise's had been. What Louise said, at least on Eudora Gavarny's surface, was only the truth. "She has the ability to appear perfect, I know." She lifted a hand as though to wave the matter away; Joseph was the one she needed to convince of Eudora's treachery, not Louise. "Enough, Louise. I would rather hear your reason for dancing every dance."

Louise settled back against the cushions again, giving a cat's smile. "Tonight my Andrew was asked to join the Cumberland Fleet! He has gone with Lord Addison, who is to sponsor him, this very night to develop some scheme they have devised should Andrew be accepted to the club."

"Scheme? I thought all the Cumberland Fleet did was to sail about the Thames, raising flags and firing cannon on celebratory days?"

"As near as I can tell, that is exactly what they do, then off to a coffee-house they go, to tell each other how clever they are. But Andrew is delighted, so I am delighted for him."

"How splendid for him," Augustine said.

The sisters shared a smile, and Louise sank back in her chair once more, settling comfortably. "Since Andrew means to neglect me for the remainder of the night, do let us share a light repast and gossip about people we do not like," she suggested. "We have not done that in ages, and it would be such good sport—"

"I admit it would. But it must be postponed for tomorrow instead, Louise. Tonight I must speak with Joseph," Augustine reminded her.

"Oh, yes, I quite forgot. About his marrying Mrs. Gavarny."

"About his *not* marrying Mrs. Gavarny!" She bit her lip, but then went on, "Louise, she is as deceitful as Meribah ever was, but at least Meribah was too shallow to hide it for long. Mrs. Gavarny is far more clever, far more cunning. I must tell Joseph, and I fear he will not believe me. He will think me mistaken, or manipulative, or jealous, I fear."

"Jealous?" Louise latched on to the one word Augustine wished she had ignored. "Why would he think you jealous?"

"Indeed, why?" Augustine said, giving a light laugh that was almost real. "I have never given him a single reason to think I might . . . that I care for him. You are right. I am being foolish. If he dismisses my words, it will be because he chooses not to believe me, not because he sees . . . he thinks—!" Augustine ended abruptly, seeing the dawning understanding in Louise's eyes.

"Augustine!" Louise declared, staring wide-eyed. "You are in *love* with Joseph!"

"Yes," she said simply, giving that forced light laugh again. "Well now. You have seen it. Eudora Gavarny has seen it. I suppose that means even Joseph will see it, if I am so foolish as to attempt to remain in his life. Thank you for helping me to realize this must all come to an end," Augustine forced her voice to remain even and calm, so as not to betray the devastation she suffered within.

She moved to her writing table, idly shuffling and moving about the attribute cards lying there. "And that means I cannot continue to assist Joseph in finding a wife, should he reject Mrs. Gavarny, not if I am so unable to hide my feelings."

"Augustine!" Louise repeated, a hand pressed to her breast in a gesture of utter surprise. "But . . . I must say, this makes sense to me. You have not been yourself since this whole matter with Joseph began! I recall how restless you were that day on the bench when Joseph was driving Lady Christina in the park. And the day you came to *me* for advice on how to introduce Joseph to a different set of ladies, well! I thought I should faint for the novelty of your being uncertain! And," she said, tilting her head, a gesture of equal surprise and comprehension, "And you said something peculiar to me then, which I found odd but did not think to question."

Augustine winced, remembering her words.

" 'You said 'some loves are not possible.' I thought you meant between yourself and Christopher, but you meant *Joseph!* But, Augustine," she went on, her brow wrinkling in puzzlement, "why must such a love be impossible?"

"I suppose I have proven such a love is quite possible," Augustine said, relying on a wry tone to get her past the moment, "except that it must be returned to be of any value, Louise."

Louise gasped. "You think Joseph could not love you?"

Augustine smiled ever so softly at her sister, not for the first time thinking Louise and Marcus had much in common, since they both were reserved with strange persons and situations, and now Louise spoke with the kind of innocence about love that Augustine would have expected from Marcus.

"Oh, Augustine, have you told him?"

"Heavens, no!" Augustine sank into the chair before her writing table, feeling the blood leave her face. "And you must not either, Louise! It is a poor enough thing that I mean to dissuade him from marrying Mrs. Gavarny, when his time in England is so short! I think I can bear to have him angry with me, but I could not bear to be avoided out of pity or aversion. Please, you must vow you will say nothing!"

Louise hesitated, but there must have been real distress writ across Augustine's features, for Louise relented. "Yes, of course. Of course I will say nothing, if that is how you say it must be. It is your affair to settle." She stood and crossed to where her sister sat, reaching down to idly touch one of the attribute cards. "I saw you at this when I came in. What do you? Do you search for some clue as to who would make Joseph a perfect wife?"

Augustine looked listlessly down at the cards, and nodded.

" 'Witty,' 'Insightful,' 'Thoughtful,' " Louise read the arranged cards aloud. " 'Patient,' 'Honorable,' 'Well-Read,' 'Sensible,' 'Gentle,' 'Loving,' 'Maternal.' " She made a sweeping gesture over them. "But, Augustine," she protested, "these are words to describe *you!*"

"Oh, Louise, there is no point in saying such things!"

Augustine protested, a blush creeping up into her cheeks.

"What words describe Augustine?"

Both ladies spun to face the open door of the parlor, where Mosby belatedly announced "Lord Sumner, my lady," with a hint of chagrin at having been unable to precede the newcomer as was his duty.

Joseph strolled into the room. Marcus, his face stained by tears, was on his father's hip. "He would not settle," Joseph said by way of explaining the boy's presence. "I thought perhaps your servants could treat him to bread and butter while we spoke?"

Augustine made an assenting sound, standing and beginning to move toward Marcus.

Louise, however, interceded, going to the lad's side before Augustine could take more than a step. "Better yet, perhaps that could be my privilege," she volunteered after one glance at Augustine's flustered expression. To Marcus Louise said, "Would you care to have bread and butter with me in the kitchens, Master Marcus? And perhaps we could talk Cook into providing a cup of tea with honey, do you think?"

Marcus looked dubious, then he gave a quick nod of the head. Joseph placed him on his feet, and the little boy accepted Louise's hand. She led him to the doorway, where she stopped for a moment. "To answer your question when you came in, Joseph: the attribute cards spread there on the table contain words that describe, to perfection, our Augustine." She turned then, leading Marcus away with soft encouraging words.

Aghast, Augustine looked down at the cards, but only in time to see Joseph had already moved to read them. He stood silent and still for a moment, then gave a nod. "She is correct. You are all these things."

"It is of no importance," she said faintly, knowing her earlier blush now deepened.

He turned to her. "You wished to speak with me. Concerning Eudora," he stated.

"Yes."

"You do not approve of her?"

"Joseph, what I have to say is not because I wish to be unkind or to frustrate your hopes, but because—"

"Because she is not all she seems," he finished for her.

"Yes, exactly," Augustine gasped, then stared. "You knew?"

"No," he said, touching one of the attribute cards briefly with his fingertip before turning to face her fully. He had well-shaped hands, hands she would miss gazing at if the evening ended poorly. Yet, there was hope to be had here that it need not end in disaster, for Joseph did not refuse what she said, seemed even to have suspected something himself. But was it a suspicion of Eudora Gavarny's motives, or her own?

"No," he said again, making her heart clench in uncertainty. "I did not know. Until tonight, I thought her the very paragon for which we searched." He began to pace slowly, sending Augustine a glance. "But, no, that is not true. Despite the apparent perfection, there was something in Eudora that I found . . . troubling. Is having no flaws in and of itself a flaw? No matter. There was something that kept my tongue between my teeth. Would I have offered for her in the end, if no evidence came forward?" He shrugged. "I think not, but who is to say?"

"Oh, Joseph! Does this mean . . . ?"

"That she is no more under consideration? Yes, it means that."

Augustine blinked back sudden tears of relief. "I am so pleased. She is Meribah all over again, and I brought her into your life! You cannot know the anguish I suffered once I saw a glimpse of her truer nature, and I did not know how to tell you of it."

He nodded, folding his hands together before him as he turned to face her fully once more. They seemed to have run out of things to say, but he stood still, watching her, as if there remained unfinished business. For herself, she had already dismissed the matter of *The Lady's Boat*—it was only stone, unfeeling, unnecessary for happiness. The only real matter remaining was the termination of their pact, and whether it must also mean the end of any continuing friendship between them.

"What was it," she asked, unable to ask the question that truly plagued her, "that made you realize what Eudora is in fact?"

"Everything, I suppose. For all that I looked for a nonpareil, I found I was suspicious of such a creature when I found her. But in truth, it was how she treated Marcus. I could have perhaps forgiven her for being shrill—what adult is never shrill with children?—but when she told a lie, it tinted all else as lies as well."

"A lie?" Augustine echoed, unable to think what he meant.

"Her gown, the one that was stepped on, the blue velvet. She said it was made of fabric—"

"—she had bought the day her husband died," Augustine supplied. "That is a lie?"

"Perhaps. But if it is not, then what she told me only three days earlier was a lie, and she knew I had heard it."

"That look of shock she had—!"

"Yes. She realized she had told me a different tale of how the fabric came into her life, that she had seen it in a shop window and that it had reminded her of the color of my eyes." His mouth slanted into an objecting *moué*. "Tonight I did not even need to ask her how she had noted the color of my eyes two years ago, since we never met before you introduced us. She realized what she had done, and realized I knew it as well. She was courteous enough not to offer me any further lies by way of some mumbled explanation."

"I wondered if she could be ever gracious to a man, where she could not with women," Augustine marveled. "Obviously not."

He gave her a sharp look. "She was ungracious to you? Unkind?"

"No," Augustine admitted, half-turning to the table to sweep the attribute cards into a pile, evening the edges between her hands. "All she did was to look at me in such a way that I knew what she was. Just as it took but one small lie for her facade to fade before your eyes." She set the cards down, tapping the top card with one finger and giving a crooked smile. "I suppose there is no point in your retaining my services. I have failed you. Twice. Do you know, Louise and Andrew move in slightly different circles than do I, so perhaps she could assist you—"

"Augustine," he said, and she was suddenly aware how near they stood to one another. He took a step nearer yet. "Whatever is the Seventh Indication of Love? You never gave me a card or told me what it was," he said.

"I never did, did I? But it is the most important one," she flustered, taking a small step back, out of the immediate circle of his presence. "It is a worthy one for today, to send you on to better fortunes, I think. The Seventh Indication is easily summed in one word: compatibility. It is desire and ability combined, supplanting all the other Indications. It is when two people seem utterly wrong for each other, but when they are together, everything is utterly right. He might give up nothing for her, or she might be even more meek than he is himself, and his habits may drive her mad half the time—but, despite it all, somehow they fit together, they make sense of the nonsensical. They love each other, cannot explain why, and do not care to try."

She hesitated, then lifted her chin and spoke directly from the heart. "*That* is what you must search for, Joseph. Search for love, that is what you are made for, and if you seek anything else it will continue to be Meribah all over again."

"So you have tried to tell me all along."

"Because I am right."

He gave a soft, slow smile. "Yes, Augustine, I admit it. You are right. I must not remarry without first finding love."

She could not breathe for a moment, for his smile had warmed her lungs, her very thoughts, so that nothing about her functioned properly for a few long moments. The spreading warmth of his smile, however, stopped abruptly when it touched her cooled heart, that center of her that knew his best, his loving smiles would be meant for someone other than her.

"So we remain friends?" she asked softly, clinging to this one last buoy in a sea of loss.

"It is my wish."

"Ah. I am so pleased." She turned away, convinced the expression on her face must be the opposite of her words.

"Augustine." He came up behind her, his hands settling on her shoulders.

"I will get Louise!" she said, shrugging away from under his touch, her voice too high. "You two may use my library to plan a strategy, if you like—"

"Yes, you will get Louise, to share your news, but not just yet," he told her, his hands once again touching her, this time on either arm. He turned her to face him.

"News?" she sputtered, trying to smile and knowing it was impossible. "That she is to assist you now?"

"What does it mean, Augustine, if all Seven of your Indications are present?"

She shook her head, at sea.

"What does it mean if I am willing to give up my cursed solitude? That I want to be in your company, even when you laugh like a charwoman in my carriage? What does it mean that, after speaking with dozens of ladies, it is only you who tempts me to consider the possibilities of love?"

"Joseph?" she said, her eyes wide, her hands coming up to touch his forearms, rather as though she needed to touch him to comprehend his words.

"What does it mean," he went on, smiling ever so slightly, "that you cared for Lord Bromleigh's dogs? Can it be I have found another soul who cannot resist the useless creatures? What does it mean that dozens of ladies can make me laugh, but it is only you who makes me smile just from thinking of you? What does it mean that sometimes I wish to box your clever little ears, and a moment later wish to whisper sweet nothings in them? And what does it mean, Augustine, that I care nothing for any of that, not if one word of it means you would not have me, would leave me to a life without you?"

Augustine stared up at him, too amazed, too filled with a sudden breath-taking joy to speak.

Instead she went into his arms, closing her eyes and then opening them again in wonder at the ready way he had accepted her into them, at how they wrapped about her in a gently possessive way.

"Augustine," he said to the top of her head, his voice thick, "I love you."

She pushed away from him slightly, to look up into his face, and spoke the truest words she had ever spoken, "Oh, Joseph, I love you, too."

He lowered his mouth to hers, sealing their words with an enraptured kiss that might have lasted longer but for the shuffle at the doorway.

They both turned to find Marcus staring at them. Louise came directly behind him, her cheeks pinkening. "He slipped away when I was talking to Cook. So sorry. Please excuse us," she said rapidly, taking the little boy's hand. "Come along, Marcus."

"Why?" Marcus asked, obviously wishing to remain.

"Because Papa and Lady Auggie are busy falling in love," Joseph said to him.

Louise beamed, but Marcus only said matter-of-factly, "Oh." He took up Louise's hand, allowing himself to be led away.

Augustine felt a blush of happiness stain her cheeks as she gazed again up into Joseph's grinning face. "Perhaps you are only just falling in love with me, Joseph, but I fell in love with you long since," she said, and trembled at the admission.

His reply was to put a hand on either side of her face, turning her mouth up to meet his in a kiss, a lengthy one that left no room for doubt in her mind as to the extent of his feelings.

He finally raised his mouth, and she would have sworn that now it was his turn to tremble. "Augustine, if I swear it is not for any good and practical reason, but because I am madly in love with you, will you marry me?"

"Well, I do not know . . . ," she teased, only to receive another long kiss, which she returned until she had to stop and laugh from pure joy. "Of course I will marry you! But, Joseph," she said, with a grin to match his, "what will Society think of me, the matchmaker, making the best match for myself?"

"You flatter me! I like that in a wife! But, as to what they will say, they will congratulate me for my great good fortune in attracting the matchmaker's discriminating regard."

"Not just my regard, Joseph," she said, her grin softening with the sincerity that rang in her words. "My heart."

He kissed her again, but this time it was a gentle thing, a promise, a troth.

"Then there is only one question that still requires an answer," he said at length. "Do you think we can yet arrange to marry before I leave England? Or would that be hurrying you too much? Marcus can stay with you while I am gone, as you have already said you would—"

"Certainly we must marry before you leave! If we did not, how could I possibly travel with you? I should have to hire a companion, to save my reputation—"

"Travel with me? Augustine—!"

"Of course I will travel with you. I am not about to remain in England, longing for you while you traipse about the Continent. I am perfectly capable of keeping Marcus safe and secure while you are about the State's business. And you have to admit that travel is so broadening, even for the very young," she said, her gaze daring him to gainsay her.

"I realize you really wish to go along so that your new husband does not spend too much time alone with the lonely and rejected Lady Quiggmore," he teased, "and not for any 'broadening' experience it might mean for Marcus."

"Well, of course that is really why."

He laughed, and pulled her close again. "And I shall allow you to come, because I do not wish to be the lonely and dejected new husband who has left his beautiful, clever, delightful wife behind," he assured her, and kissed her yet again.

AUTHOR'S NOTE

Lady Quiggmore was invented for the purposes of this tale only. While not a true person, nor even an amalgam of the various ladies who were once (in truth or speculation) paramour to the Prince Regent, her presence in this tale is in keeping with both the man and the age.

I enjoy hearing from readers! You may write to me at:
Teresa DesJardien
P. O. Box 33323
Seattle, WA 98133

Please include a self-addressed, stamped envelope for a reply.

ZEBRA'S REGENCY ROMANCES
DAZZLE AND DELIGHT

A BEGUILING INTRIGUE (4441, $3.99)
by Olivia Sumner

Pretty as a picture Justine Riggs cared nothing for propriety. She dressed as a boy, sat on her horse like a jockey, and pondered the stars like a scientist. But when she tried to best the handsome Quenton Fletcher, Marquess of Devon, by proving that she was the better equestrian, he would try to prove Justine's antics were pure folly. The game he had in mind was seduction—never imagining that he might lose his heart in the process!

AN INCONVENIENT ENGAGEMENT (4442, $3.99)
by Joy Reed

Rebecca Wentworth was furious when she saw her betrothed waltzing with another. So she decides to make him jealous by flirting with the handsomest man at the ball, John Collinwood, Earl of Stanford. The "wicked" nobleman knew exactly what the enticing miss was up to—and he was only too happy to play along. But as Rebecca gazed into his magnificent eyes, her errant fiancé was soon utterly forgotten!

SCANDAL'S LADY (4472, $3.99)
by Mary Kingsley

Cassandra was shocked to learn that the new Earl of Lynton was her childhood friend, Nicholas St. John. After years at sea and mixed feelings Nicholas had come home to take the family title. And although Cassandra knew her place as a governess, she could not help the thrill that went through her each time he was near. Nicholas was pleased to find that his old friend Cassandra was his new next door neighbor, but after being near her, he wondered if mere friendship would be enough . . .

HIS LORDSHIP'S REWARD (4473, $3.99)
by Carola Dunn

As the daughter of a seasoned soldier, Fanny Ingram was accustomed to the vagaries of military life and cared not a whit about matters of rank and social standing. So she certainly never foresaw her *tendre* for handsome Viscount Roworth of Kent with whom she was forced to share lodgings, while he carried out his clandestine activities on behalf of the British Army. And though good sense told Roworth to keep his distance, he couldn't stop from taking Fanny in his arms for a kiss that made all hearts equal!

Available wherever paperbacks are sold, or order direct from the Publisher. Send cover price plus 50¢ per copy for mailing and handling to Penguin USA, P.O. Box 999, c/o Dept. 17109, Bergenfield, NJ 07621. Residents of New York and Tennessee must include sales tax. DO NOT SEND CASH.

FROM AWARD-WINNING AUTHOR
JO BEVERLEY

DANGEROUS JOY   (0-8217-5129-8, $5.99)

Felicity is a beautiful, rebellious heiress with a terrible secret. Miles is her reluctant guardian—a man of seductive power and dangerous sensuality. What begins as a charade borne of desperation soon becomes an illicit liaison of passionate abandon and forbidden love. One man stands between them: a cruel landowner sworn to possess the wealth he craves and the woman he desires. His dark treachery will drive the lovers to dare the unknowable and risk the unthinkable, determined to hold on to their joy.

FORBIDDEN   (0-8217-4488-7, $4.99)

While fleeing from her brothers, who are attempting to sell her into a loveless marriage, Serena Riverton accepts a carriage ride from a stranger—who is the handsomest man she has ever seen. Lord Middlethorpe, himself, is actually contemplating marriage to a dull daughter of the aristocracy, when he encounters the breathtaking Serena. She arouses him as no woman ever has. And after a night of thrilling intimacy—a forbidden liaison—Serena must choose between a lady's place and a woman's passion!

TEMPTING FORTUNE   (0-8217-4858-0, $4.99)

In a night shimmering with destiny, Portia St. Claire discovers that her brother's debts have made him a prisoner of dangerous men. The price of his life is her virtue—about to be auctioned off in London's most notorious brothel. However, handsome Bryght Malloreen has other ideas for Portia, opening her heart to a sensuality that tempts her to madness.

Taylor-made Romance from Zebra Books

WHISPERED KISSES (0-8217-5454-8, $5.99/$6.99)
Beautiful Texas heiress Laura Leigh Webster never imagined
that her biggest worry on her African safari would be the handsome Jace Elliot, her tour guide. Laura's guardian, Lord Chad-
wick Hamilton, warns her of Jace's dangerous past; she simply
cannot resist the lure of his strong arms and the passion of his
Whispered Kisses.

KISS OF THE NIGHT WIND (0-8217-5279-0, $5.99/$6.99)
Carrie Sue Strover thought she was leaving trouble behind her
when she deserted her brother's outlaw gang to live her life as
schoolmarm Carolyn Starns. On her journey, her stagecoach
was attacked and she was rescued by handsome T.J. Rogue. T.J.
plots to have Carrie lead him to her brother's cohorts who mur-
dered his family. T.J., however, soon succumbs to the beautiful
runaway's charms and loving caresses.

FORTUNE'S FLAMES (0-8217-5450-5, $5.99/$6.99)
Impatient to begin her journey back home to New Orleans,
beautiful Maren James was furious when Captain Hawk delayed
the voyage by searching for stowaways. Impatience gave way
to uncontrollable desire once the handsome captain searched
her cabin. He was looking for illegal passengers; what he found
was wild passion with a woman he knew was unlike all those
he had known before!

PASSIONS WILD AND FREE (0-8217-5275-8, $5.99/$6.99)
After seeing her family and home destroyed by the cruel and
hateful Epson gang, Randee Hollis swore revenge. She knew
she found the perfect man to help her—gunslinger Marsh
Logan. Not only strong and brave, Marsh had the ebony hair
and light blue eyes to make Randee forget her hate and seek
the love and passion that only he could give her.

*Available wherever paperbacks are sold, or order direct from the
Publisher. Send cover price plus 50¢ per copy for mailing and
handling to Penguin USA, P.O. Box 999, c/o Dept. 17109,
Bergenfield, NJ 07621. Residents of New York and Tennessee
must include sales tax. DO NOT SEND CASH.*